Warning!

To avoid spoilers, be sure to read the first two books
in the Mage Web series first:

Forging the Blade

Book One

Mainly by Moonlight

Book Two

HELL'S GATE

BOOK THREE OF THE MAGE WEB SERIES

C. LaVielle

DRAGON'S EGG PRESS
Portland, Oregon
2021

Hell's Gate
Book Three of the Mage Web Series

Copyright © 2021 by C. LaVielle
All rights reserved under international and
Pan-American Copyright Conventions.

Dragon's Egg Press
Portland, Oregon, U.S.A.

Front cover illustration and design by Ture Ekroos
www.tureekroos.com

ISBN 978-0-9983260-2-3

First Edition 2021

This book is for my husband
Craig LaVielle

The demons peering out from behind the ornamental capitals
that open each chapter come from two sources. The ones
that may remind you of Tenniel's illustrations to Lewis
Carroll's Alice books are from Louis Le Breton's illustrations
to the 1863 edition of Jacque Collin de Plancy's *Dictionnaire
Infernal*, and the other demonic images are from Johann
Scheible's 1849 edition of an older German Faustbook called
Magia Naturalis et Innaturalis.

HELL'S GATE

PART I
Asmodius and Andromeda
1973–1975

PART II
Hell
2014

PART III
Damia

EPILOGUE

Part I

Asmodius and Andromeda
— 1973–1975 —

1

Adam

Adam Carnegie Morgan took a deep toke off the hash pipe and passed it back to Geoffrey Gould as Led Zeppelin's "Stairway to Heaven" began twining its gorgeous, sinuous way through his friend's apartment. He settled back, closed his eyes, and waited for the smoke to work its magic.

It kicked in almost at once. His brain relaxed out of its tight, driving focus and opened up to dance randomly through all sorts of unimportant but delightful possibilities. He exhaled slowly and was actually able to enjoy watching the smoke twist and swirl. The orange shag carpet and the moss green chairs and sofa pulsed with color. Lines of power slipped into view and danced through the room, almost begging him to reach out and weave them into a spell. This was the way the world was supposed to be.

His epiphany came in a brilliant flash.

He'd have said it was almost a religious experience, if he'd been at all inclined in that direction.

He realized that ever since he'd started working at his father's bank, he'd been one unhappy, screwed-up mage.

How could that be?

He'd had it all figured out.

He'd gone to Grant High School in Portland, the Mage Web's magnet school for magic on the West Coast. While he was there, he'd gotten his magical education at Tesseract Academy, that weird, wonderful place at the center of the circle of time where the Web educated its youth, preparing them to go forth, explore the multiverse, and protect humanity from itself.

Then he'd come home to San Francisco and gone to Stanford University. Adam was fascinated by money and the byzantine system that moves it through the world, nourishing some and starving others. He had understood quite early in life that money was power. The more money you had, the more power you had. And, of course, the more designer clothes and fancy cars you could buy. So he'd studied economics and gotten his MBA. His father and his father's father on back *ad nauseam* had been bankers, and Adam's father was keen to train him to step into his polished wingtips. And Adam had been happy to comply. What better place to accumulate money, control it, and watch it flow than a bank?

The music kicked up a notch and the lyrics caught his attention.

What was a bustle doing in a hedgerow?

Was there still time to change the road he was on?

His father had wanted Adam to learn banking from the bottom up, so he started Adam off as a teller.

He hadn't even lasted a day.

It was a simple job except for the customers. Most were tolerable, but some were insufferably stupid or just plain rude. After the third person he'd managed to either completely enrage or send away in tears they'd whipped him off the floor so fast his teeth clicked, and had him shadow one of the service managers. At the end of the first day, the service manager sat him down and gently informed him that he was not a team player.

Like duh.

They shuffled him around the main branch for a few more weeks, then finally stashed him in the Wealth and Investments Division with a job that kept him away from customers, which was fine with Adam. And he thoroughly enjoyed it—for about six months. After that, it became a monotonous routine and was no longer a challenge. He had also found all the perfectly legal tricks and hidden fees that the bank used to suck huge amounts of money out of its clients' accounts. Most of these accounts represented the hard-earned life savings of people who didn't understand investments and trusted the bank to take care of them. Sure, many of them didn't really need all that money, but that didn't justify the theft, which is what it was, pure and simple.

Every one of those deductions from a client's account made him uneasy.

And he wasn't making nearly enough money. He had two nice three-piece suites that he wore to work, but the rest of his clothes were cheap rags. He glared down at his Black Sabbath T-shirt, frayed black bell-bottom jeans, and worn leather sandals. He knew that as he advanced, he'd be making quite a bit more, but he wanted it now. Living in San Francisco was expensive.

Robert Plant howled over a pounding storm of drums and guitar.

Something needed to change.

"This is good shit," Adam said. "What is it?"

"Lebanese Red. Wanna buy some?"

Adam took a sip from his bottle of Anchor Steam and stared at his friend like he'd never really seen him before, even though they'd been at Tesseract Academy together and were both Dragon Lodge members. Geoffrey was now head waiter at the Top of the Mark, and Adam was sure his job involved much more than waiting tables. The Top was one of San Francisco's premier restaurants, and lots of financial, political, and social business—deals, liaisons, and love affairs that the Web needed to know about—got transacted there. But even with the extra the Web probably paid him, he wouldn't have made enough to live in this classy apartment with its eye popping city and bay views. And then there was his huge record collection, Thorens turntable, Bose speakers, and trendy furniture. And he always had the best weed and hash around.

As the cool, frothy beer slid down his throat, Adam had yet another epiphany.

"You're a dealer!"

"Gee! What was your first clue, Sherlock?" Geoffrey's good-natured, blue eyes twinkled merrily.

Adam grinned right back.

He'd found the answer to at least one of his problems.

The storm of music came to a crashing halt, and the last line dropped syllable by syllable into the silent room.

Geoffrey leapt up and turned off the stereo.

"We need to talk," he said, flopping back into his chair.

"Actually, I'm just a pot smuggler. The hard drugs are too dangerous—both to sell and to take. I won't touch them and I won't work with anyone who does. But there's plenty of money in weed and hash. In fact, the demand is so high that I can't keep up. I need a partner. Are you interested?"

Interested? If Geoffrey's apartment was an example of the money he could make selling his favorite form of self-medication, Adam was thrilled to his pedicured toes. The fact that pot was illegal just added spice and excitement.

"Maybe," he said. "What kind of money are we talking about?"

"If you work all the contacts I have for you, you can make fifty grand the first year."

Shit! That was more than he made at the bank.

"Could I keep my job?"

"Oh yeah. I have more contacts than that and still work at the Top. Come on, Adam. I need someone I can trust, and you'd make a great pot smuggler."

2

Adam

dam found that pot smuggling was simple in theory. His main expenses were storage units for the product, quarters for the phone booths, and gas. The contacts Geoffrey gave him included drivers who shipped stuff out and brought stuff in from Mexico and Eureka, California, and local distributors. He paid the drivers, stored the stuff, and supplied distributors.

The rules were simple too: Always deal in cash. Never let other dealers or drivers know your real name or where you live. Arrange your drops from a phone booth—preferably several different ones. Keep the location of your storage units secret.

But, at the end of the day, the whole system was based on trust. All the safeguards in the multiverse wouldn't protect you from a contact who was determined to turn you in.

He started out small. He cleared out his savings account, bought a few bricks of Lebanese Red from Geoffrey, and began working his local contact list. Within three days he'd doubled his money and was looking for more product.

Adam and Geoffrey were lounging in the Buena Vista Cafe one evening, sipping Irish coffees and watching the Powell & Hyde Street cable cars rumble by.

"I've got a truck-load of weed coming up from Mexico this week. Wanna split it?" Geoffrey asked.

A few days later, in the wee hours of the morning the two mages headed south and east to a county road just off Interstate 5. A stand of cottonwoods, the only trees for miles around, loomed up in their headlights. They drove their rental vans behind them and stepped out into the cool, dry darkness. This far from the city, thousands of stars glittered in the black velvet sky and the silence wrapped itself around them, sending Adam's nerves into overdrive. He leaned against his truck, trying to look like standing in the middle of Voodoo-black nowhere, waiting for who-knows-who was the most natural thing in the multiverse, but after a while he gave up and started pacing.

"He's late!"

"This guy's always late. Chill."

An hour later, headlights appeared in the distance and the roar of a semi engine smashed through the silence. The truck approached rapidly and pulled in beside them, breaks screeching.

The driver leapt out and headed for the back of the trailer. He bore a distinct resemblance to Oddjob in the James Bond movie, only minus the lethal top hat, and dressed in worn-out jeans and a filthy wife-beater tank top instead of a black suit. He reached up, jerked open one of the trailer doors and disappeared into its depths. It was crammed full of antique furniture and smelled like moth balls, but, after some shuffling and bumping he appeared at the door with a large, sturdy cardboard box. More boxes followed until twenty of them lay in a pile at their feet, smelling faintly of pot. He vaulted down from the trailer bed, stalked toward Geoffrey, and didn't stop until he was almost on top of him. He stank of old cigarette smoke, and Adam was sure he hadn't seen a shower or a toothbrush in days.

"That'll be eighty grand."

"Not until we've seen what we're paying for," Geoffrey said. His tone was soft and reasonable, but his shields intensified and began expanding out, pushing the driver back a step. He fished a Swiss army knife out of a shirt pocket and cut open one of the boxes. It was lined with a plastic garbage bag. The knife disappeared and was replaced by a small flashlight, which he used to examine the contents of the bag.

"This stuff's nothing but shake! And it's full of stems." The flashlight disappeared and out came a pipe.

"Aw, c'mon man. I'm in a hurry. I'm running late."

Geoffrey stopped crumbling weed into the bowl of his pipe and slowly turned a reproachful glare toward the driver. One eyebrow arched up.

"We noticed."

His contact cursed impotently as the young mage took his sweet time lighting up, taking a toke and passing it over to Adam.

"This shit's only a few notches more potent than oregano," Geoffrey said after his third hit. "Fifty grand."

"No way," snarled Oddjob.

Geoffrey shrugged and turned toward his van.

Steel glinted in the starlight as the driver pulled a knife out of his boot and grabbed for him. In one quick move, Adam kicked it out of his hand and lunged into him, sending him sprawling to the ground and the knife spinning off into the dry weeds.

"The man said 'fifty,' and that's generous. Take it or leave it," he said.

Oddjob's glare dripped venom. But when Geoffrey returned with a grocery bag full of money and set it beside him, he scooped it up and stalked back to the cab.

Adam wound up with a pile of shit weed stinking up his storage unit. Covering it with a drop-cloth didn't help much. He thanked the gods he'd had the foresight to rent a shed in a eucalyptus grove.

His distributors pissed and moaned, even though he was selling the stuff for a song. But San Francisco was starving for weed, and low-income flower children were still everywhere. They eventually sold out. He didn't double his money, but he made a nice profit.

And he'd enjoyed himself immensely.

As the months went by Adam realized how hard it was to spend all the money he made. Even after he'd started paying his landlord in cash and banking most of his paycheck, he still had shoe boxes full of money on the top shelf of his closet.

His inner banker was in a constant snit.

Money did not belong in shoe boxes. It needed to be invested so it could make more money. But investments left a paper trail, and the IRS and law enforcement were very good at following paper trails back to their illegal beginnings.

If he started a business, like a night club or a restaurant, he could run his illegal cash through it and pay himself with the squeaky-clean profits, which could then be invested. And restaurants always needed small bills to make change. He could turn some of those inconvenient ones, fives, and tens stuffed into the shoe boxes into space-and-time-saving Benjamins.

But he needed a sizable loan to finance a business large enough to launder all the money he was making.

And he knew right where to get it.

3

Adam

At the end of the next quarter, Adam got his accounts in order for the last time. He headed up to his father's office and trudged across the huge Aubusson carpet to the reception desk. Even though he'd made the appointment a week ago, The Dragon Lady, his father's formidable executive assistant, peered up at him over half-moon glasses and informed him that Mr. Morgan was busy and would be with him in a few minutes.

Actually, it had been more like thirty, but who was counting? His father's suite took up the entire top floor of the building, and the view of the city, the bay, and the Bay Bridge was amazing. Adam never got tired of it.

At last he was ushered into the inner sanctum. He and his father dispensed with the pleasantries fairly rapidly, and Adam explained that, regretfully, he was not cut out to be a banker. Fortunately, the managers he'd worked under had kept his father appraised of his disastrous progress, and he agreed wholeheartedly.

"So, what will you do?"

"I'd like to run a restaurant and night club," Adam replied, sliding his tentative business plan across the gleaming expanse of the teak desk.

James Morgan took in the whole page at a single glance—he'd probably seen thousands like it—then sat back in his elegant Danish modern executive chair and regarded his son intently over steepled fingers. His clear red aura was shot through with gold and crackled with mage energy.

Adam felt like a small furry animal gazing into the eyes of a powerful, deceptively benign predator. His father had never looked at him like this before, and he realized that, for this moment, he was no longer his son. He was a client.

"As you've noted in your plan, it will take at least six months before the business will make a profit, and you haven't mentioned how long it will take to remodel the property you buy. How will you support yourself during this time? And what do you have as collateral? And what, if anything, do you know about the food and entertainment industry?"

Adam had foreseen the first two objections, and he'd come prepared. It was a huge risk, but he had to take it. Turning his face into a mask of stone, he pushed his purple-black aura out to meet his father's and handed him the profit/loss report from his pot-smuggling business.

"Egad!" the banker said as his eyes raked through the columns and came to rest on the bottom line—net profit. He sank back into his chair, sighed.

Despite the gravity of his situation, Adam felt a small surge of pleasure. He had always enjoyed jerking his father's chain.

"This is, unfortunately, a perfect occupation for you. It's also one I had hoped you would avoid. And, yes, of course, you'll need to own something like a restaurant." He skimmed the report back across his desk and into Adam's hand. "I didn't see that," he said.

He closed his eyes and went still, but his aura lit up like a pinball machine.

Finally, he came to a decision. It probably took less than ten seconds, but it felt like forever. "Finish your research, find a property, show me a detailed business plan, and I'll consider it," he said, and glanced at his watch. The interview was over.

His father had cut right to the nub of the issue. Adam knew nothing about the restaurant and entertainment business and, although he loved eating and cooking and being entertained, he couldn't care less about the business end of it—just whether or not it was making money.

He needed a partner.

A partner he could trust completely.

And right now, he couldn't think of anyone that he trusted completely.

4

Elizabeth

lizabeth Katherine Stanhope wandered aimlessly through the bustle of the Financial District. It was her lunch hour, but she wasn't hungry. At least the fog had lifted and the sun was warm on her shoulders. San Francisco Bay sparkled blue in the distance, and a cool, salty breeze swept the synthetic office fug out of her lungs. There were worse places to be stuck.

But she was definitely stuck.

The sidewalk was packed with tourists and men in three-piece suits. A young businessman several yards ahead caught her eye. As he stalked along the sidewalk, the crowds parted as if by magic. And then she looked more closely. Of course he was able to slip through everyone like they didn't exist. He was a mage. And, even from the back, she recognized the set of those shoulders, the dark wavy hair, and the purple-black aura that shimmered around him.

"Adam! Wait up!" she yelled, pushing her way toward him.

He stopped abruptly and whipped around, sending a family of tourists in tie-dye T-shirts scrambling to avoid running into him. He ignored them and spotted her immediately. His somber face lit up with the radiant smile that had never failed to raise her pulse rate. Black silk Armani three-piece, black wingtips, blinding white dress shirt, and piercing amber eyes completed the picture. A woman, dressed to the max, stiletto heels clicking sharply, turned to stare appreciatively as she passed him.

"Elizabeth!" he said, scooping her up and twirling her around. "I thought you were in Crete!"

"I was, but the funding dried up," she replied as he plunked her back down.

Elizabeth's mother was an anthropologist, her father, an archaeologist. She'd spent her childhood traveling the world with them, working the digs and following her mother around as she got to know the people of the area and their customs, folk lore, and legends. She had loved every minute of it and so, of course, graduated from Stanford with a double major in anthropology and archaeology. Her parents had called in a few favors and got her a job on an international team that was putting the finishing touches on the excavations at the Palace of Phaistos on the island of Crete. She had been ecstatic. The Minoan civilization was her specialty. She spoke Greek and could translate Linear B, and she'd already spent a few seasons there with her parents. But after one fabulous year, the money had run out.

"That's rough. What are you doing now?"

"Shuffling papers for a bunch of lawyers and looking for another job at a dig. But they've gotten scarce. Even Mom and Dad haven't been able to find anything. What about you? Looks like banking agrees with you."

"Actually, it doesn't." His face froze. From past experience, Elizabeth knew this meant her question had pulled up a ton of intense feelings inside him that he preferred to keep hidden. She had found that the best way to deal with the frost face was to wait it out. Adam would tell her what was going on with him—or not. Questioning, cajoling, or sympathy on her part would make him clam up even more.

She waited.

"Let me buy you lunch," he finally said. "Or if you've already eaten, at least a drink."

"Lunch would be great." Her appetite had miraculously returned.

They headed into a nearby noodle shop. It was packed and loud with the babble of customers and the crash of dishes being dumped in bus trays. While they sipped tea and waited for their order, they talked about Stanford and traded stories about which of their friends was doing what and with whom. She was enjoying herself immensely. It was like they'd never been apart. By the time the food arrived they were chattering nonstop about her work in Crete. When the check arrived, Adam sat back and studied her. Then he ordered another pot of tea and leaned forward.

Yes! Her patience had paid off.

"Several months ago, I suddenly realized that I hated banking and was completely bored and miserable. So I decided to become a pot dealer."

"You're kidding, right?"

"No. I'm completely serious. I know someone who gave me a list of contacts and supplies me with the stuff. It's easy, it's fun, and in six months I've made forty thousand dollars—even with working full time at the bank."

Ah. That was it. The money. Adam loved his creature comforts. And now that she thought about it, the danger and secrecy would also appeal.

"And I've just quit my job."

"What?!"

"The problem with dealing drugs is figuring out what to do with all the illegal money." Adam poured them each a cup of tea from the pot that had just arrived. "I need a business, like a high-end restaurant or night club, to run the cash through and pull it out as profit. So I asked my father for a loan."

"What did he say?"

"He told me to find a property, write out a detailed business plan, and he'd consider it."

"But you don't know squat about running a restaurant."

"No, but if I find someone to run it for me, it might be fun to own one."

It all became crystal clear. She'd been wondering why tight-lipped Adam Morgan was telling her all this.

"And you want me to run it for you."

"Yes." He took a sip of tea, sat up a bit straighter, and eyed her apprehensively.

"Elizabeth, will you be my business partner?" His knuckles went white on the hand gripping his cup.

Holy shit! He was asking her to run a money laundering business. If they were caught they'd go to prison—for a long time. At least for most people it would be a long time. A mage could simply teleport, or jump, out of prison to anywhere in this world or any other world that they could visualize clearly. But that would mean giving up this life and creating a new identity. Which would be difficult.

She certainly wasn't morally opposed to pot. Many of the cultures she'd studied as an anthropologist had used it for millennia. And, according to Amanita, her psychoactive-ethnobotany instructor at Tesseract Academy, Cannabis was not only a great mind-altering drug with virtually no side effects, but was also a potent medicinal herb. She used it herself occasionally and so did almost all her friends.

And Elizabeth was surprised at how appealing the idea of having Adam as a business partner was. She realized that if she wanted him to be part of her life, this was her best chance. A marriage proposal was out of the question. Adam loved beautiful women of all sizes, shapes, and colors and refused to be tied down to just one, which was fine with her. She was okay with sharing.

"I don't know squat about running a restaurant," she said.

"You're a quick study. You could learn."

"Let's talk about it," she said, and reached for her cup.

5

Adam

When Elizabeth had called his name, Adam had recognized her voice immediately and felt an unreasonably large jolt of joy. And something else. It felt suspiciously like the thrill of weaving a spell and having it suddenly catch hold in the multiverse and begin to work. Had he been invoking her subconsciously? She was one of his favorite people and he had missed her. When he discovered that she was at loose ends, he began to wonder if she might be willing to go into business with him.

By the time they were halfway through lunch, he'd decided she'd be perfect. Elizabeth was sharp as the pottery shards she was constantly poring over, and tough as the crew she'd managed at Phaistos. And she was good with people—which he definitely wasn't. The problem had been talking her into it. When the dust finally settled, they'd agreed to share the profits fifty-fifty; and even though he was to remain the sole borrower, she would own a third of the value of the business.

The first thing was to find a property. They'd never be able to afford anything in San Francisco—real estate was skyrocketing—so they decided to check out Portland. They both had fond memories of the city from their high school years. Adam did some research and learned that it had more bars and discos than you could shake your tush at, and a police force that was on the take. But most important, the property costs were low. A few jumps forward in time assured them that it was definitely an up-and-coming city. They found a dilapidated, five-story apartment block on NW Lovejoy Street in the Alphabet District. This was far more property than they'd planned on, but they knew from their jumps that this would soon be an upscale area, and Adam immediately realized that they could turn it into an efficient money machine—a trendy night club at street level, three floors of apartments, and a high-end restaurant on the fifth floor. The price tag was ridiculously low, so they made an offer.

When he turned in his detailed business plan, his father had given him every penny he'd asked for. But it wasn't a "Here's the cash, son, pay me back when you can" sort of loan. It was a formal bank loan, and Adam signed away everything he owned to secure it.

"Don't get caught," he'd said as he handed Adam the signed papers. His face was grim, and the young mage knew that if he were, there would be no help from his father.

Geoffrey wasn't happy about losing his partner, but he saw the advantages of having Adam in Portland and gave him a few contacts to get him started.

6

Elizabeth

Anthropology is the study of people and the culture they live in and how each influences and shapes the other. Elizabeth understood that the restaurant and entertainment industries were cultures just like the Minoan civilization, and she studied them from the viewpoint of an anthropologist—she began talking to entertainers and people who worked in restaurants. And, as with any industry, she found that it wasn't what you knew, but who you knew. Geoffrey Gould was the head waiter at the Top of the Mark and just happened to be a mage and a friend of theirs from high school. He put them in touch with Tony Zika, a friend who was a chef at Jake's Famous Crawfish in Portland and was thinking about starting a restaurant of his own.

To Elizabeth's delight, his specialty was Mediterranean cuisine, and yes, he would be thrilled to run their restaurant.

He also put the word out that she was looking for a lead bartender and a nightclub manager. A dozen or so highly qualified people showed up for interviews and within a few weeks she had selected Nova Conner as the lead bartender and Jeff Springsteen as the nightclub manager. She had learned a few important things from managing the crew in Crete: hire the best people you can find as foremen, pay them well, and then get out of their way. Let them choose their workers and organize the shifts. So she left the set-up and hiring for the restaurant to Tony and the nightclub to Jeff and Nova. She worked with all of them on the design, décor, menus, and pricing.

Elizabeth had fallen in love with the classy but decrepit art deco, brick apartment block's exterior, so they gave it a face lift and gutted the interior.

They decided that the nightclub would be on the first floor, with another entrance to a lobby with two elevators—one that went directly to the restaurant and a keyed elevator for the tenants. Adam and Elizabeth would each have an apartment on the fourth floor. The second and third floors would be divided into twelve well-designed studio apartments with reasonable rents. The restaurant, with a glass wall overlooking downtown Portland and the Willamette River, would be on the fifth floor.

The art deco theme of the exterior would continue in the lobby and nightclub. Avocado, orange, and an awful harvest gold were the colors of the seventies, but not right for art deco. Elizabeth chose pale apricots and grays and lots of wood, glass, and stone instead. The entire building had to be well soundproofed, of course.

They called both the building and the nightclub Lovejoy Place.

Tony's family was from Greece and he remembered his childhood there fondly. When he found out that Elizabeth had worked on an archaeological dig in Crete, he suggested that they call the restaurant "The Dolphins." He'd vacationed in Crete with his family a few times, and a picture of frolicking dolphins that he'd seen in one of the archaeological sites had stuck in his mind. She knew just the fresco he was talking about and ran with the idea. She found a muralist to reproduce the dolphins on one wall and other ancient Minoan artwork everywhere else. The glass wall was framed with replicas of two huge reddish-brown Minoan pillars. Two dolphins in a yin-yang arrangement were the logo for the restaurant.

They hired an amazing contractor who, with a few magical nudges from Adam and Elizabeth, had the restaurant, nightclub, and apartments up and running in six months.

7

Adam

ortland in the 1970's was a gritty, unconventional, naughty city and Adam loved it. But compared to San Francisco, it was small-town slow and easy. And, like a small town, it was leery of new people and new businesses. Fortunately Adam had a network of friends in the city from high school—many of them mages, and many of them influential. Between Geoffrey's contacts and Adam's friends, his pot smuggling business skyrocketed. Portland was as hungry for the magic weed as San Francisco.

Elizabeth took to managing The Dolphins and Lovejoy Place like a mermaid returning to the sea. She was a natural at creating an enticing ambiance and cachet, and the restaurant and nightclub soon became hot spots for well-to-do Portlanders to see and be seen. Adam was happy to maintain a low profile, keeping the books, paying the bills, and managing the money. And he was surprised at how much he enjoyed promoting the businesses. Without letting on that he was one of the owners, he enjoyed taking friends out to eat at The Dolphins or for drinks at Lovejoy Place. He also talked several restaurant reviewers into trying them. The excellent food and service and the magical atmosphere brought rave reviews and packed houses. By the end of their first year together, the legal businesses were making a solid profit.

Adam was, at last, able to let go of his worries. Elizabeth was a joy, and he thrived on the excitement and intrigue of dealing pot. When he was arranging meet-ups and drop-offs from phone booths and socializing with his contacts—drinking with them at various bars and playing basketball at the hoops in Laurelhurst Park—the young mage knocked a few years off his true appearance and slightly shifted his features. He became a scruffy college student named Sam who drove a beat-up, blue Datsun 510 coupe. The real Adam, at age twenty-four, dressed in designer clothes, drove a black BMW, and was one of the most sought-after bachelors in Portland. His contacts would never have recognized him.

8

Elizabeth

Portland sparkled below her in the night, bracketing the gleaming black mirror of the Willamette that reflected a gorgeous full moon. Soft, jazzy background music wove through the clink of china and the conversations and laughter of her guests. Elizabeth savored the flaky-sweet goodness of a piece of baklava, took a sip of bittersweet Greek coffee, and marveled at the perfection of the moment. Adam sat across from her sipping a brandy. It had been a long, leisurely dinner, and their conversation had rambled over what their days had been like, what was happening at Lovejoy Place, what was going to happen at Lovejoy Place, and what was going to happen when Adam finally got her back to his apartment.

CRASH!!! The sound blasted through The Dolphins' smooth ambiance.

"Shit, Tara. Look where you're going!"

Elizabeth jerked around to see Rachel Stevens, the head waitress, glaring at Tara Dansk, the waitress they'd just hired. Rachel's white blouse was soaked with coffee. Her tray, broken cups, and ruined dessert plates lay at her feet.

"I was!" the new girl snapped. "But you barged right in front of me!"

She had to defuse this.

Now.

"Opa!" Elizabeth shouted, clapping and sending a surge of joyful energy into the stunned silence.

Opa. That uniquely Greek exclamation that can be used to transform embarrassing moments of klutziness into moments of laughter and celebration.

"Opa!" Yelled every Greek in the room, and everyone who had traveled in Greece, and everyone who had Greek friends. They all laughed and applauded.

The two waitresses looked momentarily shocked, and then smiled, bowed, and began cleaning up. Elizabeth sank back in her chair.

"Nice save," said Adam, raising his snifter to her and taking a drink. But his gaze flitted watchfully around the room. And he wasn't smiling.

"You feel it too, don't you?" said Elizabeth. "There's a nasty tension in the air. I didn't notice it before, but I do now."

Adam nodded.

"Rachel's been with us almost a year, and I've never seen her lose her temper. And Tara is a lovely, efficient little mouse of a girl that wouldn't snap at her worst enemy. That ugly scene shouldn't have happened. I need to do a walk through the whole building and find out what's wrong."

"I'm coming with you."

The stairwells and hallways in the apartment floors had the same jittery tension as the restaurant. Now that she was paying attention, Elizabeth sensed a dark, desperate, hunger sliding over her shields, searching for a way in.

The worst place was the nightclub. It was roaring. The music was cranked to the max and the dance floor was packed with writhing, shouting bodies. To most people, this would look like a rockin' good time, but not to Elizabeth's mage-trained eyes. The disco ball hung like a glittering, malevolent eye, shooting sparks of violence and corruption around the room. And when she looked closely, she spotted dozens of grotesque, impossibly black shapes twisting and shifting in the dazzle, swirling through the crowd like hungry predators, gorging themselves on the drunken, sexy energy. Deathly white faces with empty black eyes flashed out of the darkness and whispered into the dancers' unsuspecting ears or ran glistening black tongues over their auras. Then they would turn and disappear as if they'd walked around some invisible corner—only to be replaced by another.

A woman at the bar collapsed into her date's arms. He grinned at Nova, who was mixing drinks like a madwoman, and practically carried the staggering woman out into the night. Nova paused long enough to grin back. But her eyes were blank and expressionless. A huge light-sucking shadow surrounded her. It had two blazing red eyes that glared hungrily around the room, which was beginning to resemble a scene out of Dante's "Inferno."

Elizabeth, eyes wide with horror, grabbed Adam's hand, and headed up to her apartment. She needed to get away, if only for a short while, from the horror that Lovejoy Place had become.

"Demons!" She spat the word like a curse the moment they were safe in her shielded living room.

"We have this place warded out the yin-yang. How the blazes did they get in?" Adam was pacing like an enraged panther.

"This entire building, except for our living space is open to the public," Elizabeth replied. "A demon can't go anywhere it's not invited, but if someone is possessed by a demon, by inviting them into our club, or restaurant, or an apartment, we've also invited the demon. The wards can't touch them. I can't believe we didn't notice this before."

"We saw what we wanted to see," said Adam. "Customers spending money on maybe too many drinks and having a good time. We didn't bother to look any further."

"And, of course, the demons didn't want to be seen. Once they were in, they kept quiet and in the background. You're right, they wanted everyone relaxed, full of alcohol and lust, and feeling safe. That's why we didn't notice them. We should have been checking for nasties that hitchhiked in on our customers, renters, and workers as soon as we opened, and clearing them out a couple times a week. An exceptionally evil one has its talons in Nova, and I'd never even noticed."

"Shit! Do you know anything about exorcism?"

"A little. I'll study up on it once we get the building clear."

—

When the club and restaurant closed in the wee hours of the morning, Adam and Elizabeth did a quick check to make sure all their employees were gone and the tenants were all at home. Then they locked up the building and headed downstairs to the club. The tables were wiped clean, the bottles and glasses behind the bar sparkled, the carpet and dance floor were spotless. But the fug of old perfume, lust, sweat, and alcohol hung heavy in the air. The disco ball hung motionless, glinting moodily as shadows, visible only to mages and psychics, seethed around it. The subtle, smoky stench of demon lurked in the corners, and the room pulsed with their cruel malice.

They were watching.

And waiting.

Getting rid of them would have been a technically simple magical working if chills weren't tap dancing up Elizabeth's spine and her heart wasn't racing. She was scared shitless. Which was not a good way to begin working magic. She squeezed Adam's hand and breathed deep, calming breaths. When the fear crept to the edges of her consciousness, she turned a questioning glance to her partner, who nodded. His face was grim and unreadable.

The two mages stood in the center of the club and did a quick Middle Pillar to jump start their energy. They cast a circle, a globe of shimmering, crackling power lines, and began expanding the globe out toward the demons. Almost every demon it touched went up in flames like a bug in a bug zapper. By the time the web of power reached the circle around the building, only a few of the stronger ones remained trapped between the two fields. Instead of wasting time and energy trying to kill them, they banished them back to the Abyss and banned them from Lovejoy Place for eternity. When they were done, Lovejoy Place was psychically clean and sparkly.

Not even a hint of demon remained.

9

Elizabeth

That same morning Elizabeth parked her car across the street from Nova's apartment building, griped the steering wheel, and stared blankly out the windshield. She still couldn't believe Nova was possessed. She'd psychically scanned all the applicants as soon as they'd applied and immediately eliminated the ones with holes or weaknesses in their auras. Nova's had been clear and strong. In fact, she'd radiated health and sanity. That demon shouldn't have been able to possess her. Anyone who has any connection at all to the multiverse, or the Divine, or the Force, or whatever they want to call it, is full of power. Their auras shine. Some more than others, but they all shine. Demons know not to waste their time on them—unless for some reason they need to have that person under their scaly thumb. Instead, they turn their attention to the disconnected, abused, angry, or insane portions of humanity.

The exact sort of person who would seek comfort in a nightclub.

Which, unfortunately, means that nightclubs attract demons like picnics attract ants. The evil bastards feed off the vitality and desires of the dancers and drinkers. Whispering not-quite-audible promises of pleasure into their unsuspecting ears, and slipping in to curl possessively around the helpless souls of those rare unfortunates who can hear them and invite them in.

But Nova, along with almost everyone else in the building, should have been safe.

Adam touched her shoulder. As if he were reading her thoughts, he said, "It's not your fault Nova was possessed. The demon probably made her an offer she couldn't refuse. But she was possessed while she was working for us in a club that we'd failed to clear. We need to get in there and do the exorcism. We owe her that. Are you ready?"

She gathered her power and released not only her death grip on the steering wheel, but also all her concerns and questions and fears. "Yes," she said. "Let's get started."

Elizabeth was grateful to have Adam beside her. She knew from the one other exorcism that she'd helped with that this would probably be a terrifying, brutal, and exhausting ordeal. The basic idea is to go in with your guns blazing and don't stop until the demon is gone.

She extended her senses up into the building and was aware of Adam doing the same. They located her apartment and, literally, went through the front door into a living-dining area with a kitchen to one side and two bedrooms and a bath on the other. Nova was sitting in the kitchen drinking coffee and staring out the window.

They returned and cast a circle—a really strong, person-proof one—around her apartment. Since exorcisms are noisy, they wove in a soundproofing spell. They invoked Archangel Michael, asking him to protect them and to help them remove all demons from Nova and from her living space. Elizabeth had only noticed one demon, but there might be more—she knew of cases where the exorcist had found dozens. Then, clutching their books of invocations and commands for exorcisms, they headed into the building.

Nova buzzed them up, and as soon as she opened the door, they grabbed her.

"Nova Conner," said Elizabeth, "you are possessed by a demon and we are here to get rid of it."

"'Oh, thank God!" she said.

But the moment they began channeling electric-violet light into her and saying, "We exorcise this demon by the power of Archangel Michael," her Madonna-sweet face twisted in rage and began snarling and spitting. She went rigid as rock, and with a flick of her arms sent them crashing into opposite walls of her living room. Nova threw open her front door and smashed into the circle.

"'Begone, evil minion of Lucifer, back to the Abyss from whence you came. Never to return to Nova Conner's body!" Elizabeth screamed as they picked themselves up off the floor, fumbling to find their places in the books.

Nova snarled and leaped across the room toward Adam, her black hair writhing out from her face like snakes and her hands outstretched like claws. But when she got near him she bounced up to the ceiling like a ping pong ball. After years of doing the Lesser Banishing Ritual of the Pentagram, Adam's aura was the psychic equivalent of a Kevlar vest.

They shot electric-violet light up into the young African American woman who was now crawling along the ceiling like a bug and screaming obscenities. Her model-perfect figure morphed into a lizard's scaly body and legs, her full lips pulled back in a snarl as fangs sprouted out of her mouth, and her ears stretched up into demonic points. Her beautiful dark brown eyes rounded into empty holes that flamed with fury. She radiated cruel, vicious power. "Be gone, puny mortals, this soul is mine!" she roared and jumped toward a terrified Elizabeth, giving her an in-your-face view of, burning red eyes, grasping claws, and a gaping mouth filled with fangs. Thankfully, the demon bounced off her shield and began flying around the room, banging into walls and cursing.

"We cast you out, unclean minion of Lucifer, along with all your powers, every specter from the Abyss, and all your fell companions. In the name of the Divine One, begone and stay far from this innocent creature!" they screamed.

They called to Archangel Michael, begging him to banish the demon, who began flashing between its own scaly form and Nova's. Did this mean it was losing control? Elizabeth didn't have a clue. All she could do was keep hammering away with commands to leave, prayers to the archangel, and electric-violet light.

After what seemed like forever, but was probably more like fifteen minutes, Elizabeth was shaking with exhaustion and her throat was raw from vibrating words of power. So they began taking turns.

The light changed from late morning to early afternoon as they slammed away at the demon. The mages were literally fighting for Nova's soul. If the demon won, that divine spark would be lost for eternity in its cruel clutches—even after her tortured body died.

At last, Archangel Michael became an almost palpable presence, filling the room with sizzling, raw power and fierce love. Nova began convulsing, and a column of oily-black foul-smelling smoke gushed out of her chest, screaming like a banshee. The sound was deafening, but Elizabeth could easily hear the archangel say in a relaxed, almost conversational tone, "I need gold light now, please."

Brilliant gold light shot from the palms of both mages, but instead of going into Nova, it spiraled around the screaming column of smoke that towered above them. When the last bit of the awful stuff had trickled out of her, the beautiful spiral morphed into a translucent golden box that snapped shut with an audible click. The evil trapped inside congealed into a snarling black demon. His red eyes blazed. He shrieked hideously as he threw himself repeatedly against his delicate golden prison. His magic crackled and spat against its walls. It burned against Elizabeth's skin like a million pin pricks. Every hair on her body stood straight out. But the archangel's restraints easily withstood his last, desperate attack.

"Open the circle, please," said the archangel.

The moment they pulled it down, the gold-wrapped demon and the archangel vanished, leaving the apartment feeling empty and filled with a miasma of terror and violence.

After thanking Archangel Michael profusely and tearfully, Elizabeth collapsed and wept tears of relief. Adam lay beside her, pale and shaking, tears streaming from his eyes. A small whimper escaped from his tightly closed lips and she turned away, giving him space. Nova's battered body was an impossible pile of arms and legs in the center of the room.

10

Adam

dam lay on the floor and shook. He wasn't sure if it was from relief or fear or a mixture of both. And someone was whimpering pitifully. Oh gods, it was him. He clamped his mouth shut, but the sound still escaped. He really didn't want Elizabeth to see him like this, but he couldn't stop. The demon's cruel, calculated, over-the-top violence had completely unnerved him. He'd been just minutes away from collapsing into a howling heap, a truly humbling and humiliating experience. He sent another heartfelt thank you to Archangel Michael and continued to shake.

When at last he was able to move, he struggled to his feet and helped Elizabeth open windows and psychically sweep the apartment until it sparkled. Then they cast a protective circle around it and filled it with light. Elizabeth seemed to be in better shape than he was. And her attack on the demon had been so ferocious he'd barely recognized his calm, diplomatic partner. If it weren't for her, Adam had no doubt that Nova would still be possessed.

Elizabeth knelt beside Nova's bruised and battered body.

"She's breathing. I can see her chest rising and falling. But I'm afraid to move her. We can't call 911—they'll ask too many questions—but she needs help, so maybe we'll have to."

"I know what we can do," Adam said, and headed for Nova's phone.

"Who are you calling?"

"Estelle."

"Why? She doesn't know anything about healing, and this isn't any of her business. And besides, she hates me."

"She doesn't hate you. I need to call her to get Althea's number."

"Yes! Althea. She was the best healer in Unicorn Lodge."

Adam grinned and let his mind drift briefly back to Tesseract Academy. Things had been so simple then. Three lodges: Unicorn for the healers, Ouroboros for the magic geeks like Estelle, and Dragon for everyone else.

"She's even better now. And she lives nearby," he said, dragging his mind back to the present. He grabbed the receiver and began dialing.

Estelle picked up on the first ring.

"Estelle, I need Althea's number."

"Why?"

She sounded worried. You called a healer when someone was hurt. Of course she was going to ask questions.

"We just exorcised a demon out of one of our bartenders and she's pretty beat up. She needs Althea."

"Yikes! What's going on? How did the demon get into her in the first place?"

"Just give me the number."

"You shouldn't have told her," said Elizabeth as Adam dialed Althea's number.

"It saved time. And Althea's her best friend. She would have eventually wormed all the gory details out of her anyway."

When Althea answered, Adam got right to the point.

"We need you to come do a healing on one of our employees. We'll pay you twice your usual fee."

"What's the problem? I need to know so I can bring the right stuff."

"We exorcised a demon from one of our bartenders and she's pretty beat up."

"Crap! Adam, what have you been messing with?"

"It's a long story. Will you come?"

"Gimme the address."

Adam hung up and flopped into the only chair left standing in the living room. "She'll be here in a few minutes."

"I think she's waking up!" Elizabeth said as she patted Nova's hand and gently stroked the tangled mass of hair back from her face.

Nova cried out and grabbed Elizabeth's hand. Her eyes were so wide with terror that the whites showed all around. They skittered over the room, searching every corner. "Is it gone?"

"Yes," his partner replied.

"Who are you guys. You're not like normal people."

"Oh, we're perfectly normal people," said Elizabeth. "We just know how to deal with demons."

"Thank you thank you thank you," Nova collapsed back on the floor. "I never believed something that evil could exist."

Adam watched in total sympathy as their tough, ballsy head bartender curled up and sobbed like her heart was broken—which, perhaps, it was. He didn't even want to imagine what having that thing inside her must have been like.

As the sobs slid into sniffles, Elizabeth asked the question that he'd been wanting to ask.

"Why did you let it in?"

"My mother was dying of cancer. And I kept hearing this voice say that if I would just let it inside me, I could heal my mother with just a touch. I didn't believe demons even existed. I thought the voice was just wishful thinking, or maybe my subconscious talking to me. If it was a chance to help Mom, I was willing to take it. So I did. And I healed my mom. The docs were amazed—couldn't figure it out. By then I'd realized that I was possessed by this thing, this demon, that made me do awful things, and when it got bored, it did awful things to me."

"Well, it's gone now," Elizabeth said, "and it can't get back in unless you invite it."

"Fat chance."

"Is your mother okay? Did it possess her too?"

"No. I don't think it could have got her even if it had tried. Mom's a devout Catholic. She would have seen it for what it was and told it to get lost."

There was a knock on the door and Althea bustled in. Her brown hair was piled loosely on top of her head, and her leggings, T-shirt, and clogs were smudged with dirt. She'd probably been gardening. Adam was glad to see the bulging backpack slung over her shoulder. She'd come prepared.

"Introduce me!" was all she said, but she was already headed toward Nova, studying her closely.

"Nova," Adam said, "I'd like you to meet Althea, a friend of ours. She's a healer and understands all about demons and can help you get better."

"It's nice to meet you, Nova," Althea said plunking down beside her. "Will you allow me to help you?"

"Yes. Please."

Althea turned to Adam and Elizabeth and said, "I can take it from here. Elizabeth, would you run a tub of hot water before you go? Nova needs a sea salt and Epsom salts bath with lots of lavender."

❧

As they headed for Elizabeth's car, wrapped in each other's arms and grateful that everyone was safe, a sick feeling of fear chilled Adam's heart. He shivered and pulled Elizabeth even closer. They weren't safe yet. There were too many unanswered questions. Like why had dozens of demons suddenly decided to infest Lovejoy Place? And why had a demon powerful enough to stand up against two mages and an archangel decided to possess the club's head bartender?

He was willing to bet his shiny new BMW that the answers to these questions would not be pleasant.

11

Elizabeth

ovejoy Place was back to its classy, comfortable self. A few demons filtered into the nightclub and restaurant, but that was to be expected in establishments where the public came to drink, dance, and pick up dates. They were relatively harmless, and it was no problem for Elizabeth to get rid of them herself.

But one evening, as she was riding up to The Dolphins in the elevator, an ash-white head materialized inches from her face. Its eyes blazed wicked red, and a gray slug of a tongue slithered out of a mouth crammed with pointy teeth and began licking her aura. It growled in ecstasy as it fed. The elevator reeked of smoke and decay. Shuddering with revulsion, the young mage blasted it to oblivion and thanked the gods no one else was with her.

When the doors opened, she shot out and skidded to a halt. Rachel Stevens looked up from the restaurant's front desk in alarm.

"Elizabeth, are you okay? You look like you've seen a ghost!"

"I'm fine. I just remembered something I need to do," she said and slipped into the restaurant.

What she needed to do was check the building for demons.

And now that she was looking, she saw that Lovejoy Place was, once again, flooded with them. A dark undercurrent lurked malevolently just beneath the sophisticated glitz. Chillingly potent, but invisible to everyone except Elizabeth. Their presence made the staff edgy. Arguments broke out over things that wouldn't have mattered yesterday. The Dolphins and the bar were louder than usual and buzzed with an almost manic energy.

Elizabeth paced up and down in Adam's living room.

"We need to banish again. They're back. The whole building is crawling with them. It's even worse than last time. Horrible faces peering around corners, bat wings disappearing through doors, claws scrabbling on the walls and the whole club smells like smoke off a funeral pyre."

"Shit. I hadn't noticed. We'll do it as soon as the club closes."

12

Adam

One evening as Adam was prowling through the club, nursing a whiskey on the rocks and chatting up the customers, Leo Battaglia waved him over to his table.

"Come sit with me a minute," he said. "I have a business proposition for you."

Leo had been a regular for nearly a year and seemed to know all the movers and shakers of Portland, especially the ones who patronized the club and restaurant. And so, of course, Adam had researched him thoroughly. He owned a meat packing plant in North Portland and had a wife and the customary two kids. No criminal background. Not even a parking ticket. He was a practicing Catholic and a faithful member of Saint Michael the Archangel Parish. He and Elizabeth had liked him immediately—

Mediterranean handsome, with a hawk nose, warm smile, and an aura of quiet power.

"What's up?" Adam sat down at the small table.

Leo got right to the point.

"Your business is quite prosperous. But I'm concerned about it," he said, flicking a speck of dust off the silk sleeve of his classic black silk suit. His eyes met Adam's, and they were no longer friendly. They were the cold, mesmerizing eyes of a snake. "So many things could go wrong. What if the police were to somehow get the wrong idea about what was happening behind these beautiful glass doors? And what if your liquor shipments were delayed for several days? And your employees. They're quite vulnerable, you know. In exchange for a few favors, we could protect your business. Keep it safe."

The moment felt totally surreal. Like they were actors in a scene right out of *The Godfather*. Unfortunately, the moment passed and reality came crashing in. This wasn't a movie. He was, indeed, staring into the cold, remorseless eyes of a Mob crime boss.

And then, to Adam's horror, Leo's body shifted and was overlaid by the dense, impossibly black shadow of a demon in human form. His eyes glittered cold, gold, and reptilian in his cruel, handsome face. Ram's horns curled back from a high ebony-black forehead and enormous bat wings spread out from his shoulders. The hand holding his drink had become a scaly black claw.

A thirty-something woman at the next table shivered as the demon's right wing enshrouded her. The man she was with touched her hand and spoke. She shrugged, smiled, and reached for her cocktail.

A cold, primal fear shot arrows of ice into Adam's gut and gripped his heart with vicious fingers. Shuddering, he pulled his aura in tight and small, hid his mage energy even deeper, and thanked the gods for his training at the Academy. Secrecy had been drilled into them No one must know of their talent. They had been taught to keep their shields close, tight, and unremarkable, and to bury the zingy sparkle of light that ricocheted through their auras and marked them as mages as deep inside themselves as they could. Even then, most other mages could usually spot it, but no one else. He hoped demons couldn't either. Because if either Leo or his demon even suspected that he was a mage, their single advantage would be lost. He forced his face into what he hoped was a suitable expression for a business owner faced with paying protection money to a relentless predator and glared at Leo, carefully ignoring the demon that was towering over them and grinning with an evil hunger.

Waves of cruel power surged off him and pounded brutally against Adam's shields.

But no one seemed to notice.

The disco ball showered the crowded room with bright droplets of light, the sound system blasted out "The Hustle," the packed dance floor writhed with bodies, and the couple at a nearby table held hands and stared into each other's eyes.

"I'll discuss your offer with my partner."

"Don't discuss it too long," Leo dropped his card on the table and left.

—

That very evening, someone threw a brick at the club's glass entry door. Fortunately, it was safety glass and didn't shatter, but it was totally ruined. Tom Baxter, Portland's Chief of Police, had just walked in. Instead of taking charge of the scene and calling in the police, he looked at Adam sadly, turned on his heel, and walked back out.

Adam stared after him in disbelief, which quickly turned to fear and fury. The Mob had the head of Portland's police force tucked safely away in its pinstriped pocket.

13

Elizabeth

lizabeth stared out her living room window, but she didn't see the glittering lights of the city spread out below her and she ignored Adam's frenzied pacing. She was seeing black sedans bristling with blazing machine guns, mowing down men and turning store windows into bursts of crystal shards. Bloated dead bodies, feet embedded in concrete, floating over cold, dark river bottoms. Severed horse heads, eyes white with fear, nesting on bloody bed sheets.

And Portland's Mob, or at least one of its bosses, was possessed by demons.

She couldn't imagine a more awful combination.

Demons and the Mob would make ghastly good partners. They both have the same modus operandi: Gain control of your victim by offering them something they really want or making them an offer they couldn't or wouldn't dare refuse, and once they're in your clutches, never let go.

Unfortunately, demons are even wilier and crueler and more experienced at this game than the Mob. She had no doubt that the demons were now in complete control.

Leo's demon and the one they'd exorcised from Nova were extremely powerful.

At least now they knew who had been bringing all the demons into the building.

Pulling her mind back into the awful present, she said, "If we accept Leo's offer, we might still continue to own Lovejoy Place, but it would be run by the demons. All our guests and renters and everyone who worked for us would be at risk of possession or blackmail or both. And since some of Portland's most powerful and influential citizens come here, Lovejoy Place would become a demon-controlled Mob gateway into Portland's wealth and power. The city government and some of Portland's biggest businesses would become its puppets."

"And, besides, Lovejoy Place is ours!" Adam said, throwing himself into the chair opposite her. "We worked hard to turn it into a prosperous business that's good for the community, its staff, and of course, us."

"But if we refuse the bastard's offer, the Mob will just run us out of business and then quietly take it over. And the Police won't raise a finger to stop them. Either way, the demons win and Portland is doomed," Elizabeth replied.

Adam slammed his fist into the arm of his chair. "We can't let this happen.

"This isn't Sicily or even New York City. This is Portland.

"And we can handle the demons and the Mob. We're adept mages!"

After discussing it from yin to yang and back again, they decided they wanted to fight. They were sure they could win, even without the police.

Adam called Leo and refused his offer.

They cast a circle and wove a binding spell around Leo and the demon that would keep them from doing anything to harm the business or anyone or anything even remotely associated with it. It was a masterpiece. Strong and bright and beautiful. As long as they kept renewing the binding, they would be safe.

14

Adam

The next afternoon Tara Dansk, the new waitress, didn't show up for work.

Adam remembered Leo's veiled threat: "And your employees. They're quite vulnerable, you know."

Impossible! She was just late.

He checked the binding spell and it was gone completely. Not a shred of their work remained. Elizabeth couldn't find it either.

Adam drove to Tara's apartment building, heart racing. He ran like a madman up the steps to the third floor, and pounded on her door, which swung open. The horrible stench of blood, shit, and demon smacked into him. He almost puked on the living room carpet, which was off-white and pristine clean—except for a trail of bloody men's shoe prints leading to the door. An awful stillness gripped the apartment, making him search desperately for a sound, any sound. And there it was—deep in the background—an almost inaudible hum. Adam stared at the footprints and listened to that mysterious hum for a long time, paralyzed with fear and rage.

Tara might be in there, alive and suffering and needing help. But there was no way he was going to walk into an apartment that reeked of death and demon to check. For all Adam knew, the demon and its human might still be here. He closed the door, stood outside, and let his senses follow the footprints through the empty living room and into a hallway. The bedroom door stood open at one end of it. He followed the tracks into it, looked around and snapped back into his body with a jolt. He fell to his knees, nearly fainting with horror. Sobbing and dry-heaving, Adam prayed that no one would come up to the third floor.

Tara was definitely dead. Her brilliant red curls were fanned out on the pillow, and her vivid green eyes stared up out of a mask of pure terror. Her black lace camisole had been ripped off and thrown on the floor. Her naked body was covered with cuts and claw marks and lay in a pool of congealed blood. Her belly had been ripped open, and her intestines pulled out and draped over the bed post, the chair, the dresser, the open bedroom door, and onto the nightstand. Anyone walking into that awful room would have had to duck under a loop of them.

Her heart, which had been cut out of her chest, lay in her empty belly. She had been dead for a while, because she was covered by a seething, buzzing mass of flies.

Adam's mind spun in helpless circles, trying to come to grips with the unspeakably cruel, senseless brutality of the killing.

And it was his fault.

If he'd let that monster blackmail them and take over Lovejoy Place, Tara would still be alive.

There was one last thing he could do for Tara.

He pulled himself together, ran downstairs, and found a phone booth. Using one of his stash of quarters, he called 911 and reported a murder.

A few minutes later, Ted Baxter, Portland's Chief of Police, pulled up to the apartment building in an unmarked car and told Adam to leave. He would handle it from here.

"'Don't you want to know what happened?"

"I know what happened. You were stupid, and an innocent woman got killed."

—

Adam sat in his BMW, speechless with horror and fury. This was an evil so dark and cruel that it was incomprehensible. If it wasn't stopped, it would crawl like a malignant cancer through the city.

No one would be safe.

There was no way he was gonna let those monsters have Lovejoy Place.

Although he was truly concerned about Portland's future, horrified by the savagery of the murder, and grief-stricken that Tara had died such an awful death, Adam was well aware that his primary motivations were less altruistic and much more personal.

How dare they threaten him?

How dare they try to take over Lovejoy Place?

And he was furious that their binding spell had been swept aside like a spiderweb, and that he'd been helpless to protect Tara against a demon-ridden Mob and a crooked police chief.

He wanted revenge, pure and simple.

15

Elizabeth

hen Adam came back from Tara's place, he was livid. Elizabeth had never seen him in such a rabid state, and she didn't ever want to again. He was barely able to spit out the words to tell her what had happened.

"I want that monster dead and every fucking one of the Mob demons banished back to the Abyss," he snarled.

Elizabeth sat in stunned silence as she grieved for the young waitress and felt her own world come apart. An evil had been unleashed on the city she had come to love, and the life they had worked so hard to build for themselves was going to be its next victim. She cherished that life and Adam was precious to her. She wasn't willing to give either of them up without a fight. Anger filtered in slowly but powerfully, replacing her grief and fear, and a plan began to take shape.

The man she had just decided to risk her soul for was sitting in brooding silence, waiting for her to process his terrible news.

"Adam, we can't kill Leo, no matter how much he deserves it. It's wrong."

He sighed and nodded.

"But we can get rid of the Mob's demons," she continued.

"And more will just take the place of the ones we get rid of."

"Not if we put another binding on Leo. Once his demon is gone it will stick."

"So how do we get rid of a demon so powerful that it can rip anything we throw at it to shreds?"

"We call up an even more powerful demon, a Prince of the Abyss, and command him to clear out all the demons connected to the Portland Mob and then banish him back to the Abyss."

She had Adam's interest, but he was shaking his head.

"We can't even control Leo's demon, how can we hope to control an even stronger one?"

"Think, Adam. We studied this at the Academy. We can control this demon because we'll know his name—remember, there is great power in a name. And since we'll know this demon's name, we can create his sigil, a physical representation of him. Possession of a demon's name and sigil tips the scales in our favor, no matter how powerful the demon is."

"I haven't given demons a single thought since high school. How come you know so much about them?"

"Because I'm an anthropologist. The cultures I worked with understood demons and how to protect themselves from them. I spent a lot of time studying them."

"Ah. I see. And have you decided which Prince of the Abyss we're going to call up?"

"I'll research it. We need to do this tonight."

They collected everything they needed, strengthened the circle around the building, and wove a soundproofing spell around Elizabeth's living room. They pulled the area rugs off the hardwood floors, and drew a nine-foot-diameter pentagram with the appropriate names of power written in the double circle around it, forming a pentacle. Three feet away from the pentacle's north side they chalked in a triangle, and inside the triangle they inscribed the sigil of Nysrogh, the demon Elizabeth had decided to call. They placed a white candle at each point of the pentagram and triangle and one between the triangle and the pentacle, lit the asafoetida incense, and were good to go.

At the stroke of midnight, they lit all the candles—except for the one between the triangle and pentacle—stepped inside the pentacle, being careful not to smudge any of the lines, and performed Middle Pillar, followed by the Lesser Banishing ritual. They each magically traced over every line and name of power, invoked the entities named on the rim of the pentacle, and asked for their guidance and protection. They wove a sphere of protection around the perimeter of the pentacle and set impenetrable boundaries around the triangle. The room hummed with power.

The pentagram and triangle glowed purple white and the candles blazed golden.

Everything was ready. Once they started there would be to turning back. Either they would succeed, or their souls would be bound to a demon for eternity. Elizabeth's palms sweated and her heart raced. She was glad she'd gone to the bathroom just before they started.

Because it had been her idea to summon the demon, Elizabeth stood in the center of the pentacle and intoned the invocation.

Nysrogh immediately began materializing in the triangle. Elizabeth watched in awe as the Prince of the Abyss gradually took shape and then snapped into focus. He stood well over seven feet tall, slender but heavily muscled with a black, feathered raven's head; a black, scaly human body; hands that ended in claws; and raven's feet.

Even from behind the strong boundaries of the triangle, he bristled with a wickedly potent magic that filled her with true, unadulterated panic. It raised the hairs on the back of her neck and turned her bones to water. It was all she could do to keep from screaming and running out of the circle and away from that dreadful presence.

And all he'd done was stand there.

His flat, round eyes blazed golden, and his feathers gleamed with an evil green-black sheen. He spoke directly into Elizabeth's mind in a soft, mesmerizing voice that vibrated with force.

"I have come. And as you can see, I am more powerful than you ever imagined. I can easily break through this flimsy wall." He flicked one raven-clawed finger, and the triangle shook like jelly.

Elizabeth's whole body shook with it. "And it will be the work of moments to destroy that useless circle. After I kill you both—slowly and painfully—and devour your souls, I will be free to enjoy the pleasures of your world."

Adam gasped.

One quick glance at her partner told her he was about to lose it. She pinched him on the arm as hard as she could.

"Ow," he muttered. But the pain seemed to cut through his terror. The panic left his face and it settled into his rock-hard, expressionless mask.

"But I am willing to make a deal with you," the demon continued, relishing their terror. "I will spare your worthless lives and your worthless souls. But only if you set me free."

He was so powerful and Elizabeth was so terrified that she actually considered telling him that he had a deal. He would spare them, because demons are bound to keep their promises. Unfortunately, if he were free, he was powerful enough to destroy their world, and their lives would truly be worthless then. If they refused his offer, tried to contain him, and he escaped, he would certainly kill them and devour their souls. And he would be free anyway. She could feel the demon's power reaching into her mind, convincing her that she was weak and helpless, and that accepting his bargain was the most sensible thing to do.

It was so tempting.

She shuddered and slapped him away.

"Not a chance, Bird Breath," she snarled, "We have work for you."

The Prince of the Abyss opened his cruel hooked beak and shrieked out curses and demonic names of power that pounded into her soul like psychic sledgehammers. But fear had made her desperate and sent her into a sort of magical overdrive. She signaled to Adam, and in seconds they wove a strengthening spell around the triangle. The demon clawed viciously at his prison, which immediately began unraveling. They pumped it full of electric-violet light and called on Archangel Michael to mend and strengthen it. Nysrogh scraped his raven-clawed feet over the sigil, trying to erase it. But the sigil held firm. He battered at the walls of his prison, but they kept up a steady flow of light, keeping the walls strong and intact. This went on for what seemed like forever, but they were able to contain him, and eventually he settled down.

"Why have you summoned me?" he screamed. His anger and hatred tore at Elizabeth's heart. But Adam placed his palm on the small of her back, and his love rushed into her, fierce and bright. It gave her strength.

"By the power of the Divine One and all those named within this circle," to her relief, her voice vibrated with power, and the demon actually flinched, "I command you to clear Lovejoy Place and the Portland Mob of all demons. Kill them or banish them to the Abyss, never to return to Portland or to the bodies they possessed. You will do this and only this. You may not harm any earthly beings. Indicate that you have completed your task by extinguishing that candle." She pointed to the small candle between the triangle and pentacle, and a golden flame blossomed from its wick. "You must complete your task before that candle burns down. After extinguishing the candle, I command you to return to the Abyss and leave us and all of Portland for eternity. Is that clear?'"

"Yes. Your wish is my command," said the demon, and disappeared.

The evil, pounding terror vanished, leaving the room in peace. The pentacle thrummed with a barely audible hum and blazed with golden candlelight.

Elizabeth sagged with relief and total exhaustion.

They powered down the pentacle, released the names of power, extinguished the candles around it, but left it ready to recharge at a moment's notice. The triangle remained fully charged with all its candles burning.

16

Elizabeth

The next morning there wasn't a single demon in Lovejoy Place.

But Nysrogh's candle was still flickering cheerfully. He should have finished by now.

They powered up the pentagram and summoned him, but the triangle with its glowing sigil remained empty. Fear tap danced up Elizabeth's spine and shook her entire body. They'd lost control of a powerful demon, who was now, most likely, turning Portland into a madhouse.

As they were panicking and trying to figure out what to do, the desk called down from The Dolphins. Rachel Stevens hadn't shown up to help with the opening. Alarm bells went off in Elizabeth's head. Rachel had never missed a day of work, and she lived at Lovejoy Place, so it was unlikely that she was just late. She raced downstairs to Rachel's apartment and pounded on the door. There was no answer. Ignoring their tenants' right to privacy agreement, she projected her senses into the living room. It reverberated with violence and reeked of smoke and burnt feathers. The mid-morning sun beamed through the floor-to-ceiling window, highlighting Rachel's once sweet face. Her eyes were wide with horror and her mouth open in a silent scream. She was sprawled on the couch, her long, black hair cascading over orange, red, and green pillows, her arms and legs twisted into impossible positions. Her chest looked like something had exploded out of it. Blood was everywhere. Sliding away from the horror that had been one of her favorite employees, Elizabeth's eyes fixed on a modern art print above the couch. It was difficult to tell where the bright, primary colors of the image stopped and the gleaming spatter of blood began.

A hand touched her shoulder and she snapped back into her body, heart pounding and biting back a scream.

"Oops. Sorry. Didn't mean to scare you. Are you okay?" It was Casey Thom, Rachel's across-the-hall neighbor. Concern clouded his dark, handsome features. She took a shuddering breath and hid her face in her hands, desperately trying to rearrange it into a calm, neutral expression and figure out what she was going to tell him.

"I'm okay, you just startled me. I'm worried about Rachel," Elizabeth finally said. "She didn't show up for work this morning, and it's not like her."

"I haven't seen her today," Casey said, running a hand over his perfect Afro. "But I haven't been awake very long. She'll turn up.

Don't worry." He patted her shoulder and continued down the carpeted hall toward the stairway, flip-flops flapping in a calm, comforting rhythm.

But Rachel wasn't going to turn up on this plane ever again.

And Elizabeth was desperately worried.

Nysrogh had been in that room. And since she'd told him to remove all the demons from Lovejoy Place, Rachel had probably been possessed by a demon. And Nysrogh had killed her when he got rid of it. Actually, since Elizabeth had summoned him, she had killed Rachel—as surely as if she'd slipped a knife into her heart.

And what had happened to her soul?

And if Nysrogh had done this to Rachel, he had probably left a trail of gory Mob corpses all through Portland.

But were there other tenants or staff who had been possessed?

Elizabeth went through the club and restaurant, knocked on apartment doors and made several phone calls. They were all alive. Rachel had been the only one.

17

Adam

When Elizabeth told Adam what had happened, all they could do was sit and stare at each other in speechless horror. Two innocent women and who knows how many Mob members had died brutal, cruel deaths and there was a second-order demon rampaging through the city.

They had screwed up royally and it was time to ask for help.

Actually, it was past time to ask for help.

Adam finally managed to convince Elizabeth that they should start by calling Estelle.

"I'm coming over. Don't do anything till I get there," Estelle said.

The brilliant adept had definite opinions about how everyone should run their lives, and wasn't shy about sharing them—*ad nauseam.* Especially when it came to Elizabeth and him. But, to her credit, after they asked for her help, she offered no words of criticism.

She arrived, clutching her copy of the Librarian.

"'We need to call in the Webmasters. Fixing this requires more knowledge and skill than the three of us possess," she said, dropping the weighty, dragon-scaled tome on Elizabeth's dining-room table. It ruffled its tissue-thin pages and snorted with indignation.

The Librarian was actually a mighty dragon whose treasure trove had been the ancient Library of Alexandria. When the mages had decided, with a nudge from the Librarian, to take most of the library, spread it out into the world, and become the Mage Web, it had divided a small part of itself into many huge black books that listed all the works available to mages. All a mage had to do was touch the entry they wanted to read and the Librarian would teleport it to them from the library of the mage who owned it. It could also teleport mages, and had its scaly, ethereal claws deep in every aspect of the Mage Web.

Adam sighed in resignation as the Librarian's potent presence dominated the room. It was like getting a surprise visit from a well-meaning but overbearing parent. After a quick discussion, they agreed that Estelle was right. Unfortunately, calling in the Webmasters meant giving up any control over what would happen to Lovejoy Place. That was the rule. If you called in the Webmasters to solve a problem, you had to step aside and let them solve it.

And that was the main reason he and Elizabeth hadn't called them in much earlier. But now they had no choice.

"Done," said the Librarian after a moment's pause, and then asked for permission to explore the rest of the building, which they gave. If it was going to help, it needed all the information it could get. And they were concerned for everyone's safety and past caring about their privacy.

A few minutes later the Librarian jumped a tiny, ancient Arab—the third of four Webmasters—into Elizabeth's living room. He bowed solemnly and said, in only slightly accented English, "Ramses Abboud, at your service." He was a legend in the Web, and they all just stood there and stared at him in awe.

Estelle was the first to recover, and she introduced them.

"A pleasure to meet you although I wish it were under different circumstances," he replied, and began asking questions and examining the pentacle and triangle on the floor.

He consulted with the Librarian, sat down in a living room chair, and thought for a minute or two. The three young mages fidgeted and waited. Finally, he looked up at them in surprise and said, "Please be seated—no need to stand," and waited for them to find chairs.

"Unfortunately, there is no way that we can save Lovejoy Place," he said. "All we can do is keep it out of the hands of the Syndicate, cover your traces so you are safe from its retribution, and send the demon back to the Abyss."

He told them what he was going to do, and because he was a Webmaster and Adam and Elizabeth were Web members who had invoked his help, they had to agree.

But the Third was right, it was the only solution.

18

Adam

A few minutes later, Thomas Nicodemus and Antonio Cortese, the Web's two most talented alchemists, appeared in Elizabeth's dining room. They were an unlikely pair. Nicodemus had been Adam's Advanced Spell Casting instructor at the Academy, and he remembered him fondly. He was tall, thin, and solemn with long, black hair that was already streaked with white. His simple black robe was full of singe marks that were still smoking, and he smelled like a chemistry experiment gone horribly wrong. Alchemy is not for the faint of heart. Cortese was short, portly, and looked like a jovial Santa Claus dressed in gaudy silk pajamas and Persian slippers with curled-up toes.

They'd obviously interrupted both of them.

Ramses greeted the two alchemists, apologized for disturbing their day and said, "I need smoke gushing through this building in maybe two hours. When we've had time to get everyone out, I want it to burst into flames and to be totally destroyed by the time the fire department gets here. Please make sure the body in apartment five is completely incinerated." He asked Adam to take the alchemists over to his apartment so they could begin figuring out how to accomplish this.

Nicodemus and Cortese were grinning and vibrating with excitement, like two kids with firecrackers on the Fourth of July. But Nicodemus patted Adam on the shoulder and said, "I am so sorry that you will be losing your home and your business. Please understand, our enthusiasm is not because we wish you harm; it is because this is a challenging project that will end with marvelous flames and explosions, and a spectacular disintegration into nigredo."

All Adam could do was nod and get them the architect's drawings of the building's remodel. He left them to it, gleefully submerged in a dining-room-table-full of blueprints and arguing amiably with the Librarian over the best way to destroy their beautiful child, the thing he and Elizabeth had worked so hard to create over the last two years.

Bitter with grief and resentment, he headed down to collect yesterday's take, the petty cash, and a few crucial ledgers. When he reached their office, he locked the door, sat behind the desk, and stared out the window at the small parking lot behind the building. Elizabeth had talked him into sacrificing parking spaces for landscaping, and he'd never regretted it. A full-sized birch tree stood in its center, and rhododendrons, azaleas, and other flowering shrubs softened its perimeter. Last fall Elizabeth had planted hundreds of daffodils, tulips, and snow drops. They'd started blooming in February, when everyone was weary of the gray Portland winter and hungry for color, and had continued through April. Right now, purple, blue, and white hydrangeas glowed in the shade. The familiar morning sounds of the club filtered in through the locked door: the drone of a vacuum cleaner, the clink of glassware being unloaded from dishwashers and put away, quick footsteps, and quiet, busy voices. Neither The Dolphins nor the club were open in the mornings, so the staff used the time to prepare for the rest of the day.

In a few short hours this vibrant, beautiful place, their pride and joy, would be nothing but smoking ashes. He stole a few minutes to begin the grieving process that would continue for the rest of his life. He wept mostly for Lovejoy Place. Fortunately, his mind hadn't fully registered the loss of Tara and Rachel and all the other lives that Nysrogh had taken. If it had, he would have been a wreck.

But time was short.

Adam began collecting the ledgers and paperwork they'd need to pay off the staff and transfer the ownership of their property to a management firm that was secretly owned by the Web and run by one of its mages. He pulled yesterday's take out of the safe and crammed everything into a briefcase. Dragging his desk chair to one side, he rolled back the carpet, opened the trapdoor, and headed down the steps to the large underground safe that held the cash he earned from selling pot. He stuffed another briefcase with it. But there was still quite a bit left—enough to fill a grocery bag. And he'd saved out most of the large-denomination bills. The Web didn't need all this money, but Estelle and the kid would.

Holding a picture of Estelle's office and library firmly in his mind, Adam reached for a spot beside her desk and jumped. He set the bag on the desk and jumped back, climbed up the steps, closed the trapdoor, and replaced the rug and desk chair. He set the books for the pot business on the desk. If everything went according to plan, they would soon be nothing but ashes.

He stole a bit more time to rest from the jump and brace himself to face the rest of the day. Then, locking the door behind him, he headed back through the club with the briefcases to check on the alchemists. He tried to act like it was just a normal morning, answering questions that would soon be irrelevant.

19

Elizabeth

A burst of power exploded beside Elizabeth. Terrified, she whipped around and spotted the source of that power—a tiny young woman that the Librarian had jumped into her living room. Her dark brown, almond eyes took Elizabeth apart and put her back together in one swift glance.

"Hi," she said. "You are having problems with demons? I am here to help. My name is Ashara." Her lilting, musical accent, jet-black hair, and mocha skin suggested that she was from India. But Elizabeth had never met an Indian woman like this. She was stocky and muscular, like a wrestler. Her hair was cropped short and shaggy, and a small, gold safety pin pierced the right nostril of her delicate nose. She was dressed in a black tank top, black leather mini-skirt, black tights covered with sparkling silver spider webs, and a pair of black Doc Martens. Her well-toned biceps were tattooed with pentacles that glowed with electric-violet light, and a mesmerizingly intricate, black design formed of words written in the Devanagari, Arabic, and Roman alphabets writhed up her hands and forearms. Today, she could have walked the streets of Portland and attracted only a bit of attention. Back then, she was a bizarre and awesome spectacle.

"Ashara is one of the three demonologists in the Web," Ramses said.

Elizabeth quit staring and remembered her manners just in time to shake the young mage's hand and introduce herself. The adept's strong grip sent jolts of energy up her arm.

"Tell me about this demon and why it is here," she said, releasing Elizabeth's tingling hand. Elizabeth explained everything and showed her the pentacle, the triangle, and Nysrogh's sigil, which the demonologist examined carefully.

"This is well executed. It would have worked, except you ordered him to banish or kill the Mob's demons. With each demon he vanquished, Nysrogh gained power. And he would also have fed on the life force of each human that died as a result of a demon being ripped out of them. Technically, he didn't kill any humans—the demons he pulled out killed them. So, technically he obeyed your instructions. Demons thrive on technicalities. After just a few murders, he became so powerful that you could no longer control him. Nysrogh has been dealing with humans for millennia and has become quite adept at outwitting them. You didn't have a chance."

She closed her eyes for a moment, and when she opened them her face was grim. "He is stalking through your city wreaking havoc. We must get him confined in that triangle at once."

At that point, Tamerlane appeared beside Estelle. He smelled like the Wildwood in Damia and that gods-awful tobacco he smoked in his pipe. And looked like the quintessential mage—long black robe, hawk-like features, tall and lanky, with long black hair and beard. Elizabeth breathed a sigh of relief. She knew nothing about Ashara, but Tamerlane was hands down the most powerful adept in the Web. With him in the circle, they had a fighting chance.

As the demonologist recharged the lines and lettering in both the pentacle and the triangle, adding a few squiggles of her own here and there, they gave Tamerlane a quick version of what was happening and what needed doing.

Adam returned just as the demonologist had finished her work, and Elizabeth introduced him to her.

Gathering the adepts around her, Ashara said, "We will not try to kill this demon. It will be difficult enough just to send him back to the Abyss. There are six of us, one for each section of the pentacle with me in the center. Arrange yourselves so that you have a direct line of fire to the triangle. You will need to focus not only on maintaining the integrity of the triangle, but you must also blast Nysrogh with electric-violet light and the command to return to the Abyss and never return to this place. Since Elizabeth invoked him, she is the one who must call him back into the triangle, but once he is here, I will utter the names of power and the commands and you will back me up. This will be difficult and may take some time, so take turns. One of you rest while the others work. This is not a contest. Stop as soon as you are tired and let the others take your place. I will work continuously."

The adepts entered the pentagram, carefully stepping over all the glowing lines and names of power. When they were all in place, they wove a breathtakingly beautiful soundproofing spell around the room and extra protection around the triangle and pentacle. Elizabeth's living room hummed and sparkled with mind-numbingly complex light spells, and she felt the comforting weight and power of the angels, djinn, taras, and bodhisattvas, dancing and swirling over the names of power and around the pentacle. Marvelous, amazing things happen when six talented adepts set their minds to a single task.

Ashara gestured to the sigil in the center of the triangle. A glowing cord slowly extended out of it, swaying sinuously, like a snake charmer's cobra. "This is our connection to Nysrogh. Energize it!"

Five bolts of brilliant white light hit the cord, and it shot through the walls and into the city.

"Elizabeth, summon the demon," Ashara said.

Her heart raced with fear. Everything depended on her being able to control, if only for a quick breath of time, a demon that she'd lost control of.

"'Nysrogh, I summon you into the triangle. Come at once!' She vibrated the command out into the multiverse and felt it latch onto him. The next moment, he exploded out of the triangle like it was made of tissue paper. He towered over them, immense and crackling with wicked power. His beak gaped open and, with a roar that nearly pounded her flat, the demon sank his claws into the dome of protection generated by the pentacle and began ripping it to shreds. The adepts desperately shot electric-violet light into the perimeter of the circle. Three djinn, who looked every bit as frightening as Nysrogh, absorbed the light, materialized, and slammed into the demon, knocking him away from the pentacle.

Ashara was amazing. Like an orchestra conductor, she directed the lethally powerful light forces they created to where they were needed. She pulled the glittering webs off her tights and threw them at the demon, who was now howling with pain and rage. The delicate, gossamer nets expanded, swirled gracefully around him, and clamped shut, binding him like a bug in a spiderweb.

"'Get him into the triangle," Ashara said, and the six mages, with lots of help from the djinn, managed to levitate the howling, struggling demon into the triangle, and poured electric-violet light into its borders. Two angels wove the light into a cage, and the adepts began flooding the triangle with electric-violet light and silently commanding Nysrogh to return to the Abyss. Ashara removed the net, which reattached itself to her tights, and severed the cord that bound the demon to the sigil. Nysrogh hissed and threw himself against the cage, which held firm. He grabbed and tugged at its glowing mesh walls. Arcs of electric-violet light zapped his hands, and he screamed with rage. "When I escape your puny defenses, I will skin you alive!"

"Nysrogh, begone. Back to the Abyss from whence you came, never to return to this place!" Ashara's voice echoed and shimmered through the room, like she was using a high-tech reverb microphone. It pounded the demon with its power. "I command you by the might of Archangel Michael!"

"I will slice you open and pull out your entrails," he howled, as Ashara continued calling out names of power. With each holy name, the walls of the triangle glowed stronger until Nysrogh was surrounded by a globe of electric-violet light so bright that Elizabeth had to close her eyes as she began taking turns throwing light and silent commands at the raging demon. This went on and on, until she was well past the point of exhaustion and running on pure adrenaline.

At last, Nysrogh let out one final, brain-shattering shriek.

"I will cut out your hearts and eat them!"

And he vanished in a puff of foul black smoke.

The silence that followed was profound and breathtaking, as if an enormous hand that had been pressing down on her had suddenly disappeared. Her light bodies snapped out to their full size, leaving her dizzy and disoriented. Everyone collapsed, gasping with relief, except for Ashara, who leaped over to the triangle, whipped a cloth that sparkled with magic from a pocket, and completely erased it. But there was no way she could erase the raven's-foot scorch marks in its center. She thanked and bid farewell to all the angels, jinn, taras, and bodhisattvas who had, essentially, saved their butts; powered down the circle; erased the names of power; and finally, erased the pentacle itself.

"My work is done," she said. "I doubt that he will ever return, but call me if he does."

And she vanished without giving them a chance to thank her.

"This has been fascinating," Tamerlane said, picking himself up off the floor, "but I'm heading home for a nap."

And he vanished as well.

Elizabeth sat on the floor with Adam, Estelle, and the Third and stared at her living room in awe. The couch and easy-chairs had been tossed around like so many pieces of confetti. Everything that was breakable was broken—even the windows. The faint whiff of smoke and feathers was a disturbing reminder of the horrible demon that they had banished. A glance at her watch told her that only half an hour had passed since Ashara had appeared.

In the midst of all the destruction, a Catholic priest appeared. He wore a full length, black cassock, a white collar, and a serene, angelically beautiful smile.

His aura sparkled with mage energy.

"Ah, Father Ventura, thank you for coming," said Ramses. "We are in need of your services. The body of Rachel Stevens lies in one of the apartments below. She was possessed by a demon and brutally killed by another demon. I am told that she was not a religious person, and normally we would respect her preferences, but due to the nature of her death, we are concerned for her soul. Please do what you can for her and prepare her body for cremation."

"You are right to be concerned. Rachel's soul is her most precious possession. Death stole everything else from her, but it couldn't steal that. Unfortunately, a demon may have accomplished what Death couldn't. I will do everything in my power to make sure that she passes safely on. When I am finished, I will return and let you know what I found. Librarian, please take me to Rachel's body."

20

Adam

Adam headed for his apartment to see if the alchemists were ready. He arrived just as Nicodemus materialized beside the dining-room table.

"Ah, you're back," the alchemist said. "We've been placing the explosives and flammables. The Librarian has been unobtrusively jumping us to various nooks and crannies in the building, and I just set the last one. It also informed us that the demon has been banished."

He walked with Adam back to Elizabeth's apartment and stared in astonishment at the chaos. Apparently, the sound-proofing spell had worked. Estelle, and Elizabeth, looking haggard and exhausted, were helping Ramses, who was shaking and gray with fatigue, into the only upright chair in the room.

"Everything is ready," said Cortese. "Let us know when you want the smoke, and after everyone is out of the building, we will detonate the explosives."

"Father Ventura is helping Rachel transition," Ramses said. "We need to wait for him."

Adam and Elizabeth took advantage of the time to scoop up their important papers and a few small keepsakes and valuables. By the time they'd finished, the priest was back.

"I found Rachel's spirit sitting on the couch beside her body, terrified and confused," he said. "I gave her what comfort I could, called Archangel Azrael to guide her on her way, and committed her body to the flame. I will say a Mass for her soul. Is there anything more that you require?"

"Thank you, Father. You have eased all our hearts. Rachel's soul is safe. That is more than enough."

"Then I will be on my way. Blessings to you all."

And he disappeared.

"Start the smoke," said Ramses.

Cortese snapped his fingers.

"Done," he said.

Adam and Elizabeth went through the apartments, telling everyone that the building was on fire and they needed to leave quickly. Then Elizabeth went up and cleared the restaurant and Adam went down and cleared the club. The fire alarms and black, sooty smoke pouring out of the air vents convinced everyone to hurry. Estelle, Ramses, and the alchemists jumped to an alley across the street and made themselves inconspicuous. Adam and

Elizabeth stayed with their employees, counting heads and trying to keep them calm.

After the Librarian had made one final sweep through all the rooms and declared Lovejoy Place well-and-truly empty, Nicodemus and Cortese began lighting the flammables. Jets of flame erupted from the first-floor windows and, seconds later, from the third floor windows. Soon the building was an inferno, and no one noticed when three explosions imploded the building, dropping it in a blazing heap safely within the property lines.

Lovejoy Place died a spectacular, quick death. As they watched their beautiful building burst into flames and collapse, the horrors of the day came crowding in. Adam was so caught up in his own grief that he almost missed catching Elizabeth as she collapsed in exhaustion. He held her tight against him as she wept bitter tears on the shoulder of his smoke-smudged-thousand-dollar linen suit.

But there were no words of comfort he could offer her.

When the fire trucks finally arrived, there was nothing left but a pile of smoldering rubble. Everyone wondered what took them so long until Police Chief Baxter appeared. His clothes were rumpled and filthy. He was moving like a zombie and looked like a man who had been dragged through the Abyss.

"The city has gone insane," he said, staring bleakly at the smoking remains. "It all started around one a.m., when Leo Battaglia's wife called me in hysterics. Says Leo woke up screaming and then his chest exploded. After that, the shit hit the fan. There have been eight bar fights that have resulted in nine fatalities, five fatal car crashes, three reported rapes, and I can't remember how many muggings. And this is just in the downtown area. A car went off the Fremont Bridge. How, in the name of all that's holy, could someone drive off the Fremont Bridge? There are rumors of a huge bird demon stalking the streets. And now this. I'm sorry the fire department didn't get here in time to save the club, they've been busy. The last report I got, they've already put out six fires." Without waiting for a reply, he walked back to his car and drove away.

Adam stared after him, paralyzed with shock. So much death and destruction.

And they were to ones who had called it down.

Elizabeth clung to him. The pain in her eyes was unbearable to see. He smoothed back her hair and, using his thumbs, gently wiped away the tears that were streaming down her cheeks.

"Blast! I can't do anything right," he said. "My hands are covered with soot and now you look like a raccoon. Here." He handed her his pocket handkerchief and turned to all the people they had worked with so closely over the past few years and said, "Lovejoy Place is permanently closed, out of business, and will not reopen. You will all receive two months' severance pay. Those of you who have lost your homes will be reimbursed, and your first and last months' rent will be returned. Our accountants will be in touch."

He took Elizabeth's arm and they walked away from the disaster they had made of their lives.

21

Adam

 few days later, Adam and Elizabeth stood in front of the four Webmasters and awaited their sentence. Estelle, Tamerlane, Thomas Nicodemus, and Father Ventura were there as witnesses. They had gathered in the First's home in Sicily. The Webmasters sat with their backs to a wall of windows. The view out those windows was spectacular—gardens filled with bright flowers and dark cypress and pine trees overlooked the sparkling Mediterranean Sea. Adam feasted his eyes on that beauty because he was too ashamed to look at anyone in the room. Four decades later, he would still remember exactly how many cypress trees were in that garden and the colors and shapes of all the flowers. They'd saved his sanity.

Ramses Abboud regarded them with a look of deep, abiding sadness.

"Adam Carnegie Morgan and Elizabeth Katherine Stanhope, your decisions and actions have led to the loss of thirty-two innocent lives, unknowable amounts of pain and misery, and millions of dollars' worth of property damage. We understand that this was not your intent, but, unfortunately, that does not absolve you. You have acquired a great karmic debt, and the sooner you begin working it off the better. You are also in debt to the Web. Your assets didn't begin to cover the time and money we spent to make things as right as possible. You will spend the rest of your lives in service to the Web. This will repay your monetary debt and, we hope, begin to cover your karmic debt.

"Elizabeth Katherine Stanhope," the Third continued, "you are beginning a new life and have been advised to take a new name. Please state your name."

"Andromeda," she replied.

"Andromeda, you will become Hell's new warden."

All four Webmasters held their hands, palms out, at chest level. Power flowed, and Adam's love, his life, and his partner disappeared from his side.

He stifled a scream and focused on a cypress tree.

The Third turned to him. "Adam Carnegie Morgan, you are beginning a new life and have been advised to take a new name. Please state your name."

"Asmodius, but with an 'i.'"

He had the small satisfaction of hearing several quickly stifled gasps.

"Asmodius, you will become our agent in Damia. And to make certain you stay out of trouble, we will turn you into a cat."

In perfect unison, the Webmasters' hands traced an intricate pattern in the air, then stopped, palms facing forward.

Power flowed.

And Asmodius was a black cat lying on an easy-chair in Tamerlane's house, in the midst of the Wildwood, in Damia.

PART II

Hell
— 2014 —

22

Molly

"Stop pacing, you're driving me crazy!" said Molly Adair.

"If I stop, I will bite something," Diana Andrusko replied. Her sapphire eyes glinted dangerously. "How much longer until moonrise?"

Adam Aubrey shoved his black-framed glasses back up the bridge of his prominent nose and tapped a key on his laptop. "Four hours and fourteen minutes. And since we're just past spring equinox, you will have almost exactly twelve hours until sunrise. The nights are getting shorter and shorter." His long fingers danced over the keys. "It looks like it'll be clear. The moon should be beautiful."

The three friends were hanging out in Molly's back yard. The warm afternoon sun highlighted a magnificent view of downtown

Portland and poured onto the lawn. The oak tree in the south-west corner of the yard was still bare, and the cherry tree in the southeast was thinking about blooming. It was spring break of their junior year at Grant High School, and they had just finished their spring three-month at Tesseract Academy, the Mage Web's training school. The Librarian had jumped them to the Academy on the second day of Portland Public Schools' spring break, and, after three months of Academy classes, had jumped them back to Portland on the third day of their break. Molly and Adam were enjoying having nothing much to do except relax in the sun.

Diana wasn't enjoying anything.

"The warmer nights are so delicious! They explode with smells. Layers and layers of them. My whole body sings! I wish the long nights were in the spring and summer and the short nights were in the winter." Diana's exotic, sharp featured face was tragic as she growled softly, stirring the hairs on the nape of Molly's neck.

"That's impossible because..." Adam began.

"We know it's impossible, she was just sayin'," Molly said, saving herself and Diana from a lecture on seasons and solstices and equinoxes. She watched her friend's frantic pacing until she could stand it no longer. "You figured out how to change without the moon last month. Why don't you let Adam drive you to Forest Park right now? You could hike into the woods, go into wolf mode, and have extra playtime before moonrise."

Diana froze and stared at Molly with wide, savage eyes and said, "Of course! The obvious solution. My brain has turned to mush." Then she was on Molly with a single, blindingly fast leap, hugging her like a boa constrictor. Molly stayed perfectly still, pushing down her panic and trying to relax. She gasped when Diana released her, filling her crushed lungs with much-needed air.

"Will you take me right now?" Diana asked Adam. Her voice was gentle, but her flashing eyes said, "I will bite you if you don't."

Adam's fingers continued to dance over the keyboard. Molly didn't know what he was tracking down this time, but she had no doubt that someone's precious secrets were making their way into his possession. Adam was an unrepentant hacker, hoarding information like a squirrel gathering nuts for the winter. He tapped one final key, clicked the laptop closed, and gazed up at Diana. Eyes that were so dark it was hard to see the pupils sparkled as he unfolded his lanky frame from the lawn chair. "Sure. Call your mom and let her know that I'm taking over wolf duty this month."

"Wait!" The back door burst open and Gram strode into the yard. Asmodius, black fur and amber eyes gleaming, glided along beside her. He gave every appearance of calmness and composure, but his violet-black aura seethed and flashed as he settled down next to Molly.

"I have news." The tiny adept wore a full-length, light-blue dress that swirled and shimmered with each quick, decisive movement. Her face had only a few delicate age lines, but they had suddenly deepened, and her wispy-gray curls snaked wildly out from her head, making her look like Medusa on a bad day.

Adam and Diana plunked obediently back down. No one argued with Molly's grandmother if they didn't have to.

"I just received a call from the Second," she said, collapsing into a lawn chair. "Ramses Abboud, the First Webmaster just transitioned. His secretary, Denzel, found him dead at his desk about a half-hour ago. They think it was his heart."

This was sad news, but nothing earth-shaking. The Webmasters, talented adepts with excellent diplomatic skills, were the Mage Web's guiding force. When one retired or died, the ones below them moved up and the new Fourth was chosen by the Web.

"I'm sorry, Gram. Was he a good friend?"

"I knew him for years, of course. Ramses was a good man and I will miss him, but he was also quite ancient—over 200 years old, I believe—and death eventually comes to us all. The thing that worries me is that he's not supposed to be dead yet."

"When *is* he supposed to be dead?" Adam asked, looking puzzled.

"He should have lived for another two years. We've done countless jumps into countless futures, and we were sure that the killings would begin in two years. And in every time-line, the murders begin with the Webmasters, and the First Webmaster was always the first mage to die."

Fear twisted the pit of Molly's stomach, and when her eyes met Adam's and Diana's, she saw that same fear.

"Something has happened recently that has tangled the strands of time, creating a new future for us," Gram continued. "In this new future, the murders have already begun and we no longer have two years to prepare a defense."

Was it possible that the nightmare that had haunted every mage's dreams and darkened their days with a shadow of dread was already happening? That someone or something was killing mages and wouldn't stop until they'd eradicated the entire Web? Adam and Diana had been mages and Web members since their freshman year, and their parents and their parents before them going back hundreds of years had been Web members. Molly's parents had been normals, and she'd only begun training as a warrior mage less than a year ago. But Esoteric World Civ and other classes that she'd taken at Tesseract Academy had convinced her that without the Web's stabilizing and protective influence, the world would be even more dangerous than it was—especially if that world was controlled by someone or something powerful enough and cruel enough to kill thousands of mages.

"But couldn't it be that he just died early?" Molly asked hopefully. "Maybe it has nothing to do with the murders."

"The First's heart was dicey, we all knew that, but it wasn't that bad. In every other respect, he was in excellent health," Gram said. "It's unlikely that he died of natural causes. But there are no signs of struggle, and Denzel says there's no psychic imprint of violent death in the study. The room was clean—almost too clean, actually. It is possible that an adept could have stopped his heart so it would show up as a heart attack in an autopsy and then wiped the room's energy field."

"But they could never have gotten in," said Adam. "Morgana gave us a few patterns in Advanced Shielding that were impossible to break, and she mentioned that the shields around the Webmasters' houses were even tougher."

"Just because a class of novice mages can't figure it out, doesn't mean that a shield pattern is unbreakable," Gram said with a sad smile. "There are a few adepts that are quite capable of getting in and out of the Webmasters' homes without leaving a trace. Morgana is one of them."

"I wish we could jump back in time and see what really happened, and save the First," said Molly.

"Yeah, but we can't," said Adam.

"I can't believe it was a Web member," Diana said. She was pacing again.

"Actually, a Web member is the most likely possibility," Gram replied, fists clenched in her lap. "I doubt that anyone could have harmed the First unless they took him completely by surprise."

Sick dread slithered icily up Molly's spine. Whoever had done this had crippled the Web in one masterstroke. Since the Webmasters had almost total control over Web policy and decisions, they were chosen with care. The selection of a Webmaster was a long, drawn-out procedure that always created schisms and bad feelings among the Web's testy, opinionated members. She had heard the horror stories about when the last Webmaster had retired. It had taken them forever to agree on the new one. The disagreements had been so fierce that years later, there were still mages who wouldn't speak to each other. If the Web reacted the same way this time, the bastard had set the mages at each other's throats right when they needed to be acting together.

If the murders had really begun, they would all be dead soon.

23

Molly

Olly and Adam headed down Klickitat Street toward the Andruskos' sage-green craftsman bungalow. It was a perfect spring morning. The magnolia trees were heavy with waxy pink blossoms, and a few trees were just beginning to glow with tender green leaves. Molly decided that if newness and innocence had a color, it would be the color of those leaves. She wished, for the bajillionth time, that her life could go back to being the color of those leaves. Everything had gone black when her parents died, and she'd collapsed into grief and depression—a suicide waiting to happen—until Gram sent her on a journey through Damia with Asmodius that had transformed her into a warrior mage. She had new friends now and a life filled with magic. But that life was complicated and tended to become dangerous at a moment's notice. And she missed her parents. There was a hole in her heart that ached whenever she thought of them.

If only they were still alive and she could go back to that green newness. Life would be so much simpler.

But another piece of her heart reminded her that if they hadn't died, she would never have met Gram or Asmodius or Diana or Adam.

And she wouldn't be a mage.

And simple was a bore.

But she missed her parents.

Molly crammed these unsettling thoughts back into their closet and dragged her mind back to springtime on Klickitat Street.

"Won't she still be sleeping?" she asked as they turned into Diana's front walk. It was bordered by a flower bed bursting with early tulips, faded daffodils, and weeds.

"If she is, we're gonna wake her up," Adam said as he rang the doorbell. His dark eyes gleamed and his lanky frame vibrated with energy. "I can't wait to tell you guys what I found out last night."

Footsteps sounded behind the wood panel door. The lock clicked and it swung open revealing a sleepy Diana clutching a mug of coffee.

"Ah, greetings," she said, stepping aside. "Come in." Molly felt the soft touch of the house shields as she pushed through them. Except for Webmasters, mages didn't bother putting heavy shields around their homes. The process was exhausting and had to be renewed daily. Instead they wove what amounted to psychic trip wires that instantly alerted them to intruders and light shields that discouraged negative energies and unwelcome visitors.

Molly and Adam followed Diana through the cluttered living room. The kitchen was even more cluttered. Shelves full of exquisite, colorfully painted Ukrainian pottery lined the cheerful yellow walls, and the white ruffled curtains still carried the exotic scent of Slavic cooking. Diana shoved a pile of books over to one side of the table and scooped up a near-empty cereal bowl, a plate covered with crumbs and dried egg yolk, and some used silverware. Depositing them into an already full sink, she pointed to a coffee maker.

"I see you had breakfast already," Adam said, grabbing a mug out of the cupboard and filling it with coffee.

"That was my brother's breakfast. I fed well last night. Coffee is all I need." Diana lounged in a kitchen chair. Her features had softened, and the look in her eyes had shifted from predatory to lazy good humor. Her hair, black shot with silver, glinted in the morning sun, and she glowed with health and well-being.

"I'm glad you had good hunting," Molly said rummaging around in the refrigerator for milk and trying not to picture Diana's latest meal. "You look marvelous."

"Thank you. I feel marvelous," Diana said, watching Molly dump milk and sugar into her coffee and join them at the table. "In fact, I feel like I imagine I'd feel after a night of really good sex."

Adam choked on a mouth full of coffee and turned a lovely shade of crimson. Diana grinned wickedly.

Molly snickered. "See, the Beast is good for something."

The Beast was what Diana called the terrifying blood lust that sang through her veins as full moon approached and screamed to a fever pitch with full moonrise.

"Adam says he's discovered something important," Molly said, taking pity on her blushing friend and changing the subject.

"Excellent. I hope it will help," said Diana. Her expression became serious in a flash.

"I don't know if it will or not, but it's strange," Adam said, clearing his throat. His face was still a bit pink as he reached for his laptop and turned it on. "The Mage Web has its own cloud that holds every mage's computer files. It's better protected than a dragon's hoard. Even I couldn't get into it. But fortunately, I'm a Web member, so I'm already in, which made getting into the First's files relatively simple."

Molly and Diana gasped in horror. "You didn't!"

"I did," Adam said, looking quite pleased with himself. "I didn't know what I was looking for, but I hoped I would find something in the recently modified files. The latest one was a letter to a mage in France, and he was probably working on it when he died." Adam's fingers tapped a few keys and then he turned the laptop so they could see the screen. "The timing's right at least, and it ends in the middle of a sentence. But look, the First skipped down a few lines and typed the word 'Nysrogh.'"

"What's a Nysrogh?" Diana asked.

"This is where it gets interesting. I googled it and found that Nysrogh is either a drummer for a heavy metal band, the name of several people on Facebook, or the chief of Lucifer's House of Princes—a second-order demon."

Molly and Diana stared at Adam in horror. Molly had met two demons in her Who's Who in the Magical Realms class. They were the only creatures that Philadelphia, their instructor, had held confined in a triangle. One had been quite handsome and the other had been a monster. Both were cruel, twisted creatures that radiated dark, raw power. She still shuddered in horror at the memory.

"But the First was a really nice man," said Diana. "When we lived in Ukraine, the Librarian jumped me and my parents to his office in Alexandria so he could interview me. The Librarian had already offered me a place in the Web and I'd accepted, but the First was concerned about allowing a werewolf to be a Web member and wanted to meet me. He was very kind. It seems unlikely to me that his last word would be the name of a demon."

"You never told me you'd met the First," Adam said looking up in surprise. "What was he like besides kind?"

"He was Egyptian and very small. I remember thinking that his desk was much too big for him. But then I felt his aura. It was so strong and so bright—white shot with blue-green. He greeted us and made me feel like I'd known him for years. His secretary came in carrying a lovely brass tray with four cute little glasses and served us sweet mint tea. We talked about all kinds of things, and he took us out on his balcony that looked out over the old harbor and showed us where the lighthouse used to be. We could just barely see the white dome of the beautiful new library. I remember that he was really proud of it, that he'd worked hard to convince the city to build it. I am sorry he's dead." Diana said.

"I never met him," Molly said, touching Diana on the shoulder, "but I can feel the empty space in the Web where he used to be."

"It will be very hard to replace him," Diana said.

"I think his last word was the name of a demon because it was a demon that killed him," Adam said, shifting in his chair and running a hand through his crisp, dark curls.

"That's insane," said Molly. "How would it have gotten into his house? Demons can't go anywhere in this world without permission."

"It may be insane, but it fits the facts. You've both said that the First was a good, kind man who wasn't likely to be consorting with Lucifer's minions. So why would he type the name of a demon just before he mysteriously dies? He was obviously trying to tell us who killed him."

"Alright," Diana said, "so either the First invited in the demon that murdered him—which I absolutely can't believe—or, for some reason, Nysrogh didn't need an invitation and somehow managed to slip through a super-strong shield and kill one of the most powerful mages in the Web." Diana said. "We need to find out more about this dangerously talented demon."

"I already have," Adam said. His fingers flew over the keyboard. "I searched all of the First's documents for Nysrogh and found a twenty-two-year-old file that mentions that Nysrogh had been banished to Hell." He turned the screen toward them.

"This makes no sense at all," said Molly, studying the document. "How could a demon be banished to Hell? He already lives there."

"We need to show this to an adept," Diana said. "We don't know enough to understand it."

"They've probably found it already," Adam said. "I mean, if I could find it, so can they."

"But they probably haven't. From what Gram was saying this morning, they're doing just what we were afraid they'd do. They're arguing over whether or not the First was murdered and who should be the new Webmaster. The Web's fighting against itself and nothing's getting done." Molly gave Adam a gentle shove. "You just don't want anyone to know you've been snooping in the First's files."

"I'd say that's a valid concern," he replied. "I could get kicked out of the Web."

"Or the Webmasters could have you erased," Diana added helpfully.

"But we need to figure out who killed the First," Molly said, watching Adam's pale skin turn even paler as he contemplated having his memory wiped. "We need to give the adepts this information."

"I've got an idea," Adam said, sinking back in his chair. "This is what we'll do…"

—

Half an hour later they were at Molly's house climbing up to her grandmother's third-floor study. The click of computer keys, the tingle of magic, and the dry, green scent of money met them at the open door. Even though all the windows were open, the room was warm. Gram was poised in front of an array of three big screens that flashed columns of figures as she typed. Asmodius—big, black and imposing, even in sleep—was sprawled in a chair beside her.

"She's still trading," Molly whispered. "Be quiet when we go in. She hates being disturbed."

The air around them hummed like a flashing Jedi sword as they pushed through it on tiptoe and sank into chairs around the ancient oak library table in the center of the room. Adam pulled his laptop out of his backpack and turned it on. Diana reached for a book on Egyptian herbs that Aunt Althea, Gram's closest friend, had left on the table and began leafing through it. Molly settled back in a blue plush overstuffed chair and patted its arm. The Chair, in the form of a backpack, had been her faithful and informative companion on her journey through Damia. Her grandmother had met the Chair on one of her travels through the multiverse and it had followed her home.

So she kept it.

Molly often wondered what its real shape was, or if it even had a real shape.

What's up? it asked. Like Asmodius, the Chair couldn't speak. Instead it communicated telepathically. In this world, its voice in her head was a mere whisper. In Damia, it had been much louder.

We've got some questions for Gram and Asmodius.

Ah.

The warmth and hypnotic click of computer keys was soothing, and Molly relaxed back into the comfort of the Chair. This was her favorite room in the house. It usually smelled like the leather-bound books stuffed into the floor-to-ceiling bookcases that lined the walls, but whenever Gram traded stocks, it smelled like money. Estelle was a stockbroker, and worked not only for herself and her regular clients, but also for the Web. The fact that she could jump into the future made her a very successful trader. She made mistakes—even Gram wasn't able to find the right future all the time—but she did better than most.

A large silver scrying mirror hung on the wall opposite the three windows overlooking the quiet, tree-lined sidewalks of Alameda Street. Gram had created it as her Magical Weapon's class project back in the day when she'd gone to Grant High School and attended Tesseract Academy. It was shaped like a horned owl's head, wise and all-seeing. Each feather was etched in perfect detail, and its eyes were polished obsidian disks the size of small saucers. She had used it to follow Molly's progress as she traveled through Damia with Asmodius and the Chair last summer.

Her gaze shifted to the comatose cat on the chair next to Gram. It seemed like all Asmodius ever did anymore was sleep. And lately he'd been moving like his joints hurt. How old was he anyway? Cats didn't live all that long. Molly's mind shied away from the next obvious question. She loved the irascible animal with all her heart. As they'd fled through the kingdom of Damia searching for Molly's way home, Asmodius had taught her the basics of working the power lines that formed the web of light that connected everything to everything else in the multiverse. He had also saved her butt more times than she cared to count.

She remembered the forge by the River Selene in Damia. She could still feel the heat of the furnace and the intense power of the warrior goddess, Brigga, as she stoked the fire. They had been about to begin work on Molly's sword. As payment, Molly had promised to be Brigga's servant for life. Asmodius had tried to talk her out of it, but she'd wanted that sword more than anything. Brigga had just cut Molly's wrist and spilled her blood on the raw steel, binding her to the blade and to her service, when Asmodius had come tearing toward the forge, chased by a howling pack of wild dogs. As he'd leaped into the rafters he'd sliced Brigga's wrist with a razor-sharp claw and directed a drop of her blood onto the steel to mingle with Molly's. Brigga had been so distracted by the dogs that she hadn't noticed, and once the forging began it was too late, Asmodius had bound the Goddess to the blade and to Molly. Brigga no longer had a helpless servant; she had what amounted to an obedient little sister. The furious Goddess had cursed Asmodius and vowed revenge.

Molly shivered with dread. As long as Asmodius stayed in this world, he was safe from Brigga's wrath. The gods were weak here, unable to communicate with most humans and unable to appear in physical form. But what would happen when the Webmasters found someone else for him to guide through the magic-rich world of Damia where gods and dragons and all sorts of magical creatures could actually materialize?

"There, I'm finished!" The magic level in the room plummeted, and Gram's voice snapped Molly out of her painful musings. She looked up as the tiny adept shut down the screens and spun around in her desk chair to face them. "And what can I do for you three?"

"We were thinking about the First's death and we have a question," Adam said as he closed his laptop. "Do you know if anyone's looked at his recently modified files? There might be something useful in them."

"No, I don't," she said, looking suspiciously at Adam over the tops of her reading glasses. Molly's friend shifted in his chair and she felt true empathy. She hated it when Gram did that to her. "But I can call Denzel and ask," she continued. "Alexandria is ten hours ahead of us, but he'll still be awake. Denzel sleeps in small naps." She scooped her phone off the desk and placed the call.

There was no answer.

"That's strange." Her grandmother's hand shook slightly as she dropped her phone back on the desk. "He always answers his phone. That's part of his job."

Asmodius was suddenly wide-awake. He reached out and patted her knee. Fiery gold and ice blue eyes locked for a tense moment and Gram turned to them.

"We need to make sure he's okay," she said. "Wait here."

And they vanished.

"I don't think so," Molly said. "Chair, do you know the jump to the First's office?"

Of course. Estelle usually goes there on her own, but I've taken her a few times.

"Will you take us there?"

I was hoping you would ask.

Molly reached into the pocket between the worlds that Gram had created so that Flick would always be with her, but invisible, and grabbed her sword. Diana and Adam piled on top of her, and she felt the familiar lifting sensation as the Chair teleported them to the secretary's office in Alexandria.

24

Molly

They landed in electric blackness that screamed with dark, brutal magic.

Oh dear, said the Chair and immediately morphed into a cushion. This was fortunate, because as they fell down on top of it, a fireball sizzled through the space where they'd just been and slammed into the wall behind them, setting it on fire. Molly blessed the Chair's quick thinking as her eyes swept the now well-lit, blazing room.

A demon crouched in a corner. One clawed, scaly hand was still extended and smoking from hurling the fireball. A raven's head atop a black-scaled, well-muscled human body glared at them out of two blank, luminous blue eyes. It stretched its beak open wide and hissed viciously.

"Shit," said Adam and rolled under the desk, followed almost immediately by the Chair. Diana sprang to her feet and before they'd touched the floor, she had warped into a monstrous wolf that shimmered and flashed with awesome power. Her thundering roar shook the room as she bared her fangs and leaped for the demon's throat. This was the first time Molly had seen Diana in wolf form, and she couldn't decide who terrified her more, the demon or her friend. But she had to trust that the black nightmare was, indeed, her friend, and she leaped forward right beside her, wielding Flick, who glowed with power and sang steely songs of death.

The demon materialized a silver ax and threw it with lethal accuracy at Diana's head. Molly screamed in horror and reached out to deflect it. A silver weapon of any sort was the only thing that could kill a werewolf. It whirred toward Diana, a dizzying wheel of lethal silver light moving with incredible speed. "No!!!" Molly screamed as she realized she wasn't gonna get there in time to deflect the spinning, silver death.

A bolt of raw power flashed across the room and smashed into the ax, sending it crashing to the floor. Asmodius, fluffed to twice his already large size and hissing venomously, crouched in front of Gram in the opposite corner. His golden eyes blazed with anger as he leaped toward the demon, claws extended and teeth bared in a blood-curdling snarl.

Molly's sword plunged into the demon's chest, Diana's jaws clamped over its throat, and Asmodius's claws ripped at its face...

At least they would have, but the demon vanished just in time to save its scaly hide from certain death. Instead, the three mages crashed into the wall and landed in a heap on the floor.

Molly! Get me out of here! Yuck. This isn't demon blood!

Molly untangled herself from Diana and Asmodius and pulled Flick out of the plaster wall. She checked it over anxiously, while the sword complained bitterly about how nasty plaster tasted. There wasn't a mark on it.

"Sorry, Flick. I wish we would have gotten the damned thing too. He's killed the First's secretary."

Denzel's lifeless body sprawled over his desk. Streams of blood ran from his nose and mouth and his sightless eyes were wide with terror. Adam was already pulling the secretary's laptop out from under him. Gram extinguished the burning wall with a wave of her hand, plunging the room into darkness once more.

"We need to leave. Now," she said.

—◆—

Back in Gram's study each mage gave the others time to recoup from the horror they had just faced. Diana's clothes were in shreds, but still usable. Molly grabbed her and hugged her close as she growled and trembled herself back into herself. She wasn't used to changing so quickly. Adam turned on Denzel's computer and began checking its files. Asmodius looked like he was ready to kill anything that came within reach. His amber eyes glittered wickedly, and his claws flexed in and out of the chair cushion. Gram sat bolt upright, tears streaming down her cheeks. She and Denzel had been close friends. The room was silent except for the click of computer keys.

"Got it," Adam finally whispered, then slumped back in his chair with a sigh. His face was pale and etched with sadness.

"What?" asked Gram.

"The thing we went to ask Denzel about. It looks like he was wondering the same thing. When I checked his recent files, the latest one was a download of a file from the First's computer. It's a letter," he said, turning the laptop so everyone could see. "And it was modified about the same time he died. See how the First ends in mid-sentence, then skips down a few lines and types the word 'Nysrogh?'" He looked straight at Gram and Asmodius. "You need to tell us about Nysrogh."

The warm spring sunshine faded abruptly. A cold wind set the curtains flapping, and Molly ran to close the windows.

The air between the two adepts shimmered with emotion as they locked eyes once more. The moment passed and Gram slumped back in her chair, swiping away tears. Asmodius sank back on his haunches and began washing his face. But his movements were quick and jerky, and his aura simmered with rage.

"You just met Nysrogh," Gram said. "A very powerful and very dangerous demon. At least he was." Ominous rumblings reverberated from the cat. "About forty years ago, he slipped out of the control of the adept who summoned him and began a reign of terror. The Web finally managed to confine him and send him back. Years later, Lucifer sent him to Hell."

"But wasn't he already in Hell?" Diana asked.

"Hell is a concept the Christians borrowed from pagan mythology. But they can't agree about exactly where it is, what happens when a soul gets there, or even if it has to stay there forever. As far as the mages have been able to determine, it's quite real, but it's not a physical place—it's a state of mind, a place between the worlds.

"Now, think back to your Who's Who in the Magical Realms class. You were taught that demons live in a corner of the Abyss, a vast space that separates the Divine from our world. Their master is Lucifer, an angel who has been around since the dawn of time and holds power over the material world. People tend to confuse Hell and the Abyss because the Christians have made Lucifer the master of Hell, except they usually call him Satan, or the Devil, or the Father of Lies. Different names for the same being. He is our archenemy because his job is to convince humanity that physical reality is the only reality that exists. Once someone believes that, they can't believe in magic, let alone use it, and Lucifer has them right where he wants them—stuck in the physical world and under his power. And, unlike Hell, the Abyss isn't a place where sinners and unbelievers go after they die. The only people that wind up there are the ones who, for some reason, have actually sold their souls to Lucifer or one of his minions.

"But since the word 'Hell' is often used in everyday language to describe an awful place or state of mind, the mages assigned that name to the place Nysrogh came from, which is a terraformed moon. Actually, it's an asteroid captured by a planet's gravitational field. It's so small that we call it an asteroid instead of a moon. Lucifer and the Web send demons and magic users there that are too dangerous and too powerful to be held in normal confinement."

"But any mage that powerful could jump from an asteroid just as easily as a prison cell, and a demon could be invoked from there as easily as anywhere else," Adam said.

"There is no escape from Hell," Gram replied. "All prisoners are jumped into a gate that rips away their magic. After passing through Hell's Gate, humans can't jump or do any other kind of magic, demons can't respond to invocations, and souls lose the ability to travel. They can't even free themselves by dying because Hell is able to resurrect even the most mangled corpse from its DNA and energy patterns and reunite it with its soul. In other words, Hell is a magical place that negates magic, rendering its inmates relatively harmless to themselves, each other, their keeper, and the rest of the multiverse."

Molly stared at her grandmother in speechless horror. As a mage, she was intimately aware of magic at both an intellectual and a gut level. It's the force that connects everything to everything else in the multiverse. That fills people's lives with joy and purpose and reminds them that they are not only a body of blood and bone but also an immensely powerful, luminous being. It allows them to do the impossible. She knew that everyone is filled with magic, but most people don't notice it or call it something else—like energy or love. Molly, however, used it every day for everything from making things happen, to understanding and communicating with others, to reaching out to the Divine. Taking away her magic would be like blinding and deafening her, numbing her out, and then breaking her heart. Her life would be a living Hell. And if she was actually in Hell, it would last for eternity, with no hope of redemption.

"Gods!" Diana finally said. "I can't think of anything more cruel!"

"That's why we call it Hell," Gram replied.

"The Web should be ashamed of itself. No wonder you never talk about it!"

Molly said, glaring at Estelle and Asmodius.

Both adepts nodded in grim agreement.

"Who was the monster that created this place?" Adam asked.

"Nobody knows. We know it was there long before the Web existed because the Librarian discovered it in its travels through the multiverse thousands of years ago. It was attracted to the asteroid because it radiated magic, but was unable to pinpoint the source. It concluded that the asteroid itself possessed a powerful sentience that energized the Gate and controlled the living conditions on its surface. The Librarian realized that if or when someone found it, they might walk through the Gate and be trapped there. Or they wouldn't understand the true horror of the place and use it to make undesirable people disappear. Even the amoral Librarian couldn't stand the thought of this. It considered the matter for quite a while and eventually decided to tell the mages about the asteroid. Not because it believed in their innate goodness, but because, if the mages controlled the asteroid, it would ensure that nobody else could. And, since the Librarian has quite a bit of influence in the Web, it would have some control over its use."

"How did Lucifer find out about it?" Adam asked.

"Lucifer finds out about everything eventually, since he's lord of the material realm. He pointed out that it would be in both our best interests if we gave him the ability to send his most intractable minions to the asteroid. His request was well-timed—or perhaps, well-planned. The adepts had just spent a miserable two decades dealing with a few powerful demons that had somehow figured out how to leave the Abyss without having been invoked. They were too wily and strong to destroy, and once they were banished, they'd return. The Web agreed, but not before they made him promise to only send demons and only those under his direct control. Lucifer is a wily bastard, but he always keeps his promises. We haven't regretted the decision."

There was a moment of silence while the young mages assimilated this unappetizing piece of Web history. Molly shivered as the sky darkened even further and the wind howled outside the window.

"Okay," Adam finally said, bouncing to his feet and pacing. His hair was rumpled and one rebellious curl fell onto his forehead, "Then we have yet another problem. We know that demons can't go anywhere unless they're invoked, and the only magic they can do on this plane is what the person who invoked them commands them to do. We also know that Nysrogh is a demon and that Lucifer banished him to Hell, where all his magic was stripped away. So how did Nysrogh slip inside Denzel's apartment shields, shoot bolts of fire, materialize silver axes, and disappear without a trace?"

Molly and Diana gasped, but Asmodius and Gram just nodded. They'd probably asked this same question the moment they'd laid eyes on Nysrogh.

"We haven't a clue," said Gram.

Asmodius's growl rumbled through the study. His eyes blazed with anger and, perhaps, a touch of fear. *Nysrogh is no more intelligent than most of the residents of Hell. If he could figure out how to escape, the others won't be far behind.*

Daylight faded to near darkness. Lightning flashed, followed by a deafening crash of thunder, and sheets of rain battered the window. Fear shimmied up Molly's spine. If Asmodius was right, nowhere, either on earth or in the Abyss, would be safe from the vengeance of Hell's denizens.

ANDROMEDA!

Usually Asmodius's thoughts were barely audible, but his anguish smashed the name loud and clear into everyone's head. The cat's eyes were wide with fear, as he turned to Gram. Between one heart-beat and the next, Molly felt a lifetime of love, grief, and rage pass between the two adepts. It left her breathless and afraid.

SHE'S IN TROUBLE! I'M GOING TO HELP HER!

"NO! WAIT!" Molly screamed as her beloved teacher vanished.

"Let me go with you," she said to Asmodius's empty chair.

Molly, Diana, and Adam stared at each other in confusion as lightning strobed through the study and thunder boomed.

"Who is Andromeda?" Diana finally asked. Her words were nearly lost in the storm.

"Andromeda is the Queen of Hell," Gram said.

25

Asmodius

Asmodius stood at the top of the barbican tower that guarded the gate into Andromeda's castle. Everyone who jumped in to visit her landed here, then walked down the steps inside the tower and through a narrow hallway to the castle's entrance. The castle itself was so heavily shielded that only Andromeda could jump directly into it. This arrangement gave her advance warning of surprise attacks or dangerous visitors and kept friendly arrivals safe from Hell's denizens.

The castle was perched atop a tall, sheer cliff that spanned the end of a vast, oblong plain—rolling green hills dotted and crossed by sparkling blue lakes and streams. Actually, it was a valley, since it was surrounded on its other three sides by picture perfect snow-capped mountains that sloped down into lush, wooded foothills.

Asmodius peered anxiously down into the valley through a gap in the barbican's stone parapet. The scene would have been idyllic, except the land near the castle was burned over, gouged, and pitted like a war zone. Large swaths of forest had been clear-cut. The tiny houses dotted sparsely around the countryside were drab and ramshackle. Smoke drifted listlessly out of chimneys, casting a pall over the landscape. He noted the occasional ant-sized demon or human wondering through the ruined landscape.

Hell's inmates were not gentle with the land.

Hell's Gate, formed from two massive, black stone columns joined at the top by a black stone lintel, stood safe and sound at the base of the cliff. A sick fear stirred in his heart as he remembered that this wasn't just a physical gate. It was also a spiritual gate. Condemned prisoners were teleported from wherever they'd been sentenced directly into the Gate. Their first step was onto the plain of Hell. That step also stripped them of their magic, which was their link to the multiverse, condemning them to a life of hopeless isolation and spiritual poverty. They were denied even the mercy of death.

Asmodius pulled his gaze away from the Gate and shook off the horror of it, beginning with his head and ending with his haunches, removing the last trace with a graceful flick of his tail. Everything looked about the same as it had several decades ago—the last time he'd been here. Relief washed through him and his heart settled down to a normal beat.

He'd gotten here in time.

"Asmodius!" Andromeda's smoky voice surrounded him. "If you're done sight-seeing you may come in." A rectangle of bright white appeared around a few of the floor blocks just inside the parapet. They glowed, sparkled briefly, and disappeared, revealing a stone staircase cut into the barbican's inner wall. It was narrow, and there was no handrail. Anyone afraid of heights or prone to dizziness would have problems.

Asmodius contemplated the forbidding downward spiral.

Was it a trap?

Highly unlikely. Everything seemed calm and normal here, and that was definitely Andromeda's voice. He'd know it any-where, he even heard it in his dreams. She wasn't worried or fright-ened. All he had to do was go tell her that one of her charges had escaped, and she would figure out what needed to be done.

So why was he hesitating?

Because it had been decades since he'd seen her and they hadn't parted under the best of circumstances. After all they'd been through together, was she angry with him? Did she hate him? He couldn't bear it if she hated him. And he would know her feelings the moment he saw her.

He was hesitating because he was afraid of what he might see in her eyes.

Enough of this! he growled to himself. The only way you're going to find out how she feels is to walk down those steps and into the castle. Asmodius hated weakness, especially in himself, and so he trotted down into the chill, musty-smelling darkness. When he reached the ground, he headed into the tunnel-like hall-way lined with small, skinny windows that connected the tower to the castle. The iron-spiked portcullis crashed down behind him, closing off the only entrance—and the only exit. The tunnel opened into a courtyard. If this would have been a real Medieval castle, it would have been an empty, paved area—perfect for receiving large parties of mounted guests. Since Andromeda had very few visitors, and none of them arrived on horseback, she had turned her courtyard into a lovely garden, complete with trees and flowering plants from all over their world, and a fountain composed of three hideous demon faces and one hideous human face spitting streams of water to the four quarters.

Trembling with equal parts of excitement, hope, and dread, he moved through the sweet-smelling greenery toward an iron-bound oak door. His pride and self-control were such that anyone who might have been watching would have only seen a huge, menacing, black cat stalk confidently through the garden and up to the castle door. As he approached, it opened slowly, its massive hinges creaking and groaning as if they hadn't been oiled in years.

Nice touch, Andromeda. He stepped over the threshold and surveyed the entry hall. Gray, stone-block walls hung with brilliantly colored tapestries of the mages' coats of arms soared up three stories. He noticed that the Adair silver gryphon couchant on an azure field commanded a prominent place. The floor was paved with the same gray stone and spread with a huge, intricately patterned Turkish carpet. Four burgundy leather wingback armchairs grouped around a low center table, graced with a vase of white lilies, were the only furniture in the room. Behind and to either side of the chairs were two bronze stands filled with an armory's worth of spears and lances. To Asmodius's right was the door to the Great Hall. On the left side of the wall facing him was the door to the kitchen area. Straight ahead, an elegant oak stairway spilled down into the hall.

Footsteps tapped and pattered and clicked above him as Andromeda strolled into view, surrounded by her pack of Hell Hounds—massive, fierce, white dogs with red ears and paws and glowing red eyes. They looked like Doberman Pinschers, only with larger heads, broader chests, and longer fangs. She paused on the landing, framed in front of a stunning floor-to-ceiling stained glass window of angels and demons locked in vicious combat.

Asmodius's heart leapt with gladness at the sight of her. She'd hardly aged since he'd last seen her. One of the advantages of life in Hell. She stood tall and proud, her long, shapely legs encased in knee-high boots with iron buckles and fold-over tops. A serviceable, black leather corset with buckles instead of laces topped a ruffled mid-length black skirt, slashed with burgundy and cut high in front, exposing her knees and a black-and-white striped lace underskirt. The neckline of her white cotton shirt plunged into the top of the corset and over-sized cuffs clinched its wide, flowing sleeves at her wrists. The outfit suited her. Molly would have said she was "totally steampunked." But it was her eyes that held his attention. Framed by crisp, flaming red curls and an exotic mask of make-up, those oh-so-familiar emerald eyes stared down at him, alive with shrewd intelligence, but absolutely no emotion. They held no welcoming smile, no love, no joy. They held neither anger nor hate.

Asmodius watched in confusion as she motioned to her dogs to stay, and glided down the stairs like a model on a runway. The only sound was the slow tap of her boots on the gleaming oak steps. What was she feeling? Andromeda had always been so alive, so joyous, so passionate. Was this what life in Hell had done to her?

Her boots tapped sharply on the stone floor, but fell silent when she reached the plush Turkish carpet

"How kind of you to finally come visit," she said. Like her face, her smoky voice was beautiful but expressionless.

I'm sorry. I should have come earlier, but I was afraid. For Asmodius, this was an unprecedented statement. He rarely apologized, and he *never* admitted to being afraid.

"Afraid? Of little ol' me?" she asked as she strolled toward him.

"Well, you should be!" With a move so quick that he barely saw it, she snatched up a boar-hunting spear from the weapons rack and hurled it with deadly force and accuracy straight into his heart.

Asmodius felt the blow and, after a moment's assessment, realized with horror he had collapsed into a most undignified position. The spear was sticking out of his chest and his life was draining away quickly—a gush of red on the cold, gray stones.

Andromeda continued to stroll toward him.

The last things he saw were her cold, beautiful eyes gazing into his.

The last thing he heard was her lovely voice saying "Goodbye, Asmodius."

The last thing he smelled was her spicy, sweet scent.

26

Molly

A few hours after Asmodius left, Molly wandered into the kitchen in hopes of finding something for dinner and found her grandmother at the kitchen table, clutching a cup of tea. Her blue eyes stared blankly ahead, and her face was pale as cold ashes. Fear, not concern, twisted Molly's gut. Anything that would reduce Gram to this catatonic state had to be bad. Very bad.

"What's wrong?"

The tiny adept took a deep, shuddering breath and her eyes slowly focused on Molly. Her face remained deathly pale.

"Asmodius is gone."

"Of course he's gone. He went to Hell."

"No, he's completely gone. He's not in this world. I can't feel him anymore," Gram said, clutching at her heart. "I've searched and searched and I can't find him anywhere."

Molly's vision narrowed to a tunnel and her legs turned to Silly Putty. She grabbed blindly for the table and dropped into the chair beside her grandmother.

"No! He can't be dead."

"He may not be dead, but he's gone."

The world collapsed into darkness. A thick, cold darkness that wrapped around her, sucking away her strength and squeezing her heart. She felt Gram's arms tighten around her, but the darkness remained.

—

Molly had no idea how long she and Gram clung to each other, shaking with grief and trying to imagine life without Asmodius. And then hoping against hope that he wasn't dead and would find his way back. But the kitchen had grown dark, and the city lights were glittering outside the family room windows when a soft knock sounded on the front door.

"Oh, they're here already," Gram said, hurriedly scrubbing at her face and fluffing her hair. She reached out and gently brushed the tears from Molly's cheeks and smoothed back her wild curls. "Now maybe we'll have some answers."

They heard the door open and Aunt Althea's voice ask, "May we enter?"

"Yes, you are welcome," said Gram.

Gram's closest friend stepped into the darkened kitchen.

"The best trackers in the Web have looked through this world and all the other worlds open to us and we can't find his soul. He's dead, Estelle."

"If he's dead, why can't they find his soul?"

"He may have gone to the Divine One."

"Asmodius? You've got to be kidding."

"Yes, it's unlikely, but possible. He probably went between the worlds to rest. Many souls do that after a particularly difficult life."

Pain. Pure, and cruel, and untainted with the specter of hope wrenched at Molly's heart as footsteps shuffled into the kitchen and the darkened room filled with shadowy figures. Only the occasional sniff or sigh broke their anguished silence.

One by one, they each lit a votive candle with a spark of mage light. And one by one their tear-streaked faces appeared out of the darkness. Aunt Althea. Diana and Adam and their parents. Master Lieu, her weapons instructor. Ophelia Pettygrove, her friend from Grant. Principal Rathkin. Detective Fox, who had saved Molly from being killed by Tamerlane. And last, but certainly not least, Micah Ortiz.

Molly's breath caught when her eyes met Micah's, and right on cue, her stupid heart started lunging against her rib cage, trying desperately to escape and fling itself at his feet. Closing her eyes, she spoke to it sternly. Keep this up and you're gonna get stepped on. This dude is trouble. He's a gang leader and there's no place for you in his life. He doesn't really care about you, so settle down.

When it had settled down to simple flip-flops, she opened her eyes.

Micah's chiseled, perfect features were not tear-streaked.

They were tight with barely suppressed fury.

His purple-black aura flared and reached out for her, wrapping her in a tight, warm, cocoon. Molly gasped. Maybe he did care. She struggled to blast out of his embrace, but then stopped. Micah's blazing aura warmed her aching heart and filled her with comfort. Right now she needed every bit of comfort she could get, so she relaxed and smiled her thanks to him.

Her heart continued doing flip-flops.

One by one, the mages set down their candles and filed past Molly and Estelle, touching them on the shoulder. Each touch sent waves of love and healing light into Molly's pain-wracked body. And each touch was unique. Some were soft and loving, some were filled with strength and courage, and some just said, "I'm so sorry." Aunt Althea was a healer. Her touch sent waves of light coursing through Molly, sweeping away pain and replacing it with love.

And then Micah was beside her. She looked up into the mirror lenses of his aviator sunglasses and groaned. Her puffy face, wet with tears and snot, stared back at her. Oh gods, she looked like a pathetic, sniveling zombie. Micah would never speak to her again.

Micah's angry features softened, as if reading her thoughts, and he knelt beside her and hugged her. Jolts of not-so-comforting but definitely exciting energy ricocheted through her.

"Don't worry," he whispered, "We'll get whoever did this." His lips brushed her forehead, sending hot tingles surging into her brain and down her spine. If she'd been standing, her legs would have melted out from under her.

And then he left.

Molly suppressed the urge to run after him, cling shamelessly to his strong shoulders, and bury her face in his leather jacket. Instead she sat tight and savored the memory of his kiss.

Stop it! Asmodius is dead, you should be grieving.

When everyone had gone, Aunt Althea began puttering around the kitchen, which was no longer dark. It glowed with tiny, magic-packed golden flames that radiated warm, soothing love. She started the tea kettle, grabbed mugs from the cupboard, popped a casserole in the oven, and began wiping down the already spotless black quartz counter tops.

"How did everyone know?" Molly asked as Aunt Althea plunked two mugs of strong, milky, sweet tea down on the butcher-block kitchen table.

"When a Webmaster is in trouble, every adept in the Web knows," she replied, sinking into a chair across from them and taking a sip of her tea. "Adam and Diana had told their parents that Asmodius had gone to Hell to see if Andromeda was okay, so we guessed that something happened to him. Unfortunately, we were correct."

Molly nodded and sipped at her tea.

And then gasped as the sense of Althea's explanation suddenly sank in.

"You're a Webmaster?!" Molly's stomach cramped with fear, and she glared at her grandmother as if she'd just sprouted horns.

Gram nodded.

"Which one?"

"The Third—at least for now."

"Do they get killed in order?"

"Yes."

"If we don't stop this, I'll lose you both!"

"If we don't stop this, losing us will be the least of your problems."

27

Molly

I'm going in to find out what happened to Asmodius." Molly crossed her arms over her chest and glared at her grandmother.

"Yes, you must," Gram replied.

"What?" Molly gasped. Two more startled "Whats?" came from Adam and Diana, who were perched on the edge of the couch.

For the space of a heartbeat Molly felt betrayed.

Didn't Gram love her?

Why was she so willing to send her only living relative to an asteroid crawling with the cruelest, meanest demons and humans in the multiverse? And then she noticed the tears streaming down the tiny adept's cheeks.

"I don't want you to go," she said, swiping impatiently at her face, "But if we're ever going to figure out who killed Asmodius—and we really need to find out who killed him, our lives depend on it—someone needs to find out what's happening, and it needs to be a warrior mage. Unfortunately, there are only a few of them in the Web, and they are all well past middle age—except for you. Master Lieu has informed me that although you have much to learn, you are in peak condition and are formidable. If Diana goes with you, the two of you will be the most powerful team the Web can send. You were also very close to Asmodius, and are more motivated to find out what happened to him than any of the other warrior mages. But you don't need to fix the problem—if there is a problem. Just find out what happened and come back so we can figure out what to do. And, if possible, bring back Asmodius's body."

Molly collapsed into an easy chair and stared at her grandmother in astonishment. For once they were on the same page.

Amazing.

The three friends had already decided that Molly and Diana needed to go find out what had happened to Asmodius, and had come to let Gram know they were going and, hopefully, learn more about Hell and what to watch out for when they got there. They had expected her to forbid Molly to go—not agree with them. Adam and Diana sank back on the couch in astonished relief.

"We need a way to communicate," Adam said, dropping his words into the stunned silence. "We need to know what you're finding and what's happening around you and to you so we don't wind up in the same mess we're in now. The Librarian has actually been quite helpful. It showed me how to create an app for our cell phones so we can call each other between here and the asteroid. If you give me your phones, I can install it and show you how to use it."

"I need to find mine," said Gram. "Now where could I have left it?"

"What color is it?" Adam asked as everyone got up and went phone hunting.

"Bright blue," Molly replied. This was not even close to the first time she'd helped Gram find her phone. Like, the woman could keep track of hundreds of stocks, but could she remember where her phone was? "You better not lose it while we're in Hell," Molly said. "We may need you."

"Here it is," Diana called from the kitchen. "It was on the table under *The Wall Street Journal*."

"Jeez, Diana," Adam said as she handed him the phone. "How did you find it so fast?"

"I smelled it. Cell phones have a sort of buzzy, electric smell, but each one's different from the others because its owner's scent is on it."

"Ah," Adam said. "Estelle, what's your pass-code?"

Gram recited six numbers and Molly smiled. It was her birth date.

Minutes later, Adam sat down beside Gram. "Okay, a spell is woven into this app." He handed her the phone and pointed to the screen. "It's the icon with the pentagram with air waves coming off it. I've put all our numbers into the it. Any number in the app can call any other number in the app from anywhere and anytime. Cool, huh?"

"Amazing," said Gram.

"The Librarian is totally amazing. So, here's how you use it. Tap the icon."

Gram tapped the icon.

"See, a contact list comes up. Now select a name."

Molly's phone rang and she answered it.

"Hi Gram!"

"That's easy!" She waved at Molly and closed the call.

"One more thing. See that clock on the bottom of your screen? It's your recent calls on this app. Tap it. See? There's your call to Molly. If someone called you, even if you didn't answer, it would show up here in red."

"Perfect. Exactly what we need.," Gram said. "The Librarian isn't usually this helpful. The snot-brain must have finally noticed how much trouble we're in."

As Adam was installing the app on her phone and Diana's Molly said, "And that's not all! The Librarian told us a secret way into the castle from the outside. It says it can jump us to the surface and we can explore around and see if the prisoners are still there, or if anything's wrong. And then we can sneak into the castle and maybe find out what happened to Asmodius."

"It didn't want to risk jumping them onto the barbican tower like Asmodius did. It may be perfectly safe, and whatever went wrong happened after he arrived, but I don't want to take chances," Adam said, casting a worried glance at Diana.

Of course he didn't want to take chances! Diana meant the world to him. If anything happened to their exotic friend, he'd be a basket case.

"We contacted Andromeda last night and she had no idea that Asmodius was even there," Gram said.

"She must have known he was there! From what the Librarian tells me, the castle's security is so tight that you can't even fart on the barbican without her knowing it," Adam said.

"Maybe he never got there," Diana said.

"Or maybe someone's messed with the security system," Molly said.

"Or maybe she's lying," Adam said.

"She sounded grief-stricken and surprised when we told her Asmodius was dead, and very sincere about not knowing he was there," Gram said. "Andromeda and Asmodius had an intense relationship—they were very close. If she knew anything, I'm sure she would tell us."

"We're just guessing," Adam said, as he launched himself off the sofa and began pacing. "We don't have enough information to draw any conclusions. That's why Molly and Diana need to go and check things out. Then maybe we'll be able to figure out what's really happening and how to stop it."

"All the same, keep under Andromeda's radar for as long as you can," Gram said. "Now, have you figured out what you need to take besides your phones?"

"We've got some granola bars and jerky, water bottles, hiking boots, spare clothes for me and lots of spare clothes for Diana— she's hard on outfits if she has to morph in a hurry," Molly said as she took Adam's place beside her grandmother. "But we were hoping you could tell us some more about Hell. I mean we know it's dangerous, but some details would be good."

"I thought you'd never ask," Estelle said, sitting up even straighter. "I couldn't sleep, so I did some research and pumped the Librarian for all it knows about the godsforsaken place. Because the Librarian has never been able to find a central power source or computer, it thinks the asteroid is a sentient being capable of controlling the Gate and monitoring and changing conditions on its surface. It orbits a red planet that orbits a yellow dwarf sun much like our own, but it's a bit farther away from its sun than we are. The days are now twenty-four hours long. The Librarian says they were originally much shorter, but as soon as we began sending human prisoners through the Gate, the day-length changed to twenty-four hours. The asteroid wobbles slightly on its north-south axis on a forty-day cycle, which keeps the temperature range of the terraformed area between forty and ninety degrees Fahrenheit.

"That's good," said Molly. "We won't have to lug around heavy coats. Which reminds me, can I take the Chair?" The Chair would be quite useful. It could morph into a backpack and a tent and probably tons of other things. And besides, she was fond of it.

"Yes, of course. And it can jump you back here if necessary."

"What does the surface look like?" Diana asked.

"It has snow-capped mountains, forested uplands, grassy plains, a few lakes and rivers, rain, sunshine, wind, and clouds."

"It sounds heavenly," Diana said with a grin.

"It's not. Unfortunately, a bunch of criminals live there, and they've pretty much trashed the place," Gram replied. "But Andromeda's castle is quite lovely. It's built on a sheer cliff overlooking the plain."

"Where, exactly, is it?" Adam asked.

"The Librarian wasn't very forthcoming on that topic. It's the only one who knows the location and it wants it to stay that way."

"Could it be in this solar system?'

"Maybe."

"Or it could be clear across the galaxy?"

"Maybe."

"Or it could be in another universe ?"

"Maybe."

"It creeps me out. Once they jump, we'll have no idea where they are. What if they can't get back?"

"Even if you did know where it was, that wouldn't help you get them back. We've only made it to the Moon, last time I checked," Gram replied.

Adam's face drained of color and his eyes went wide as the reality of Molly's and Diana's situation sank in.

"Gram, that wasn't helpful."

"Yes, I can see that."

"Look at it this way," Molly said, patting Adam gently on the shoulder. "We've all jumped to Damia and never thought twice about it, and nobody knows where Damia is either. Not knowing this asteroid's exact location is the least of our problems."

"Yeah, I suppose," Adam said. A trace of color crept back into his face.

"I think we've got everything we need," said Diana, flowing to her feet and stretching luxuriously. "It's time for us to go. Spring break won't last forever, and I would like to be back in time to enjoy at least some of it."

"Gram, is there anything else we need to know?"

"I'm pretty sure I've told you everything. If I think of anything else, I'll call you."

"We'll be careful and when we come back, we'll have some answers," Molly said, hugging her grandmother tight. "I love you lots."

The three mages gazed down at the Librarian as it snoozed in the middle of the oak library table in Gram's study. Its black, dragon-skin cover expanded and contracted rhythmically, giving the impression of restful breaths, and its onion-skin-thin pages occasionally shifted and riffled as if it were gently snoring. Such a harmless, comfortable shape for the fierce, proud dragon who had its claws sunk deep in all aspects of Web business, made books from the extensive Web library available to all the Web mages at the blink of an eye, and had created Tesseract Academy, the Web training school at the center of the circle of time. Many adepts and every magnet high school had a copy of it in their libraries.

"I guess this is it," Adam said, gazing into Diana's eyes and reaching for her hand.

"Wait!" said Molly. "I gotta text Micah and tell him I'm going to find Asmodius."

"I don't understand what you see in that creature," Diana growled. "He's nothing but a common criminal."

Molly ignored her friend and headed toward the opposite end of the study to send her message. This gave Adam and Diana some extra moments to say goodbye.

And then it was time.

Molly and Diana stood side-by-side in front of the Librarian. The Chair had become a small, gray GORE-TEX backpack which somehow managed to hold all their belongings. They'd decided that Molly would carry everything. If Diana needed to morph in a hurry and she was wearing a backpack, she'd rip all the straps off it.

"Okay, we're ready," said Molly. "Jump us to Hell, please."

28

Micah

Damn, damn, damn!

Micah Ortiz gripped his cell phone hard to keep from flinging it on the sidewalk and stomping on it. At the candle-lighting last night, the sight of Molly's anguished, tear-streaked face had sent a storm of messy, painful emotions tearing through him. There had been nothing he could do except complete the rite and send her all the love and support he could. It had been agony. And now she was headed off to find out what happened to Asmodius. She hadn't bothered to mention where that might be, but if a talented adept with decades of experience had died there it was bound to be dangerous.

And why in all the gods' names did he even care?

Why did her steady, steel-gray eyes haunt the edges of his consciousness, sneaking into his unoccupied mind like an internet pop-up ad?

And how had he somehow come to know the location of every freckle on her face and every sweet curve of her tiny body?

And why was it that whenever they were close, he could feel their auras swoop around each other, leaving him breathless with longing?

Simple.

Because they belonged together.

Cursing silently, he jammed his phone into his hip pocket and continued down Martin Luther King Boulevard. Unlike most gang leaders, who traveled in the back of expensive black cars and were always surrounded by their top men, Micah preferred to be invisible. He moved like a shadow, quick and silent. Only the most observant of his fellow pedestrians noticed him.

But Micah noticed everything.

Usually.

Right now, that wasn't happening. His brain insisted on reminding him, for the bajillionth time, of the reasons why he and Molly did *not* belong together.

First off, she was majorly and painfully distracting.

Just the thought of seeing her hurt made him tremble with anger. And Molly wasn't just a pretty face. She was a trained fighter who could take down even the toughest gang member. And she served a warrior goddess. He knew from personal experience that the gods got their money's worth out of their servants. She was gonna be in and out of deep shit for the rest of her short life. And there wasn't a damn thing he could do about it.

And there never would be.

With a shudder, he remembered when Shandra Sheehan, her best friend, died last fall. Murdered with Flick, Molly's own sword. He had watched in helpless horror as she became a prime suspect, and then the killer's target. He had become so stuck in Molly's drama that he hadn't paid attention to business. One of his Ravens had been killed because he'd been so out of it that he'd missed the call that would have saved his life.

A total fuck-up. Even if the slime-ball who took him out did wind up face down in the Willamette River, stabbed through the heart, Jamal's death would torture him for the rest of his life. He couldn't be screwin' up every time Molly was in trouble. He needed to be on top of things twenty-four seven. His life and his men's lives depended on it.

But it was her curiosity that scared him the most. He'd tried again and again to keep her out of his business, making useless threats and snarling a lot. Not because he was afraid of what she would find. Everyone knew he was a gang leader and dealt drugs, and he was fine with that. And he doubted that she would be able to find anything truly incriminating. Detective Fox had been trying for years.

Micah was very good at what he did.

But he couldn't control everything. The streets were dangerous, treacherous places, crawling with hate and dark shadows. Regular people didn't see it, but gang members lived it and breathed it. One day Molly's curiosity might bring her too close to a nervous dealer or a flipped-out user and it'd be all over.

And finally, she was a danger to him. If any of the rival gangs ever found out how much he valued her, she would be a hostage in the flip of a switchblade. His life or the life of one of his Ravens would be the price of her release. When he'd formed the Ravens, he'd begged his mother to leave Portland, for this very reason. She'd refused, but agreed to move to the condo he'd bought her in the West Hills, assumed a new identity, and laid low. Well, sort of low. She was a prostitute and still took in the occasional client. It made him crazy. She didn't need to work, he gave her plenty of money.

Attachments were dangerous.

He didn't need another one.

Micah growled in frustration and pulled his full attention back to the street. A movement that was out of sync with his surroundings had caught his eye. Without turning his head or breaking his step, he shifted his gaze. Oh yeah. A Red Cobra Blood. Why did the numb-brains insist on wearing those red windbreakers? So easy to spot.

This would not do.

He was meeting a client.

His father had sent him a coded message from Mexico. There was a huge shipment of black tar due this week—enough to make the Ravens rich. Micah needed to find buyers in Portland and figure out how to ship the rest of the heroin to Chicago.

The young mage put two people between himself and the Blood across the street, imagined himself becoming one with the sidewalk, and hung a quick right onto Killingsworth. A glance back told him that the dude didn't have a clue that he'd turned. After a few more random rights and lefts, he headed off to meet his client.

29

Micah

icah allowed himself a moment to raise his face to the sun and breathe in the sweet spring air. His client had just agreed to buy most of the Portland stuff. The Ravens could easily move what was left. Life was good. Figuring out how to ship the rest would be a bitch, but still doable. Now if Molly could just get back from wherever she was in one piece, everything would be perfect.

At least for a while.

"I need to talk to you, Ortiz."

Micah stifled the impulse to turn and pound the intruder beside him into the sidewalk. No one had ever managed to sneak up on him. Who was this asshole?

He turned his head slowly and glared at the man beside him.

Shit! It was Detective Fox. The only man on the Portland Police Force that actually made him nervous. The dude was smart, tough, and, unfortunately, not on the take.

And he was a mage.

But he wasn't looking particularly tough or magical right now. He looked pale and terrified.

What in all the universes could have happened? Micah was suddenly curious, but appearances and working relationships had to be maintained.

"That's too bad, Fox," Micah replied, "cuz I don't wanna talk. Especially to you. Either arrest me or beat it. You're messin' with my street cred."

"I'm not looking forward to this conversation either. But it has nothing to do with you, dirt-ball. It's about Molly. Meet me at the Caffe Vita in half an hour." Before Micah could answer, the detective turned abruptly and stalked away.

—

The Portland Caffe Vita was a simple, chill coffee house at the east end of the Alberta Street business district. It was a popular neighborhood hangout, probably because it was laid back, unpretentious, and made the best coffee in Portland. Either the cop knew Micah came here a lot, or he came here himself. Neither option pleased him. Micah strolled along, trying to look cool. But what he really wanted to do was run there. As fast as he could.

And find out what had happened to Molly.

And why his archenemy was coming to him about it.

He spotted the cafe's iconic neon sign, a hunchback in a rounded-off dunce cap, pajamas, slippers, and beak-nosed half-mask, climbing a ladder and waving his coffee cup at the world. A great image of the tarot Fool—a perfect logo for his favorite coffee house.

He was fifteen minutes early. Micah made it a point to arrive at any meeting early. That way he could check out the place and make sure he got a seat with his back to the wall, facing the door.

The gang leader stopped just inside the entrance and checked the place out. There were only a few customers in the roomy cafe, and their eyes were glued to their laptops. The decor, permanently infused with the rich aroma of roasting coffee, was minimalist—no cozy easy-chairs and sofas here, just plain wooden tables and chairs. The clink of silverware and china echoed off the polished concrete floor. Harry was pulling shots. His salt and pepper spiked hair looked totally manic, and the lower part of his pristine white dress shirt was even more coffee spattered than usual. Someone must have missed a shift.

Micah strolled in and ordered a cup of coffee. The mad scribbler had been at work on the bananas on the fruit tray. Each one was covered with pen and ink sketches and quotes and cryptic flow charts done in ornate Gothic script. One in particular caught his eye. It said, "Time flies like an arrow, but fruit flies like a banana." Micah rolled his eyes and suppressed a smile as Harry poured his coffee and set it on the counter with his usual small stainless steel pitcher of milk beside it.

"He's in back," the barista said.

Shit, of course the cop was gonna be early, but this early? The dude must be psychic. Well duh, he *was* psychic. Not all mages were, but Fox definitely was.

"Thanks, Harry." Micah paid up and stalked into the back room. The cop was sitting at the only table, hidden from the front, with his back against the wall, nursing a cup of black coffee.

Bastard.

Micah slipped into the chair across from him, which had a view of the front door, and forced himself to calmly pour some milk into his coffee and watch it swirl through the bitter blackness. He firmly resisted the urge to grab the detective, shake him till his teeth rattled, and scream "What's happened to Molly?"

Instead, he growled, "I'm here. Talk."

"I just had lunch with a colleague in missing persons," the detective said. He sat still as a stone, fists clenched. His tortured eyes stared numbly at a spot just over Micah's shoulder. "She has a case with very few leads that's rapidly heading toward a dead end. One of the groundskeepers at Portland Public Schools has disappeared. He was last seen over a month ago, working in one of the beds near the science block of Grant High School. No one's seen him since, his bank account is untouched, none of his credit cards have been used, and neither has his cell phone."

"So what's this got to do with Molly?"

Fox's eyes and all their agony locked onto Micah's, making him want to cringe and look away. But he managed to retain his bored expression and stared calmly back.

"Tamerlane took Molly to the forensics lab in the science block to kill her," Fox said. Instead, Molly killed him, and he turned to dust. Nothing was left but his boot knife and his signet ring. The ring was radiating so much magic that it would have screwed up every test in the crime lab. To keep it away from the techs, I stuck my pen through it and buried it in one of the plantings outside the lab."

Micah clutched the edge of the table as understanding began to creep in and fear seeped into his belly.

"I was going to tell the mages to retrieve it and deal with it properly, but I completely and totally forgot until Riley started to tell me about her case." The detective's bleak stare returned to that spot just over Micah's shoulder.

"Tamerlane's out there somewhere," Fox said.

"And he's looking for Molly," Micah replied. His heart began to pound.

"And he can move from one body into another—all he has to do is touch it," Fox replied.

"Shit!" Micah said, slamming his hand down on the table so hard the coffee cups jumped. "You'll never find him because you won't know which body he's in. That grounds-keeper is probably nothing but ashes now, scattered to the wind."

"Exactly."

"So why are you telling me this?"

Actually, he knew exactly why the cop was telling him this, but how had the son-of-a-bitch known?

"Good question. I haven't a clue."

Micah wanted to slump back into his chair in relief, but he didn't.

"You are the last person I'd ever admit a mistake to. I'm telling you this because Brigga told me to, and you don't argue with Brigga."

Of course Brigga would know all about him, she was a freakin' goddess. And, of course she would want Micah to help Molly.

Because he was the only person who could.

"She also said that you need to talk to the Librarian."

"And you need to let Estelle know about this right now," Micah said, gazing at the unfortunate detective with true empathy. He knew the agony of realizing that he'd made a mistake, and that because of that mistake, good people had been killed. He could only imagine how painful it would be to tell an adept, or anyone, for that matter, that their beloved granddaughter was in mortal danger because you had screwed up.

He almost told the cop that his screw-up was unavoidable. That there was no way he could have known that Tamerlane had put his entire being into that ring. That it had been a simple matter for the adept to wipe the intention to tell the mages about the ring from the detective's unsuspecting mind—a mind distracted by the horrors of that night, with fear for Molly, and with making the crime scene as safe and unremarkable for the techs as possible.

He almost told the grieving man that he was truly sorry.

But he didn't.

This was the enemy. The one person in all of Portland who could put him behind bars.

The detective's misfortunes were Micah's advantages.

"I'll tell her," Fox said, interrupting his thoughts.

"Sucks to be you," Micah replied. "I'll visit the Librarian."

The gang leader stalked out of Caffe Vita, leaving his coffee untouched.

30

Molly

Molly felt the familiar lift of the Librarian's teleport. Moments later her feet touched down on the soft leaf litter of a forest floor. Diana's back was pressed up against hers, and Flick sang in her hand. Every hair on her body stood at attention and her heart thudded.

Something wasn't right.

The forest was tense with an unnatural stillness. Nothing moved, no birds sang. Not even a breath of a breeze stirred the leaves on the trees.

They were strange-looking trees, unlike any that Molly had ever seen. But they were still trees, with brown trunks and branches and leaves. And yet the trunks were too smooth, and their bark was too evenly patterned, the branches were too symmetrical, and the leaves were too perfectly oval. In fact, as she scanned the area for danger, she noticed that each tree looked almost like every other tree, and instead of the messy forest floor she was used to, with tons of different plants crowded together fighting for light and space, there were only a few bushes dotted here and there, and they were covered with bright red, perfectly round berries. It looked like someone's garden, or maybe even a stage set, not a forest.

But nothing to be afraid of.

"I smell demon," Diana's voice was a low growl, so soft Molly could barely hear it, but it sent a stab of fear through her heart. Oh, get a grip, she told herself. Of course there are demons. You're in Hell. They're everywhere.

Unfortunately, this didn't make her feel safer.

And then her brain helpfully added that they weren't just demons, they were demons that were so wicked and so dangerous that even Lucifer couldn't deal with them. And any humans they might meet would be just as bad.

Her heart thudded even harder, and cold sweat iced her skin.

"Do you see anything?" Molly asked as she slid Flick into its scabbard.

"No. Let's get moving. We need to get out of these trees. The map shows the area around the castle as plains surrounded by hills with forests. If we go downhill, we'll get out of the forest and maybe we'll be able to see Andromeda's castle."

"Why is it so quiet?"

"I don't know and I don't care. We need to get out of here."

Diana's predator instincts were probably on overdrive, but Molly wasn't going to argue. They headed downhill at a quick, silent trot, with Diana in the lead.

They hadn't gone farther than the length of half a soccer field when a white hand tipped with long, filthy claws appeared out of nowhere and snatched Flick and its scabbard out of Molly's belt. She whirled around and faced a nightmare.

The demon was smaller than she was, but what he lacked in size, he made up for in nastiness. His white, scaly body pulsed with malice and hatred. He was definitely a he. It was white and scaly too. And barbed. Molly almost made the mistake of looking away in disgust. His eye sockets were empty as a blank computer screen, but still managed to glitter with an evil hunger. His bat-like snout quivered with excitement.

"You're from outside!" he hissed, staying well out of their reach and weaving threatening patterns in the air with Flick. He held the sword with practiced ease, and Molly had no doubt that those intricate patterns would have been lethal if the asteroid hadn't stripped away his magic. She was facing the demon equivalent of a warrior mage.

MOLLY! Get me away from this monster. He's disgusting and he wants to kill you! Flick's voice tore at her heart.

"I know because the trading post doesn't have weapons like this beauty." The demon's tongue slithered out of a lip-less mouth that barely had room for all the fangs sticking out of it. The long, gray worm-like thing stretched, quivering, toward Molly and then retracted.

MOLLY, PLEASE!

"I think I will kill you both." The demon hissed. "And, unlike me, you will stay dead, because I do not think that you have walked through Hell's Gate. I will do it slowly—death by a thousand cuts. Oh yessssss." The monster moaned in ecstasy. "I haven't actually killed anyone in centuries."

Flick! Come to me! Molly reached for her blade and the next moment, her beloved sword was in her hand.

"Magic!" the creature snarled. His face contorted in a terrifying mix of greed, rage, and hopelessness as he made a desperate lunge for the sword.

In one swift, elegant reflex, Molly cut the demon in two.

"Shit!" Molly said, staring in horror at the gruesome, still-kicking corpse and plucking Flick's scabbard from its unresisting hand. "I didn't want to kill him."

"You didn't have much choice." Diana put a comforting hand on her shoulder. "He would have killed us."

Molly, you didn't *kill him, which is too bad because that demon is even more wicked than Tamerlane, and much, much older, so he has even more amazingly horrible stories! It will take me months to savor them. But they taste flat and sad, like they didn't really happen to him, but to someone else. Someone else who really mattered. Let's leave before I need to taste him again.*

Molly wiped her sword clean on the demon's corpse and shuddered at Flick's mention of her former weapon's teacher. "Flick, I don't see how you can get any peace with all that evilness inside you. But you're right." Turning to Diana, she said, "We don't want to be here when he revives."

"And Flick's right about the way the demon tasted, too," Diana said as they headed downhill at a mile-eating lope. "That demon didn't smell as strong as the two demons in our Who's Who class. Those guys smelled intensely intense, potent, and evil. And when they moved, I could never be sure which way they were going to go or what they were going to do next. They screamed with danger and soul-shrinking evil. It was their magic that made them that way. That demon was ugly and mean, and I wouldn't trust him any farther than I could kick him, but he didn't have any of that powerful, jittery, twisted magic—that's why I didn't realize he was so near. I won't make that mistake again."

"Yeah. He was ugly and nasty, but he wasn't on fire with evil like a real demon. And, come to think of it, neither was Nysrogh. I mean, he used to be a Prince of the Abyss. If he would've had his normal powers, we'd be toast. Instead he ran away rather than fight us. But we still need to be careful. Even if they don't have magic, if they're here, that means these guys are the wickedest of the wicked and the brightest of the bright."

They ran in silence for a few minutes and then Diana said, "Um, maybe you should put Flick away. It's a beautiful weapon and this is a place ruled by violence. I do not want to fight every inhabitant of Hell for that sword."

Molly sighed. It felt so good and so right to have Flick pressed up against her side and to feel her sword's strong, steely magic mingling with her own. She had hoped to be able to wear it while they were here.

"Sorry Flick, I wish you could stay, but you're just too good looking." Without breaking stride, she tucked her sword back into its pocket between the worlds.

"Did you notice how strong Flick's voice was?" she asked Diana, who was ahead of her on the trail, setting a quick pace.

"Now that you mention it, yes."

"It's as strong as it was in Damia, which has much more magic than our world. Which means this place has at least as much magic as Damia—maybe more."

"Which means," Diana said, "that it's probably something like a spell that removes the prisoners' magic when they walk through the Gate. They are starving for magic in the middle of a thick soup of it! But that would mean that if anyone escapes from here and gets far enough away from the Gate, their magic would probably return. That might explain why Nysrogh was able to do magic."

"Yeah, but that doesn't explain what he was doing in Denzel's and the First's offices. First off, he had to somehow escape from this asteroid and return to earth; and second, demons, even the strongest ones, can't go anywhere they're not invited. I can't believe either Denzel or the First would invite a demon into their space, especially one who was supposed to be in Hell.

"But anyway, since this place is pulsing with it, doing magic should be as easy for us here as it is in Damia. We should practice jumping. We'll probably be doing lots of it."

Out of necessity, Molly had gotten good at jumping while she was traveling with Asmodius in Damia. It was much harder at home, but fortunately, she had been able to teleport there as well.

"See that bush up there that's right next to the trail? I'm gonna see how hard it is to jump to it."

She mentally reached for a line of power near the bush and willed herself to be there.

After a heartbeat of swirling blackness, her feet landed on leaf-litter. The bush was beside her and she turned to see Diana standing on the trail, mouth open and eyes wide.

"You did it!"

"And it was freakin' easy! You need to learn how. We'll be a lot safer."

It took Diana about five minutes to master the art of jumping. Molly decided it was even easier than in Damia, but still tiring.

They cut Diana's practice time short so they could keep moving, and the forest soon turned into tree stumps. Without the trees, the view was amazing. The hill, dotted with tree stumps and brush, sloped down and down into a broad valley. Huge swaths of it were black, like they'd been burned. The valley, surrounded by snow-capped mountains, was flat and dotted with small, ugly houses, some off by themselves and some in village-like groups. A few ant-sized figures moved along a network of paths. The castle stood atop a cliff at one end of the valley. It was everything a castle should be. Huge, square, and foreboding. A tall tower with a pointy roof anchored each corner. Built of the same gray stone that formed the cliff, it perched like a vulture, dominating the landscape.

Watching…Waiting.

The cliff face soared straight up. It would take some serious climbing skills to make it up that smooth surface.

"Whoever chopped down all these trees sure made a mess," Diana said. "The ground is all cut up and gouged and there are dead branches all over. Let's go back into the forest—walking is easier there."

"And we'll stay hidden." Molly pointed down to the valley. "If we can see them, they can see us. And I'd rather not be seen. But the good thing is, they're still here, so not everyone's figured out how to escape."

Senses on alert, and every nerve on edge, they headed back up into the forest, searching for a trail that paralleled the valley.

31

Molly

Night didn't just fall here. It pounced. One minute it was dusk and the next minute it was dark.

Sort of.

A shadowy-dim, blood-red light flooded the asteroid. It beamed down from the red planet that had become visible on the horizon. Ominous and brooding, it blocked out a huge chunk of the starry, black sky. Molly could see its surface details through the tree branches—craters and slowly swirling surface storms, and streaks of darker red. The temperature dropped suddenly from warm to decidedly cool, and ground fog snaked through the forest like a living thing.

"Do you think that's Mars?" Molly shivered and pulled a jacket out of her pack.

"It might be," Diana replied. "I do know that it's not our moon. Lady Moon makes my blood sing and sends me strength. This planet just watches like an evil eye, waiting for a chance to strike."

They proceeded carefully, tense with fear. Because as it got darker, things got busier. Hell's denizens were definitely nocturnal. Screams and snarls of fury, anguish, terror, and every emotion in between echoed up from the valley, setting Molly's heart pounding and her nerves jangling.

Then the awful noise stopped.

The tense, expectant silence was even more terrifying than the screams and snarls.

And the jolt when they started up again was heart-stopping.

Quick footsteps thudded on a nearby trail coming up from the valley, fleeing whatever madness was happening for the quiet of the woods.

"What's happening down there?" Diana snarled. Pulling Molly off the trail and back into the trees. She still looked like her cool, exotic human self, but she was in total predator mode, radiating don't-mess-with-me danger and brutality.

"I don't even want to think about it," Molly whispered, hunkering behind a tree as a panicked, blood-soaked human ran by, followed moments later by a blood-soaked demon. One of his bat wings was shredded, and the claw on the other was covered with blood. And blood dripped from his fangs. His breath came in quick, ragged gasps, punctuated by low, guttural growls. Was he chasing the human or were they both fleeing the same nightmare? Impossible to tell.

"Everyone here is afraid. I can smell it in the air." Diana's voice was a soft, edgy rumble. "They travel alone because they don't trust anyone, and they hate everyone. I can smell that, too. Come, the trail is clear now."

Fortunately, the demon and the human were headed away from the castle, so the two mages trotted quickly in the opposite direction. Several minutes later, Diana skidded to a stop. Her eyes swept up and down the trail. "Someone's coming, but I can't tell which way they're coming from. Off the trail. Now!"

Diana slipped into the forest on one side of the trail and Molly disappeared into the other.

A frighteningly short time later a demon loped silently into view and stopped exactly at the point where they'd left the trail. It stood perfectly still, wolf-like snout quivering, drool dripping in strings from wicked-sharp fangs. Its hungry, mean eyes darted from one side of the trail to the other, and its claws flexed, anticipating a kill. It turned around slowly, searching, trying to figure out where its dinner was hiding. It stopped. Its evil, yellow eyes glared through the forest and focused directly on Molly, who was plastered against a tree, heart pounding, doing her best tree imitation. Its jaws opened and its tongue flicked out like a snake's, tasting the air in confusion. It could smell her, it knew right where she was, but it couldn't see her.

A huge Amazon of a woman came slinking along to trail from the opposite direction, silent and swift. Her brown, heavily muscled body was naked except for a dirty leather loin cloth. Her face contorted into a mask of cruel anger when she spotted the demon. Without a pause, she drew the bronze knife tucked in her belt and slid it up under the distracted monster's back ribs and into its heart.

"Out of my way, Lobo," she snarled, kicking the corpse aside. "Steenking demon!"

As the woman disappeared around a curve in the trail like a malevolent shadow, Molly stood paralyzed with horror at the senseless brutality of this place where death didn't exist. By the time she was able to move, Diana was back on the trail waiting for her.

"Next time follow me to the downwind side," she whispered as they continued to jog toward the castle. The forest pressed in on either side, the planet-light highlighting the trees and casting black shadows that shifted in the blood-red mist. Molly shivered as her gibbering brain began imagining, in terrifying detail, all the things that might be lurking nearby.

They were still heading toward the castle.

At least they hoped they were.

Diana stopped suddenly and Molly slammed into her. It was like hitting a solid wall of terror.

"Another demon?"

"I smell cheeseburgers," her carnivorous friend said, and drew in a deep, ecstatic breath.

"You're crazy! There aren't any Burger Kings in Hell."

"There must be, because I smell Whoppers."

"How can you tell they're Whoppers?"

"I know a Whopper when I smell one. My nose doesn't lie," she said as she loped into the forest.

"Come back here! You have no idea what's out there. It could be a trap."

"I *do* know what's out there. Whoppers. I am hungry."

"Then eat a granola bar!"

Diana growled, made a rude sound of disgust, and continued into the woods.

Shit! What kind of nightmare were they headed into? Because by this time, Molly was sure that there could be nothing but night-mares in this gods-forsaken place. All she could do was follow her friend and try to protect her.

Diana slipped swiftly through the forest, making a beeline for the burgers, and Molly stumbled over roots and bushes, swearing softly and trying to keep up.

Diana finally stopped, and Molly crept up beside her.

"They're in there," she said, her voice thick with hunger, but barely audible. She pointed into a small clearing, glowing in the red planetlight and striped with the pitch-black shadows from the huge tree trunks that surrounded it. It was empty except for the shadows and shrubs.

"Let's get out of here," Molly said grabbing Diana's arm.

She didn't budge.

A human form emerged from the shadows and into the ghastly red light.

It was holding a Burger King bag.

"Micah!" Molly breathed, and sprinted into the clearing, Diana right behind her. Molly flew into his arms and Diana grabbed the bag. He tensed, and then wrapped his arms around her and held her close. She buried her face in his shoulder, breathing in his familiar scent of leather and peppermint and reveling in the feel of his warm, safe body, of her heart pounding because of something besides terror and the total cruelty of this world. She began weeping in great, choking sobs. Micah stroked her hair and rocked her gently.

Oh jeez. She was finally in his arms, the place she'd been dreaming about for months, and it felt even better than she'd ever imagined. And what was she doing? Crying like a baby and sniffling and getting his leather jacket all slimy. The realization made her cry even harder. When she at last got her sobs under control, he hugged her close and then gently pushed her away. She looked up, saw her face reflected in his damn mirrored aviator glasses, and cringed. Her hair was a mess, her eyes were all puffy. Tears were streaming down her cheeks, and snot was dripping out of her nose. Yuck. No wonder he'd pushed her away.

Micah produced a handkerchief from somewhere and offered it to her.

A handkerchief? Micah? Who'd a thunk? She wiped away the tears, blew her nose, and, as an afterthought, wiped the slime off his shoulder. She tried to give it back, but the corners of his lips quirked up as he regarded the soggy fabric. "You can keep it."

"Um, thanks," she mumbled, shoving it into her jeans pocket. "What are you doing here?"

"Eat your burger and I'll tell you. That is, if there are any left."

Diana was sitting cross-legged in the middle of the clearing happily devouring Whoppers. "Here," she said, holding the bag up to Molly.

The three mages sat back-to-back in a circle, bathed in red mist and black gloom, scanning the woods for trouble. Molly and Diana gulped down their meal. When they were finished, Diana gazed hopefully at Micah and sniffed.

One corner of his mouth curved up, but his eyes remained inscrutable behind the dark, mirrored lenses. "Yes, I brought you these as well," he said, fishing two large, dark-chocolate bars from his coat pocket. "You might want to save some for later."

"Thanks, you are a prince," Diana said, breaking off a piece of chocolate. "There may be hope for you yet. But you are also a fool. Some demons, as you know very well, have an acute sense of smell. You could have gotten yourself killed."

"I don't think so. And besides, I was counting on your nose finding me before they did. Now listen up, ladies. I have bad news." And he told them about his disturbing conversation with Detective Fox and his visit with the Librarian.

Molly was glad he'd let them eat first because the mere thought of facing Tamerlane again made her gut clench with fear. Tamerlane was more powerful than any of the adepts in the Web. And not only that, he was an eternal, a creature capable of sucking the life force out of anything living and making it his own. Eternals were faster and stronger than any vampire, and like a vampire, could live forever. When their body wore out, they simply found another suitable human, touched them, kicked out their soul and aura, and moved into their body.

"That's impossible!" Molly could barely choke out the denial through her terror. "He's dead! I killed him. I saw him turn to dust. And he didn't touch anyone. And he couldn't have moved into a ring—it's not alive."

"You killed his *body*," Micah said. "When you die, your soul and personality hang around for a while. The stronger your identity, the longer you can stay in close touch with the physical world. Tamerlane is an eternal. The body he inhabits at any particular time means nothing to him; it's his original identity that matters and it's had centuries to become strong and vibrant. Think about what his aura looked like."

"Yeah," Molly said, "It was amazing. So bright and complex that it almost hurt to look at it."

"So, when you killed the body he was in," Micah continued, "he wouldn't just die, even if there was no one to touch. According to the Librarian, it's possible to enchant an object so that it will house your soul and identity for awhile. Tamerlane didn't live to be centuries old by being careless. In the unlikely event that someone did manage to kill him, he enchanted his ring, which he always wore, so he could move into it. The ring is solid gold and beautiful, so he was confident that someone would pick it up and he could take them over. They don't teach us this at the Academy—for obvious reasons."

"But Tamerlane wouldn't be here, would he?" Diana asked Molly's next question for her.

"Maybe not, but he might be. The Librarian said Tamerlane's been to Hell before, so he could jump here again. It sent me to warn you and keep an eye out for the bastard because it didn't want to take chances."

And then an even more frightening thought occurred to her.

"How will I know it's Tamerlane? He could be anybody."

"You'll know because I know what Tamerlane's soul looks like. I can tell if he's taken over a body because I'll see his soul in it."

"You can see people's souls?!" Diana stared at him in horrified fascination.

Micah nodded sadly.

"That's kinda creepy," Diana said.

Oh jeez, that is totally creepy, Molly thought. I'm in love or lust or whatever with a guy who can see my soul.

Shit.

I don't even know what my soul looks like.

He knows more about me than I do.

She shivered as she remembered that awful night last fall when Micah had found her in Wilshire Park and shaken and slapped her out of a deep, deadly stupor. When she'd come to and looked up at him, he wasn't wearing his glasses, and she'd seen his eyes. They were two swirling pits of blackness, pulling her relentlessly into their depths. What would have happened if she hadn't scrunched her eyes closed. She'd forgotten all about Micah's eyes until now. Had she blocked the memory? Or had he somehow made her forget? All she knew for sure was that Micah, the guy that made her heart race with a single glance, the guy she never stopped thinking about, was even darker and more terrifying than she'd thought.

She shrank away from him in fear.

And then froze.

Micah had been watching her closely, and when he saw her fear, he'd crossed his arms over his gut and bowed his head so she couldn't see his face.

Shit. You are such an idiot. Micah just handed you a piece of himself. A very private piece. A piece that makes him vulnerable. Which is the last thing Micah Ortiz ever wants to be. And what do you do? You look at him like he's some sort of monster. He's never gonna trust you again. You'll be lucky if he even speaks to you. Shit. Shit. Shit.

"I didn't want to tell you, but I had to," he said, interrupting her self-recriminations. "If Tamerlane is here and we find him, he will probably attack—at least I would if I were him. I need you both to believe me immediately when I tell you it's him or none of us will survive. But please don't tell anyone else. Not even Adam. Especially not Adam. I don't trust hackers."

Of course, he didn't want anyone to know. Micah wasn't exactly mister popularity at school, but if this got out, everyone would avoid him like a bad case of zits. And if the Ravens found out, would they still follow him? Molly was struggling to figure out how *she* felt about him, and she was one of his biggest fans.

"What does seeing someone's soul tell you about them?" Diana asked. Her horror had vanished. She now looked curious and sympathetic.

Of course she would be sympathetic.

When the mages at Grant found out she was probably a werewolf, they'd backed off in fear—like Molly had just done to Micah. Diana knew how much this hurt, and she also knew that even though someone has power, that doesn't automatically make them evil or mean. And the only way to get a clue if someone is evil or mean is to talk to them about their power—and listen carefully.

Duh.

"Not much. We actually get more useful info by reading auras," Micah said, sitting up straighter and leaning toward Diana, obviously relieved to explain. "Your soul is sort of like your higher self. It chooses a body, personality, and family for each of its lifetimes so it can learn the stuff it needs to and repay its karmic debts. When someone dies, their personality gloms onto their soul as it leaves. But while they're alive they're separate. So when I look at your soul, what I see isn't you, or your personality, or even your thoughts. I see the being behind you and all the identities it chose before you."

"And what does that tell you?" Diana asked again.

"I can tell how old a soul is and whether or not it's content with the way its person is leading their life, which gives me clues about that person. Each soul is unique. It can't be disguised. A person's soul identifies them even more positively than a fingerprint."

"But seeing someone's soul doesn't let you read their mind or see their future or even know whether or not they like you?" Diana asked.

"No." His mouth curled up into a grim smile.

So maybe seeing a person's soul wasn't as intrusive as Molly had thought. But in a way, it was even worse. Micah could see who you really were and all your past lives. It must have been confusing for him when he was a kid.

"Have you always been able to see souls?" Diana asked, anticipating Molly's next thought.

"No. Remember when we tranced out and invoked the gods in our Greek Mythology classes? Did you ever notice anyone who seemed really out of it when they came back from one of those trips?"

Yes, she had. When they'd returned from their visit to Apollo, Ophelia Pettygrove had been lying face up amid the red poppies and golden grasses of the Greek hillside, eyes staring blindly up at the clear blue sky. Krios, their instructor, had closed her eyes, thrown his outer robe over her, and dismissed the class. Ophelia was always getting involved in a project or piece of research and forgetting to eat. And, since brains use up humongous amounts of sugar when they do magic, Molly had figured she'd skipped a meal or two and fainted from low blood sugar.

"They'd been totally possessed by the god you were visiting," Micah continued, "not just talking to them like everyone else in the class. When a god possesses you, you become that god's agent in this world for the rest of your life. They tell you what you're supposed to be doing for them, and they usually give you a gift to help you accomplish it. They don't ask if that's okay with you, they just do it. You have no choice. The adepts never mention this, probably because they don't want to freak us out so bad we won't trance. But when it happens to you it's a total freak-out anyway. The Lord of the Underworld, He Who Must Not Be Named, possessed me and gave me the ability to see souls, although I wouldn't call it a gift."

"Demons!" Diana whispered, leaping to her feet. "They've surrounded us."

Oh jeez. They'd smelled the Whoppers.

The three mages stood back-to-back in the dusky-red clearing and scanned the forest that loomed chill, dark, and nearly invisible all around them. Not a twig snapped and neither foot nor claw rustled the leaf litter. Diana had morphed into a monstrous, black nightmare of a wolf, snapping and sizzling with sapphire-blue magic. Molly drew Flick and heard the snick of Micah's opening switchblade.

They waited...

"Maybe they left," said Micah, his voice a hopeful whisper.

"Not a chance," Molly said. "They have nothing left to lose and a sword to gain." Make sure you kill them."

Right on cue, five demons erupted out of the forest. A goat-headed, cloven-hoofed monster twice Molly's size headed straight for her, sword in hand, golden eyes blazing with greed. As he snarled and slashed the blade down toward her neck, Molly somer-saulted between his legs, swiveled on her butt, and sliced through the tendons just above the back of his knees. The demon roared and dropped like a puppet with cut strings. Before he even hit the ground, Molly drove Flick through his back and into his heart.

Micah was fending off a demon with a lizard's body and man's grotesque head. His tough scales protected him from Micah's knife. Meanwhile, a creature with a snarling lion's head and black bat wings had worked his way behind the young mage and leaped for his unprotected back. Molly lunged forward and swept her blade through the creature's neck. With her next step, she kicked it aside to keep both the body and the black blood spurting out of it from hitting Micah. She looked up just in time to see him throw his switchblade into the lizard demon's eye. The beast howled and grabbed at the knife. As it raised its arms, Molly lunged forward and drove Flick through a gap between its scales and into its heart.

Diana had torn the throat out of a jackal-headed demon and snapped its neck. Another demon with huge wings and clawed feet and hands had jumped on her back and was about to drive a wicked-looking knife into her neck. In one swift motion, Micah plucked his knife out of the lizard demon's eye and threw it. It drove into the space between the demon's wings with a thunk, and the demon toppled off Diana's back. The snarling werewolf, who was as vicious and dreadful as any of the demons attacking her, spun around, grabbed the demon's neck in her huge, bloody jaws and snapped it with a quick jerk. The crack echoed through the clearing like a gunshot.

In the eerie silence that followed, Molly and Micah stared at each other in shock, their breath smoking from their lips in the chill night air. Diana scanned the forest for something else to kill. When nothing presented itself, she growled. It was a soft growl, but it came from deep inside her. Molly shuddered as it vibrated through her chest. The werewolf shook herself, blue sparks of leftover savage energy flying off her coarse, black coat. Then she stretched—a perfect downward facing dog. Digging a hole with her huge fore-paws, the werewolf gazed pointedly around the clearing littered with hamburger-scented trash and bloody demon corpses, nudged Molly's pack, and trotted into the forest.

Molly could feel Micah's presence like a magnet, tugging on her heart till it ached. She knew if she'd just walk over and put her arms around him it would stop hurting. She wanted to tell him that yes, she'd been weirded out when he'd said he could see souls, but after he'd explained, she was okay with it. She'd met Hades, and he wasn't nearly as scary as all the myths keep saying.

In fact, she'd sort of liked him. Unfortunately, Micah was ignoring her, busily gathering up the greasy papers, stuffing them in the hole, and covering them over with dirt. Molly choked back a sob, grabbed her pack and began picking her way through the trees. She'd try to patch things up later. They needed to put as much distance as possible between themselves and all those dead demons, or there might not be a later.

When they'd all reached the trail, they loped silently toward the castle, Diana in the lead.

32

Micah

After just a few minutes of the quick pace Diana set, Micah's breath was getting short, and he was forced to acknowledge the sad fact that the werewolf and the warrior mage were in much better shape than he was.

With a ragged sigh, he focused on the terrifying, black wolf in front of him so he wouldn't have to think about Molly. Diana's soul, however, was far from terrifying. It was a dazzling fountain of multicolored light that sprang from her heart and coursed through her light bodies. It was younger than most mage's souls, but just as powerful. And it was happy with the fact that its human had somehow managed to embrace not only the part of her that thrived on a predator's joyous, violent life, but also her rational, gentle part that wanted to be a naturopathic doctor. He had always been fascinated by the Ukrainian mage and would have liked to know her better, but she'd made it quite obvious that she hated his guts. Bringing the Whoppers to Hell had not only been a way to locate them, it had also been a peace offering to Diana. It had worked. He was pretty sure that he was at least off her shit list.

But he'd lost Molly. Her look of horror when he'd told them he could see souls was burned into his brain. He'd been afraid this would happen, but he hadn't had much of a choice. Tamerlane was alive somewhere in some-body, and Micah was the only person who could tell Molly which body that was. Unfortunately, he'd had to tell her how he knew so she'd believe him; so he could give her a fighting chance at staying alive. As far as Micah was concerned, the trade-off was worth it. He couldn't even begin to imagine a world without Molly, even a Molly who thought he was a monster. At least he'd had the chance to hold her close, to breathe in her fresh, woodsy, cinnamon scent, to feel their auras click together at last, like two pieces of a talisman.

But then she'd started sobbing.

He hated it when women cried.

It triggered memories of his mother's heartbreaking sobs when his father had come home roaring drunk and mad at the world and taken it out on them. He'd been helpless then, and he was helpless now. Because this place, where hate and fear and despair hung like curses in the bloody night, was awful enough to make even a warrior mage cry. And there wasn't a thing he could do about it.

Sounds of struggle erupted behind him and Molly gasped in pain. Micah whipped around to see her twist out of the grasp of a snarling crocodile with a human legs and vulture wings. As she was backing away and reaching for Flick, Micah leaped forward and plunged his switchblade through the demon's leathery back scales and into its heart.

The creature had clawed Molly's jacket and T-shirt to shreds, leaving four bleeding gashes across her right breast. If he'd been paying attention, it wouldn't have happened. He'd screwed up again. They stared at each other over the still-twitching demon. One of its wings brushed Micah's ankle sending chills crawling up his leg.

Rage washed over his fear and helplessness, and with it came the urge to snarl and scream and kick the now quiet corpse of her attacker. Diana's growl was a low, ominous rumble as she edged between Micah and Molly. The wolf's piercing blue eyes locked onto his. Their message was clear. Don't even go there. But there was understanding in them as well. Who could understand uncontrollable rage better than a werewolf? Diana probably dealt with it all the time and knew that even uncontrollable rage could and must be controlled. Micah growled softly, unclenched his fists, and stepped back. Shoving his rage back into its flimsy cage, he stood facing Diana, breathless and shaking. The wolf nodded and touched his foot with her paw.

Maybe he couldn't control this place or its cruel inhabitants, but he could control his temper. And there was another thing he could do to make things better.

"Molly, you're hurt. Hold still," he said.

Micah began clearing her aura over the vicious claw marks, trying, with absolutely no success, to ignore the well-formed piece of anatomy they disfigured. As he began adding healing light, he stepped back in surprise and awe. Hell's dense magic shimmered green and sparkling along the light path he'd made and flooded into the gaps in Molly's light body, busily weaving them together. Within minutes, the bleeding had stopped, and tender, pink, new flesh had filled in the deep gashes in her physical body.

"Wow! Thanks." She quickly turned away and shrugged out of her backpack. Her cheeks were definitely flushed, and her breathing might have been a bit faster than normal.

"It was the asteroid. Its light went into you through the link I made. Way cool, but kinda scary," he babbled, trying to hide his embarrassment. "This place is like a control freak on steroids."

And it takes one to know one.

"Yeah. But I'm glad I don't hurt anymore," she said, pulling on a clean top and sweatshirt and stuffing her bloody, shredded clothes into a pocket that conveniently appeared on the side of her pack.

Then Molly touched the shoulder of the black nightmare beside her. "I feel much safer when you're in your wolf form, and I know you do too, but I think your magic is so strong that it's somehow attracting demons. You've gotta switch back." She carried her pack a short distance off the trail and set it behind a tree. "Here. And use the wipes in the side pocket." A half-growl, half-whine of protest followed her back to the trail.

"I wonder how long it takes for them to come alive again," Molly said, gazing down at the corpse.

"It probably depends on how badly the body is damaged," Micah said, relieved that she had found something safe for them to talk about while they waited for Diana.

"It starts with a few little sparkles of green light, and more appear until the body is completely surrounded. Then gold comes in. But that's the most we've dared to watch," Molly replied.

The first green spark had just begun to dance over the corpse as Diana emerged from the forest; every hair in place, clean, neat, and dressed in jeans, blue sweatshirt, and a purple Polartec vest. No one would ever suspect she was just seconds away from being a huge, vicious wolf that fought and killed with savage glee.

And no one would suspect that just a short while ago the lovely, fragile-looking girl shrugging into her backpack had dropped and killed a demon twice her size and skewered another one in a matter of seconds. Micah had caught a glimpse of her deadly grace and efficiency and her grim, merciless face—the face of a practiced, skillful killer. He had known she was a warrior mage, but the reality was now beginning to sink in. The warrior Molly was completely different from the Molly he was used to. The warrior Molly was tough, unyielding, and aggressive, the sort of person you'd want to have your back in a fight, but not the sort of person you'd want as a girlfriend. Which one was she really? Or was she both? And if she was both, did the two Mollies overlap? And if so, by how much?

And what would it be like to kiss a girl who could kill you in a dozen easy ways? Micah shivered, and then shivered again because he couldn't tell whether he was shivering from fear or desire.

At least now he was beginning to understand the Dr. Jekyll and Mr. Hyde nature of his companions and was totally amazed at the ease with which they flipped between the two personalities. Together they were a badass, lethal force. Micah reluctantly let go of any remaining thought that he could protect this deadly duo and simply hoped that he wouldn't distract them or get in their way if they needed to fight again. His job was simple—keep an eye out for Tamerlane's soul and let Molly know in time to defend herself.

"Let's go!" Diana said as soon as she spotted the sparkle.

They moved out at a slower pace, much to Micah's relief, and soon arrived at a crossroads made by another trail coming up from the valley. Diana stopped and sniffed.

"Off the trail," she whispered. "This way."

Micah and Molly followed her as she disappeared into the forest.

No sooner had they settled into their hiding place than two humans walked by on the trail leading uphill.

"Good-by, Rasputin," said one as he turned onto the trail that paralleled the valley. "I'll see you in a few centuries."

Rasputin, a tall, gaunt man in a long brown robe waved half-heartedly at his companion and continued uphill. His narrow, black-bearded face was a terrifying mask composed of equal parts of anguish and malice.

"I want to see where he's going," Diana whispered when the mad monk was out of sight.

The three mages crept soundlessly along the trail. The trees here were huge—much larger than any other trees they'd seen. Their branches formed a dense canopy that blocked out the planet's light. Much as Micah hated that ominous red glow, this quiet, brooding blackness was even worse. It left him breathless and nervous, jumping at every real or imagined sound, braced for an attack that could happen any second or never come at all. Fortunately, Diana had no trouble seeing in even the darkest dark. He gripped the tail of her vest to keep from losing her and felt Molly hanging on to the back of his jacket. They moved through the thick silence for what felt like forever. Then, far ahead on the ruler straight trail, red light beamed through enormous tree trunks. They crept forward cautiously, blending into the forest until they were nearly invisible. A large clearing surrounded by a tall fence made of wickedly barbed iron poles opened up ahead of them. A gate in the fence faced the trail and stood ajar, the key still in the lock. Above the gate swung a sign made of simple iron letters that spelled out "Peaceful Rest Cemetery." The red planet hung menacingly just above the treetops, turning the mist that snaked along the ground into swirls of blood.

Inside the fence, rows of black coffins perched atop sawhorses. A powerful, vibrant soul was tethered to each coffin by a silver cord, but Micah was pretty sure it was really attached to the body inside. He now noticed what he'd missed on the other demons he'd seen. A strong field of electric-blue light shimmered around each soul and down its cord. It looked almost exactly like the electric-blue stasis fields that adepts wove around people or things they wanted to freeze so they couldn't move or change. The blue light was probably generated by the asteroid and was what it used to trap the soul in its body and isolate it from the multiverse. This, of course, would completely cut off the person's magic.

The awful reality of Hell became achingly clear.

A soul was supposed to be free to roam the multiverse, making all its resources and light available to its physical body. When the body dies, its personality and memories become part of the soul, which is supposed to move on, rest, recoup, and if it chooses, continue its evolution in a new body. But here were dozens and dozens of beautiful souls isolated from all of creation and trapped in their bodies' rotting remains. The seething mist that coiled around them pulsed with their grief and misery.

This was cruel, unnatural, and evil.

He shuddered as he scanned the cemetery for Rasputin, and spotted him gliding silently through the coffins behind a giant demon dressed in a sleeveless tunic made of the same coarse brown cloth as the monk's robe. Muscles rippled along the demon's broad shoulders under pale, snake-like skin. He had human hands and reptilian legs and feet. His head was a human skull.

This place terrified him and made his heart ache, but the bodies and souls that were here were trapped in coffins. Micah couldn't see how it had anything to do with the escaped demon that murdered mages. They should go back to the crossroads and head for the castle. But there was a mystery here and he wanted to know more about it. Was the answer worth the risk? As he turned to ask Molly and Diana what they thought, they were already tiptoeing through the gate. Micah shook his head and followed them, only more cautiously.

As they moved closer, they heard the demon snarl, "I am full up. Perhaps I can find one whose time is over." He stalked through the coffins, glancing at the foot of each one as he passed. Micah stopped to examine the nearest coffin. It was metal, probably iron. And so were the sawhorses. A metal tag, deeply incised with a series of numbers, had been bolted onto the foot of the coffin. A date, maybe?

"Ah, here," said Skullface, stopping beside a coffin. "And you will fit. I won't have to cut you up." He turned to the human. "How long?"

"Two centuries."

"Then you owe me two thousand gold wardens," the demon said and held out his pale, scaly hand. The monk poured a pile of golden coins into it. Skullface's eye-sockets glowed an even brighter green as he counted out each one. They clinked cheerfully as he slipped them into a pouch on his tool belt. Then he pulled out a wrench and began removing the large bolts in the lid. When he was finished, he lifted the lid and tipped the coffin on its side, dumping the desiccated remains onto the ground. A huge, grinning cat skull with goat horns and a jaw full of fangs stared vacantly up into the starry sky from the center of a jumble of bones. The soul followed, attached to the bones by its silver cord.

The demon gestured to the empty coffin and Rasputin climbed in and lay down.

"Now?" asked the demon.

"Yes," replied the human.

Skullface reached into the coffin and snapped Rasputin's neck with an echoing crack.

The three mages watched in horror as the demon, humming tunelessly, replaced the lid and began bolting it down over the human, whose heels were still drumming on the metal coffin.

Diana grabbed Micah's and Molly's arms and began tugging them toward the gate. Her face was a mask of horror and revulsion. They slipped silently out of the ghastly graveyard, and then ran like all the inhabitants of Hell were after them, tripping and stumbling in the darkness, until they reached the crossroads.

33

Micah

The werewolf, the warrior mage, and the gang-leader stood at the crossroads and stared grimly at each other.

"Shit!" said Molly. She was actually trembling. "I can't believe what I just saw. We need to talk."

"Let's get off the trail then," said Diana, sniffing the air and peering up and down both paths. The malevolent red eye was now at about the ten o'clock position in the sky. It gleamed down through the trees with vicious brilliance, casting shadows that writhed and danced in the slight breeze.

They slipped down-hill through the forest like the shadows that surrounded them and soon found a tiny clearing that was well away from both trails. They were near the slashed and burned area, so Micah could see that they'd almost reached the castle.

Beside and below the castle, he could just make out a large, thick-edged outline of a rectangle set on its short side.

That had to be the Gate.

"How could Rasputin have just laid there and let that demon break his neck?" Molly asked, drawing his attention back to the clearing.

Micah gazed at her sadly. Of course, she would be freaked out. Molly was all about life. Her aura gleamed with the red of vitality and passion, not anger and death.

"Maybe after all this time in Hell, he was happy to pay a fortune for a few centuries of oblivion," he replied. "And he wasn't the only one who needed a break. Skullface is running a booming business. What a racket! I bet his partner was in one of those boxes, and when he gets tired, Skullface'll dump him out and get in himself."

"I guess," said Molly. "But I remember when *my* life was a living hell. Even though there were times when I could have just given up and died, I still fought it."

"Yes, but could you have kept doing it for a hundred years? If time runs the same way here as it does on earth, Rasputin's been living in Hell since the early 1900's."

"There is no way I could let someone kill me either," Diana said. "But, after a hundred years of Hell, perhaps things would look different." She unzipped a side pocket of Molly's pack and took out her cell phone. "I'm going to see if this app Adam installed on our phones works and let him know what's happening. He's probably frantic by now. I'll be back. Don't go wandering off." And she headed into the trees.

Micah watched her leave and tried to think of something safe that he and Molly could talk about.

A small, calloused hand slipped softly into his and held it with an iron grip. Startled, he whipped around and found himself staring into Molly's sad, upturned face. If his reaction surprised her, she didn't show it. If anything, her grip on his hand tightened. His heart shuddered and thought about stopping. This was it. She was gonna tell him to leave her alone. But that would be stupid. Where was he gonna go? And she needed him to watch out for Tamerlane.

"I'm okay with you being able to see people's souls. Really I am." she said. "It just kinda freaked me out at first. But when you explained about it, it wasn't so scary. I mean, Diana and I can be pretty scary too, but you seem to be okay with that. It's like all three of us are dangerous freaks, controlled by someone or something bigger and more powerful than we are. Something that makes us do things that we'd never even think of doing. Awful things. All we can do is hope that thing controlling us is looking at the big picture and is really on our side. We need to stick together, because who will understand us better than us?" Her soul continued to sparkle and swirl and her aura stayed bright and steady. If anything, it got brighter. Micah knew she was telling the truth. Or at least she thought she was. Relief surged through him like warm sunlight into a cold, dark room, and life was suddenly good again. But all his stupid, numb brain could think to say was, "I'm glad you're okay with it." Which didn't even begin to say what he was really feeling.

But it was enough, thank the gods.

He felt her relax just a little, and she looked up at him and smiled. It was a tiny smile. It didn't light up her eyes, it just softened them. "I'm so glad you're here. This place is the pits. It's cruel and evil and it makes my heart hurt. Diana is wonderful, but when she's edgy and ready to morph, which is like all the time here, she's not the sort of person you can go to for comfort. Would you put your arms around me and tell me everything's gonna be okay? Even if it's not?"

Her straightforward honesty and trust took his breath away. On the street, nothing was straightforward and you didn't trust anyone—especially with something as fragile as your feelings. But he managed to mumble, "Of course," and took her in his arms.

Her hands slid under his open jacket and around his waist. As he pulled her tight against him, every one of their light bodies clicked together and he was at peace. Suddenly he could say with complete honesty, "It's okay. Everything's gonna be fine."

"Thanks." She sighed and melted into him. But her embrace was fierce and tight.

Micah didn't know how long they stood wrapped in each other's arms and auras, but when Diana returned and said, "Um...you guys...I'm back," he decided that it wasn't nearly long enough.

"It worked, and I was right. Adam was frantic," she said as they turned toward her. "Almost as soon as we'd left, Estelle got the news that they'd found the Second Webmaster dead in his living room. Shredded to bits."

"Oh, gods, that's awful," Molly said, her face a mask of horror and grief. Micah knew it wasn't just because she was grieving the Second's death. She was deathly afraid for Estelle. Molly's parents had died less than a year ago, and now Asmodius was dead. Losing her grandmother would be devastating.

"Was it Nysrogh?" she asked. "The First and his secretary weren't shredded, they died of heart attacks."

"They're pretty sure it was. There was a black feather on the floor."

"We're running out of time," Diana said. "Everything seems to be normal here, at least as normal as things probably get. Let's go straight to the castle and see if Andromeda has any clues about how Nysrogh escaped and where Asmodius is."

"Fine, but how are we gonna get there without being seen?" Micah asked. "That valley is where everybody lives. It'll be way crowded."

"There was hardly anyone on the trail we were on, and maybe it will take us all the way to the castle," Molly said.

"Okay, fine," said Diana and headed up hill to the trail paralleling the valley.

Diana set a fast pace and they found that the trail did, indeed, continue to the castle, or at least to the small mountain it was built on. Its sheer, rock sides soared hundreds of feet straight up out of the valley and up past the highest of the hills behind it.

"The door into the castle that the Librarian told us about is up that way, I think," Molly said, pointing to a small path that climbed almost straight up along the side of the pinnacle to the top of the hill they'd followed around the valley. The same path led almost straight down to the valley floor.

"Someone's coming," Diana said. "Off the trail. This way!" She began climbing uphill.

They had just settled in behind one of the large, fruit-bearing bushes an easy stone's throw from the trail when a figure appeared around a curve in the path. As it came closer, the bat ears, claws, and bristling fangs made it obvious that it was a demon. It was also definitely male. He was moving at a fast trot, but suddenly skidded to a halt. Twitching his huge, furry ears he turned and scowled at the trail behind them. Soon another demon appeared. Bat-ears hissed like an angry tom cat.

"What are you doing at this end of the valley?" he snarled. "I thought I'd seen the last of you a year ago."

"Well, you thought wrong, asshole," said the other demon. "I'm back." His human face was crisscrossed and puckered with scars, and two fangs protruded from his upper jaw, giving him a slight lisp. "I want to find out if Crazy Moloch has really found our ticket out of here."

Bat-ears and Scarface looked down at the ominous, black Gate. Micah could see a few tiny figures walking toward it through the swirling mist.

"Everyone's arriving early. He said he'd start at midnight," said Bat-ears.

"We might as well go down. It's not like we have anything else to do," said Scarface as he continued toward the downhill trail.

They waited in tense silence until Bat-ears and his acute hearing had disappeared down the trail as well.

"Shit! They *are* escaping," whispered Diana. "We need to find out how they're doing it and stop them."

"Yeah, but whoever this Moloch is won't be starting until midnight," Micah said, gazing up at the angry red planet that was close, but not quite at its highest point. "That won't be for another hour or so. We have time to find this entry-way."

As they headed uphill, Micah decided that Hell's inhabitants probably didn't spend a lot of time at this elevation because the forest here was pristine and park-like. Walking was easy. The trees were huge and the bushes heavy with luscious-looking fruit. Molly reached down to pick a berry. Micah grabbed her wrist.

"That might not be a good idea," he said. "Remember the story of Persephone? She only ate a few pomegranate seeds when she was in the underworld, and she was stuck there for half of every year."

"But they look so good!" Molly protested, gently twisting her wrist out of Micah's grip and reaching for the bush. It took all of Micah's self-control to keep from pulling her away again. You're not sure anything will happen, he told himself sternly. Back off.

"Stop!" Diana said, running back toward Molly. "Micah's right. Why risk it? It's not like we're starving."

"Oh, alright."

Micah sighed with relief.

"Here, have some chocolate," he said, pulling a bar out of his pocket.

The air up here was clear and crisp. The planet glared down out of a black velvet sky filled with millions of sparkling stars. When they reached the ridge line, they walked along it until they came to the base of the castle's mountain. Its rocky sides glowed red orange in the planet-light. Looking up, they could just make out the castle walls, which were built with the same rock and glowed the same ghastly orange. Looking down, the mist-filled valley was a roiling sea of blood. Micah shivered and turned his attention back to their immediate surroundings. The ground along the base of the mountain was cleared to gravelly dirt for the width of a four-lane highway, but the side of the mountain was screened by a thick line of bushes right at its base.

"We're supposed to be able to see the outline of a door in the side of the mountain," Molly said as they scanned it from the cover of the forest. "But we can't see the side of the mountain."

"It will take forever to paw through all those bushes until we find it. I have a better idea," Diana said. She followed the tree line to where it met the trail that followed the mountain up the hill and began sniffing. She continued along the clearing until she was almost at the other end of it. "The door is here," she said, pointing to a spot behind the bushes.

"You can smell doors?" asked Micah.

"No, but I can smell whoever goes through a door. Several hours ago, probably more than six but less than twenty-four, a demon walked up that trail and along here and walked into that bush. He either walked all the way up here to relieve himself, which he didn't because I don't smell pee, or he went through the door on the other side of that bush."

"Wow," said Micah, "that's amazing!"

"No, it's just what werewolves do. But what's really amazing is that I know this demon, but I can hardly believe my nose. It's Nysrogh!"

"It can't be," said Molly. "He's not here anymore. He threw a fireball at us in Denzel's office almost two days ago. We couldn't have imagined that."

"But he was just here. My nose doesn't lie. He smells like burning feathers—very distinctive."

"But he wasn't on fire," said Molly.

"All demons smell smoky, like they're on fire. It was Nysrogh."

"And he's shown us where the door is," said Micah.

They scurried across the clearing into Diana's bush and found the faint outline of a door into the mountain.

"Let's not try to open it yet," Molly said. "We need to get down to the Gate. It's almost midnight."

They slipped silently downhill through the forest like three shadows and stopped when they got back to the trail.

"How will we get down there without being seen?" Diana asked as they stared down at the Gate. Dozens of tiny figures were clustered around it. A circle of torches flickered golden on the mist that swirled like a living thing through the crowd and made the Gate ripple like a dark, lurking shadow.

"They're all on one side of the Gate, and it looks like they're all facing it. So Moloch's probably going to stand in front of it," said Micah. "See that bush that's close to the Gate and on our side of the crowd? We could jump down to it because we can see the ground behind it, and it would hide us from everyone. Do you know how to jump yet?"

"Yes, and it's really easy here. That's a great idea. But let's jump one at a time," Molly said. "They say that you unconsciously correct and don't materialize inside anything, but I don't want to test it if we don't have to."

"Okay, but..." Before Micah could finish his sentence, she'd disappeared.

And reappeared behind the bush beside the Gate. A moment later, Diana materialized beside her. The gang-leader sighed and raised his eyes to the starry sky. Dealing with people who acted independently and without his say-so made him nervous, and traveling with Molly and Diana was like following two puppies through a mine field. He took another minute to make sure they were well hidden, then jumped to join them.

Dozens of demons and maybe ten or fifteen humans stood surrounded by torches that sent strobes of gold light and black shadow across their grotesque features. The humans kept well apart from the demons, and everyone pointedly ignored everyone else. The resulting silence was potent. Micah could feel the waves of anger, fear, and hatred surging and crashing around them. They made the hairs on the back of his neck stand up and his heart race with fear. One misplaced word or move and this quiet, brooding scene would turn into a battlefield. It was even edgier than when two opposing gangs met to organize a truce.

The Gate loomed just to their left.

It was twice as tall as the tallest demon. A door that went nowhere. Walking through it would just put you a few steps farther in that direction.. It looked to be made of satin-smooth stone. The flickering torchlight picked out the figures of demons and human-like creatures carved into its sides. The ones on the right side were screaming in agony and falling. At the bottom, only their legs and hips showed as they plunged into the depths of the earth. On the left bottom side, heads, arms, and torsos of the creatures were climbing out of the ground, reaching up with peaceful expressions. Three winged figures stood on top of the

Gate, carved from the same satiny-smooth, black material. They were stern-looking, inhuman, and beautiful. The one on the right had what looked like a sword in one hand and was in the process of throwing a screaming humanoid down after the figures already falling into Hell. The figure on the left held one hand out in a gesture of welcome and was helping a demon up out of the Gate with the other. The one in the middle stood gazing upward with both arms raised. The flickering gold torchlight shining through the shifting, swirling mist brought the Gate to life, demons and humans writhing and twisting down one side of the Gate and up the other.

It radiated a severe, alien magic—not exactly cruel, but unfeeling and relentless. It pounded into Micah's chest and turned his bones to jelly.

This wouldn't do.

He strengthened his shields.

The pounding decreased.

Molly and Diana were staring at the Gate in horrified fascination. As he watched them, they both snapped up their shields and relaxed, but their looks of horror remained.

"How can they stand it?" asked Diana. "And why would anyone want to give a speech in this horrid place?"

"They can't feel it," Micah said. "To do magic, you have to be able to feel it. And the Gate took away their magic. But they were once all powerful magic users, so they have enough savvy to know that this is a special place."

"Yes, and Moloch probably figured that since they all came in through the Gate, this would be a good place to tell them how to get out," Diana said.

"Oh shit! That's Nysrogh!" Molly whispered, pointing to a bird-headed demon. "I thought you said he'd gone into the castle."

"He might have been coming out of it. But if he escaped, what's he doing back here, and what was he doing in the castle?" Diana asked.

"Nysrogh is a big, badass demon," said Micah, "but his soul is surrounded by the same blue stasis field as everyone else in the crowd. There's no way he could have escaped and no way he could have killed a Webmaster or any other mage for that matter."

"Ah," said Diana, "so that's how it works. A stasis field."

"Or something like it," Micah replied.

"But he *did* escape, and he *did* kill Denzel, and he *was* using magic. Diana and I both saw him!"

"We obviously need to find out more," Micah said.

34

Micah

When the red planet had centered itself exactly over the Gate, a figure appeared out of the mist and glided silently toward the waiting demons. It crossed in front of the Gate and stopped between its two sides, perfectly framed and totally dwarfed by its terrible blackness. He had a bull's head crowned with a crescent of wicked-looking horns. His body was human, but it was also built like a bull—solid, muscular, and larger than life. The swirling mist curled around his legs and hips, making it look like he was floating, godlike, above the ground. He swept his audience with a piercing gaze as he gathered their attention. When every eye was upon him, he spoke.

"I bring you great and wonderful news!

"I died.

"And if I died, so can you!"

There was a great, joyous roar and everyone started talking at once.

Thank the gods! This wasn't a real escape. Moloch was claiming that he'd found a way to die, which judging by the enthusiasm of Hell's inmates, would be a close second to actual escape. And maybe he was telling the truth. His aura looked brighter than the others', and Micah could see that Moloch's soul had only a faint trace of the blue stasis field around it.

And the demon shimmered with magic.

Then, from the midst of the crowd, a voice boomed. "If you died, then what the hell are you doing here, numb nuts?"

Everyone fell silent, except for a few angry growls and mutterings. Micah figured the speaker had only had a few seconds before they attacked.

"I'll tell you why," Moloch continued in a calm, unhurried voice. "It's a fantastic story."

At the mention of a story, demons and humans alike leaned forward in anticipation.

Micah was amazed.

Life in Hell must be really boring if just the promise of a story was better than a good fight. And then he realized that he was hooked too. Even though Moloch's story wouldn't give them any useful information about how Nysrogh had managed to escape and kill three adepts, he still very much wanted the hear it. And it looked like Molly and Diana did as well. Their attention was riveted on the powerful demon at the Gate.

"As many of you know," Moloch continued, "about a year ago I moved up to live in one of the rough shelters on the hillside. And as one of you knows," he looked pointedly at a demon in the back of the crowd, "someone came by and demanded all my food stores. When I wouldn't hand them over, that someone killed me. I expected to float awhile in the soft, pleasant void while my body regenerated and then awake to an empty larder and a ravaged garden.

"But that didn't happen."

The audience rumbled in disbelief and surprise.

"Instead, I started speeding away from my body, watching it get smaller and smaller. Up ahead there was this brilliant light. It was the whitest white I've ever seen, like it was full of nothing and everything all at once. I couldn't wait to be surrounded by it. But then Her Nibs appeared beside me and stopped me with a touch of her hand."

"You saw the Warden?" a demon in the front howled in astonishment.

"And she touched you?" a human over to one side whooped in disbelief.

"It probably wasn't the flesh-and-blood Warden, because I wasn't in my body, but yes, I saw her. And yes, she touched me."

Then they all began yelling, "What did she say? What did she do?"

"What was she wearing?" asked a woman.

"She was smiling and dressed in a white, flowing gown the same color as that amazing light.

"'Congratulations, Moloch,' she said. 'You've graduated from Hell. I came to wish you safe journeys and to ask a favor of you. Would you be willing to go back and tell my other charges that you died and how you did it? You don't have to, but you could save some of them from eons of suffering.'

"I was going to refuse. The thought of returning to this horrible place, even for a short time, made me cringe. And why would I want to make this sacrifice for beings who had been nothing but cruel to me and wouldn't listen anyway?

"And then I realized that I had to.

"Because it was the right thing to do.

"But just out of curiosity I asked what would happen if I said no.

"'Then you would continue on your way,' she said. 'You don't have to do this, and I would understand if you decided not to.'

"So I said yes, and here I am."

All Hell broke loose.

"Liar!"

"What a load of shit!"

"You expect us to believe that?!"

"Who do you think you're talking to? A bunch of fools?!"

Moloch just stood gazing defiantly back at them.

Finally, someone up front said, "How did you do it?" The voice was soft, but somehow it carried over all the outraged cries.

Silence fell with an almost audible thud, and Moloch gathered up that silence until he had just enough, and then he spoke.

"All I can tell you is what I did. But I suspect that the way out may be different for each of you.

"It all started one day as I stood looking over the valley and thinking about how truly ugly it was. My next thought was that it was only ugly because we'd made it ugly. With a little care and attention, this place could be beautiful. You all know what beauty is. I've been inside some of your shelters. Most of them are quite attractive.

"But I wanted the whole valley to be beautiful.

"I began with my own place. I cleared away all the dead plants and stumps and dug up the soil. On my next trip to the trading post, I bought my food for the week and with the wardens I had left, I bought flower seeds and planted them all around my shelter.

"They grew and bloomed and brought color and joy until someone crept in one night and pulled up every last one of them." Moloch looked regretfully at one of the humans. "They died a painful death."

"Yeah," said a voice in the crowd. "After that we all kept out of your garden!"

Everyone laughed—except for the human.

Micah had been having real problems wrapping his mind around the concept of a demon flower gardener. But a demon flower gardener who grabbed anyone who hurt his flowers and tortured them to death made a bit more sense—sort of.

"However," Moloch continued, "some of the flowers had already gone to seed, so I piled the dead plants in back of my shelter, smoothed over the soil, and spread their seeds. I soon had more flowers. And not just flowers from the seeds I'd planted. There were all different kinds of flowers. It was like Hell suddenly decided to grow a beautiful garden in my space. A miracle!

"And then I bought paper, pens, and watercolor paints and began drawing pictures of the flowers and anything else that caught my eye. I practiced and practiced and eventually got quite good. I had pictures tacked up everywhere and stacks of them on my worktable. It occurred to me that maybe others would like my pictures to brighten up their shelters. So I began leaving them on your doorsteps."

"Yeah, thanks," growled a lion-headed demon. "They made great fire starters."

The crowd roared with laughter and Moloch smiled.

"But I know some of you liked them and displayed them. It made me happy.

"One day I overheard a neighbor bitching to another neighbor that someone had broken into his shelter and stolen his food. His neighbor laughed and walked away. I had extra food, so I offered him enough to tide him over until next week. He looked at me with suspicion but accepted the food and lived comfortably until he could buy more. Oddly enough, this simple act also made me happy."

The bull-headed demon sparkled with magic as he paced between the sides of the Gate.

Too bad nobody could see it.

"This is insane!" a voice from the back howled. "Why are we listening to this drivel?"

Moloch smiled sweetly. Unfortunately, demon faces are not designed to smile sweetly.

The effect was terrifying.

"Because you want to hear the end of the story," he said.

And, of course, they all did, and there was an expectant silence.

"After that, whenever someone needed something," he continued, "I did what I could to help; and I noticed that my heart became lighter and life was no longer a burden. Why this was happening was a total mystery to me, and I moved up the hill so I could be alone and think about what was going on inside me. I concluded that beauty is a healing thing, and so is kindness. Creating beauty and being kind doesn't just benefit others, it heals you. I haven't a clue why, but it does.

"So, if you want to die, create beauty, open your hearts, and be kind to one another."

The crowd muttered and growled. This was definitely not what they had been hoping to hear. They had wanted an easy way to escape from their agony, and instead all they'd got was Crazy Moloch gushing about beauty and kindness.

"I'll open your heart!" snarled a red demon in the back row. The torchlight flickered over his goat horns, blazing eyes, and wicked fangs as he drew back a huge long bow and released the arrow. It slammed into Moloch's chest, pinning him to the Gate. "Now die—if you can! And quit pestering us with your stupid stories."

Moloch looked down at the arrow and up at his murderer. "Thank you," he said and slumped over. The arrow held, and the demon hung suspended on the ascending side of the Gate.

"Is he dead?" Molly asked.

Micah could barely hear her over the cruel laughter.

"Oh yeah. I don't think I've ever seen a soul leave its body so fast."

Micah was grinning like a fool.

"That is so awesome!" Molly said. Her steel-gray eyes had softened to silver and they danced with joy. "There is an escape from Hell after all!"

Snarling and snapping and pushing and shoving, demons and humans alike began to leave, firmly believing that the idiot would revive and go back to his shelter in the hills. But a few drew closer to the sad remains and settled down to wait and see if Moloch had been telling the truth.

A group of demons passed uncomfortably close to their bush, and one glanced at it suspiciously.

"Time to jump back to the door before someone spots us," Diana whispered.

35

Molly

The three mages stood in the shadow of the castle's cliff and stared at each other in amazement. The night was still. Not a soul stirred in the surrounding forest, according to Diana's nose and Molly's mage sense.

"Holy shit!" said Molly.

"Exactly," Diana replied.

"Do you think anyone believed him?" Molly wondered.

"How else are they gonna explain the corpse hanging on the Gate?" Micah said. "And it's not going away anytime soon. Like, they'll be able to say, 'If you don't believe me, just go look at the Gate. How many corpses have you seen around here lately?'"

"If they respond to miracles the way humanity usually does, I'm sure they'll eventually come up with a logical explanation,"

Diana replied cynically. "What I'd like to know is how an arrow managed to stick in that black stone."

"I have a feeling that the Gate can be anything it wants to be, and when that nasty red demon shot the arrow, it decided to be made of something softer for a few seconds," Molly said. "Yet another miracle for everyone to think about. And I think it's way cool that Andromeda cares enough about the prisoners to ask Moloch to go back and tell them there's hope of escape and how to do it. It doesn't exactly make me feel warm and fuzzy about this place, but at least it's not quite the nightmare I thought it was."

"Yeah," said Micah, "It's still Hell, but it's got an exit door. Fine. Now let's figure out how to open *this* door." He began running his fingers along the tiny crack in the stone wall. "Any ideas?"

"The Librarian told us that there would be a tiny indentation where the doorknob would be," Diana said, "and that only a mage's touch could open it."

"Here it is!" said Micah. "Now what?"

"Touch it, summon your magic, and tell it to open," Diana replied.

But then Molly realized that Nysrogh had opened that door and he wasn't a mage and he didn't have any magic. Fear flared through her. Something was wrong. What if it electrocuted him? Or triggered an alarm? Unfortunately, they needed to get into the castle and this was the only way. Stifling the urge to nudge his hand out of the way and do it herself, she watched helplessly as Micah fit his finger into the small notch in the stone face. The crack began to glow, and the glow shimmered toward the center of the door until the whole thing was glowing.

And then it disappeared, revealing a staircase.

"Shit!" snarled Diana as something on the stairs clicked. She leapt at Micah and knocked him to one side.

Molly stood petrified as everything warped into a slow-motion nightmare. Three daggers flew out of the door and thunked into her friend while she was still suspended in mid-air. One pierced her throat, one pierced her heart, and one pierced her gut. They sent her flying, and she flew for what seemed like forever, arms extended and her lips twisted in a snarl until she landed in a broken, bloody heap.

There was a thud as Micah landed safely on his butt well away from the door.

Molly ran toward Diana as blood gushed from her friend's mouth and the life began fading from her eyes.

It was like running through water.

This was too much. First her parents, then Tamerlane, then Asmodius, and now Diana.

She couldn't do this anymore.

A scream of agony shaped itself in the back of her throat as her heart shattered.

Strong arms grabbed her. She tried to jerk free, the arms tightened. There was no escape. A hand covered her mouth, cutting off the scream that would have echoed through Hell, bringing every demon within hearing range down on them.

"Hush now. And breathe."

It was Micah.

She continued to strain against his hold. Why wasn't he letting her go to her friend. Tears of grief and frustration flowed down her cheeks and over his hand. Her eyes never left Diana's face.

"Remember your 'Who's Who in the Magical Realms' class," he said. "There's a reason they taught us all that stuff. What did you learn about werewolves?"

Realization dawned and she slumped into his embrace. Micah took his hand away from her mouth. He was probably wiping it off right now.

Moments later Diana shimmered moonlight-white and went almost transparent. The daggers fell to the ground, and she continued to shimmer as her body slowly morphed into a huge, black wolf. Electric-blue magic cracked and sizzled around her as Diana lunged to her feet, struggling for breath and balance.

With a cry of joy, Molly sprang forward to support her. It was like hugging a solid wall of black, coarse-haired terror, but she held on, weeping with relief until her friend's breathing steadied and her body quit wobbling.

"I thought you were dead!" she sobbed. "It was awful. I'm so glad you're a werewolf!"

Micah touched Diana's shoulder and looked into her fierce, blue eyes. "You saved my life. I owe you."

Diana growled softly, pulled away from Molly's embrace and Micah's touch, and headed for the now open and, hopefully, harmless door. But before she could reach it, bright points of light glittered in the opening and then flashed.

And the door was, once again, solid rock.

Diana sniffed at the dent Micah had touched to open the door and continued to sniff along the tiny crack. She stopped when she reached a point about three feet above it. She was up on her hind legs, front paws braced against the wall, and the part of the door she was sniffing was about eye level. Molly stared in awe at her friend as she realized just how huge she was. At her height of five feet, four inches, Molly could have just reached that spot—but only if she'd stood on tiptoe. Diana looked down at them to make sure she had their attention, pointed at the spot again with her nose, and then sat back on her haunches.

"Diana's nose comes to the rescue yet again!" Micah said. "There's another dent up there just like the first one. See it?"

If she got up close, Molly could just make it out.

"It's so high up we would have missed it. But Diana could smell it because it smelled like Nysrogh. And I'm betting that the place I touched didn't smell like Nysrogh. Am I right?"

Diana nodded.

"Wait a minute! Let's back up." Molly said. "The Librarian said that if a mage touched that spot the door would open. It didn't say anything about daggers shooting out and killing you. So either the Librarian wants us dead, or it didn't know about the daggers. And I'm not willing to believe it wants us dead."

"Someone's booby-trapped this door since the Librarian was here," Micah said. "But why?"

"They probably did it so Nysrogh could get into the castle," Molly replied. "And they booby-trapped the original way in because they didn't want a mage to come in. And it had to be Andromeda who set the trap because she's the only one who could have, since she's the only mage in Hell," said Molly, pulling her phone out of her pack. "I'm calling Adam and letting him know about Andromeda and the door—just in case we don't make it back."

After she'd placed the call and assured a frantic Adam that Diana was alive and well, Molly's brain began skittering around the next obvious question of why Andromeda would allow a demon into her castle.

"Okay, let's see if we can get in this time," Micah said, interrupting her thoughts. He stood beside the door, out of range of the daggers. When Molly and Diana had moved behind him, also out of range of the daggers, Micah held one index finger over the upper dent.

Just like before, the crack glowed and the light moved into the center of the door until the whole thing sparkled with light and the door disappeared.

They waited.

And waited.

Micah waved a stick in front of the opening.

No daggers.

The three mages hustled inside just before the sparks appeared and the door reformed with a flash.

36

Molly

The door re-materialized and everything went dark—or at least it tried to. The silhouette of a wolf writhing with violent surges of electric-blue light glowed in the blackness. It illuminated metal stairs that spiraled straight up the center of a metal tunnel and disappeared into more blackness above.

Molly gazed at her monstrous friend and her insides clenched with fear. Diana may have escaped death this time, but she wasn't invincible. A lethal wound made by anything silver would kill her as quickly as a normal person. And then there was Micah. She could feel his edgy presence close beside her. He wasn't invincible either. And yet, here she was, leading both of them toward a very possible death. How could she live with herself if one or, gods forbid, both of them died? But if they didn't go up those stairs and figure out what was going on, they'd die anyway, and so would all the rest of the Web.

Okay fine. They were gonna do this thing.

And she was gonna make sure they all came out of it alive and well.

She sucked in a shuddering breath. "Wait! Nobody move. We need to think about this." Her voice echoed sharp and harsh off the unforgiving metal walls.

"A touch more light will help." Bright, white light flared and steadied, exposing every dismal detail of the space around them. Micah stood with his right hand extended. A small globe of mage light floated just above his palm.

Molly blinked and firmly stifled a pang of jealousy. She hadn't taken the time to figure out how to call up mage light yet, but right now, she was glad Micah could. The Academy taught all the cool stuff—like jumping, time travel, calling up mage light, dimension travel, and advanced spell casting—the last quarter of senior year. Micah wouldn't be taking those classes until next term. The fact that he already knew how to jump and call up mage light spoke volumes about his magical ability.

"Much better, thanks," she said. "Diana, has Nysrogh been in here?"

Diana snorted and rolled her eyes. Molly sniffed the air. She was surprised Diana wasn't gagging. The faint, but still nauseating, reek of burnt feathers in the close quarters of the stairwell brought back the horror of Denzel's office and made the gleaming metal walls feel like they were collapsing in on her.

"Okay," she said, taking a deep breath to calm herself, which, of course, only made things worse, "we know Nysrogh has been in and out of here at least once, and that means he managed to go up and down those stairs, because the only reason to be in here is to use those stairs. And since we just saw him down by the Gate he knows how to avoid any traps on them. I doubt that there are very many, because he has to remember them all."

All her practical magic instructors made a big deal about observation. "Think about the Sherlock Holmes stories," Aunt Althea, her 'Auric Healing' instructor, had said. "It's a mistake to rely completely on magic. If you look, really look, at the light bodies you're working with and really think about what you're seeing, you can discover an amazing amount of important, life-saving information. This is true of situations and places too. Observe carefully before you act." For Molly, this was much more easily said than done, but she was getting better at it.

First off, where had the daggers come from? There should at least be an empty rack or something. She examined the walls near the door and found what she was looking for. A thin rectangular crack at the two o'clock position from the door outlined where the rack that had fired the daggers had slipped back into the wall. And it was probably already reloaded and ready to fire again. But what if the mage—and only a mage could have sprung the first trap—managed to survive the daggers and figure out the trick of opening the door? Molly had no doubt that there were other traps farther up the stairs. And, because she was almost sure the silver metal that cruelly reflected Micah's light over and over again was either iron or steel, anyone killed by a trap in here wouldn't be reviving anytime soon. The stairs made a gleaming spiral straight up past the mage light and into absolute darkness. An iron pole ran through the center of the shaft, and the stairs were welded onto it and onto the walls of the shaft.

Two perfectly smooth crevices, an inch or so deep, were cut into opposite sides of the pole and exactly followed the spiral of the steps. She hoped they would never find out what those were for. The floor was iron too. She looked for faint lines in it that would indicate hidden doors and had almost given up when Micah shifted his light, revealing a thin rectangular crack positioned under the second step. Aha! And then she noticed that the step wasn't attached to the pole and there were cracks all around it on the wall. There were no strings or lights on the step, so the trap was probably pressure-activated. Any weight would cause it to retract into the wall, and something nasty and probably very sharp would shoot up out of the floor into anyone unlucky enough to have stepped on that step.

"Here's a trap," she said.

"Totally wicked," Micah said as he examined the step. "I don't even want to imagine the mind that invented this place."

Micah felt it too. The evil menace that oozed out of the cold, echoing stairs and walls and filled the shaft with so much venom and malice that you could almost feel its thick sliminess coiling around you. Molly shuddered.

Almost as if she'd read her thoughts, Diana growled softly and put one paw on the first step and examined the second step.

"Nysrogh skipped that one, didn't he?" Molly asked.

Diana nodded and sniffed the third step.

"Oh Jeez, this is gonna take us forever," Molly said, gazing up at the seemingly infinite spiral of steps. "I wish we could just jump."

"Yeah, me too. But we can only jump to the steps we can see, and if one of them is booby-trapped, we're toast. We gotta do this one step at a time," said Micah.

Their progress was mind-numbingly slow, but they didn't dare go faster. Even the slightest mistake meant death. Diana was in the lead and would survive if the trap involved just the step she was on, but if it didn't, Micah and Molly would die.

The twenty-third step was, indeed, a trap, like the second step, so they skipped it.

After what seemed like forever, they were checking out step number one hundred eight, and Molly was going crazy. The cold, hard walls seemed to be pressing in on her, twisting every sound and word and echoing them back as malevolent whispers. She wanted out of this cramped, deadly place so bad she was ready to scream. Micah laid a gentle hand on her shoulder and said, "Chill out, Molly. Take a breath, stop for a minute, and think of something nice."

Freakin' freaky! How had he known she was about to explode? Had he lied to them? *Could* he read minds? Or was she that obvious? Well, duh. He could read auras and hers was probably all over the place. And, yes, she was that obvious. She'd never been able to hide her feelings. And his advice was good. Going bonkers was not going to help her concentrate on keeping them safe. So she closed her eyes, slowed down her breathing, evened it out, and imagined Micah's hand moving down from her shoulder and his arms wrapping around her waist, pulling her up tight against his body. And she imagined his lips touching the base of her neck with gentle kisses. Her breathing sped up again, but, yeah, she felt way better. She smiled and opened her eyes.

Just in time to see a tiny, luminous red dot appear on Diana's head as she sniffed the next step. With a terrified gasp, she jerked her friend's massive head back.

"Laser," Molly cried, and braced herself for the daggers or swords or whatever that were gonna kill them all. But instead, something clicked in the darkness above. A moment later, something whirred like an old electric toy train moving over its metal tracks. As she was peering up and trying to figure out what it was, her trained ears picked up the unmistakable sound of not one but at least two wicked-sharp blades slicing rapidly through the air.

Shit. That's what those grooves were. Tracks for a murder machine. As if she had summoned it, a glittering, whirling propeller of blades the width of the shaft appeared in the mage light above them.

There was no escape.

It was gonna chop them into bloody bits.

"Quick. We gotta jump out of here," she screamed.

"No!" Micah grabbed her arms. "Stop! I have a better idea."

What better idea? Couldn't he see the steely death that would slice through them any second now? But Micah hadn't survived years on the streets without being able to think on his feet.

And she trusted him.

She trusted him with her life.

Molly stopped. And felt the familiar lifting sensation of a jump. But when she touched down and opened her eyes she was still standing between Diana and Micah on the iron steps, staring at the same nearly invisible, hair-thin laser beam. Micah's mage light still glowed just above them. But there were no deadly, whirling swords. She peered down through the gloom and could just make out the floor. There were no swords there either.

"I didn't want to walk up all these steps again," said Micah as he let go of Molly's arm and Diana's tail.

"Shit! When did you figure out how to time travel?"

"I didn't," Micah confessed. "The Librarian taught me before I came here. It thought at least one of us should be able to do it. I took us forward an hour, so the blades are probably back up there ready to slice and dice the next person who trips that laser."

They traced the laser beam up to its source on the wall over their heads. From there it ran diagonally through the gap in the spiral and down to the opposite wall. They had been so busy scanning the steps and walls at their level that they hadn't noticed the danger shining down from above.

"I can just get by without tripping it," Molly said, "but you probably can't, and Diana can't. Nysrogh is bigger than either of you. He could never make it through here. But he did, so there has to be a way to turn it off."

Diana was way ahead of them. She was pointing with her nose to the bottom of the hundred and eighth step.

"There's a switch there because Diana can smell Nysrogh on it. But is there another?" Micah said.

Diana was already sniffing the entire area, carefully avoiding the laser. At last she returned to the point under the step and stopped.

"That's it?" Micah asked. Diana nodded, and he reached under the step. "Ah, here it is." His hand moved slightly and the beam disappeared, and no deadly blades came whirring down on them. When Molly, impatient to be moving, started to step up, Micah touched her arm. "Wait a sec. It's probably gonna come back on and we need to know how long it'll stay off. And we need to make sure of the next few steps. Did Nysrogh step on them?" Diana nodded. A short time later, the laser sliced through the air once more. There would be plenty of time for all of them to slip through. Micah switched the beam off again and they continued their nerve-wracking climb.

Andromeda must have figured the helicopter sword blades would finish off anyone trying to climb up to her castle, because when they made it to the top of the steps there had been no more surprises. Unfortunately, the steps ended at a blank, solid rock wall. Diana was already sniffing, and located two spots that Nysrogh had touched. They were marked by two bumps in the rough carved wall that stood out just a bit farther than the others, but not far enough to be noticeable if you didn't know what you were looking for.

The bumps were on the right side of the step and the top one was out of Molly's reach, so Micah moved as far to the right of them as he could and Molly and Diana went down a few steps until their heads were below the bottom of the door.

Micah held a finger over each one and pressed them both at the same time.

A door-shaped outline of brilliant white light flashed into being and filled itself in, until the whole rectangle glowed. Micah slid even farther back as it began to sparkle. Then it vanished, revealing a single room, cut into the rock and divided in half by floor-to-ceiling iron bars.

"Yes," Molly said, doing air punches. "We're in!"

"Not yet," Micah said as Diana crept carefully up the steps, stuck a paw, then her head through the opening, sniffed, checked for traps and nodded. Nysrogh had gone in, and, hopefully, it was safe. She moved into the room, followed closely by Micah and Molly.

Almost as soon as the mages crossed its threshold, the door vanished, leaving behind a blank rock wall. The mages stared in confusion at the bars, which were only a few steps away. Beyond them, a cot with a blanket thrown across it hugged the opposite wall, and beside the cot was a closed door. The room was chilly, and featureless. The gray rock walls and floor and ceiling sucked away the warmth and brightness of the mage light. But compared to the killing chamber they'd just left, it was heaven. Muscles Molly hadn't even realized were tensed to the breaking-point relaxed. Diana had already sniffed her way around the space on their side of the bars and then jumped past them into the other side. After a careful examination, she sat down and stared at her companions expectantly.

"Lemme guess," Molly said. "Nysrogh was on our side of the bars but not on yours."

Diana nodded.

"That explains the bars. They're supposed to keep someone out, not in. And that someone would definitely be Nysrogh. I totally get that Andromeda doesn't want him in her castle, but why let him in this far?"

"Someone has used that cot," Micah said. "Do you know who it was?"

Diana shook her head.

"Then it was probably Andromeda. Who else could it be?"

"But why would Andromeda come down to her dungeons and take a nap on a cot?" Molly asked.

"We need to find Andromeda. Our list of questions is way too long, and she's the only one who can answer them," Micah said.

They jumped past the bars and headed for the door, which, of course, was locked. Micah tried his lock picks, but wasn't even able to push them into the keyhole.

"Wait a sec," Micah said, as Molly began dealing with the hard fact that the guy she was trusting with her life carried a set of pick locks. His hands started weaving a spell. Magic was so dense here that bright white lines of power immediately converged with a flash to form a bright white, functional-looking arrow. With a snap of his wrist, he directed it into the door. Shards of light in every color of the spectrum scattered every which way as it hit, and suddenly the door was gone and they were looking at a blank rock wall. Micah stared at the wall with a strange expression.

"Last summer, before I'd met either one of you, I was sitting at my computer signing up for fall quarter classes. When I moved the cursor to click on my last 'Native American Mythology' unit, something pushed my hand past it and made it click on 'Illusions and Shape Shifting' instead. When I undid it and tried to move my hand back to the Myth unit, it froze and re-clicked the Illusions unit. So I took Illusions instead of the Myth unit. If I hadn't taken that class last fall, I would never have spotted that perfect illusion, let alone figured out how to break it."

And they would never have gotten into the castle.

Diana nudged them aside and began sniffing the wall. After a thorough inspection, she stopped at a faint stain about four feet off the floor and several feet away from where the illusion had been.

"Okay, you guys, stand over here against the wall. I'm gonna try the door this time." Molly said. Standing as far to the right of the stain as she could, she pressed her hand against it.

Nothing.

Not even a bunch of daggers screaming down at them.

Shit. Now what? They couldn't jump through the wall because they couldn't see what was on the other side of it. Maybe there was no opening. Andromeda wouldn't need one because she knew her castle. She could jump from here to anywhere inside it, or to anywhere in Hell for that matter.

"Remember the outside door?" Micah said. "The one the Librarian said could only be opened by a mage? Maybe this one hasn't been changed and is still like that. Maybe you need magic to open it."

Duh. Of course.

Molly touched the spot once more, only this time she gathered up the ambient energy, channeled it into the wall, and commanded it to open.

A line of light traced a doorway and the wall inside the line began to glow. They ducked back and waited. Seconds later it sparkled and disappeared with a flash.

No daggers.

Diana stood in front of the door.

No daggers.

They waited several seconds and the door became a rock wall once more. When Molly opened it again, they rushed through.

37

Molly

The stink of sewage, fury, and despair slammed into them. It was all Molly could do to keep from puking on the heels of Micah's boots. The mage-light revealed a passageway carved from the living rock of the cliff face. It was narrow, forcing them to walk single file, but the ceiling was so high that the mage light barely reached it. A faint, heart-rending moan to their right and a vicious growl in front of them vibrated through the close, fetid air, sending her heart into overdrive. Impossible! They were the only ones in the passageway.

"Look up there," Micah said, sending the light higher.

Howls, screeches, vicious snarls, and the sound of flesh pounding against stone thundered around them as the light neared the ceiling. Molly and Micah drew their weapons and prepared for an attack.

But none came.

The mage light revealed what looked like a row of pigeon-holes a few inches down from the ceiling. They were clustered in groups of three and ran the entire length of the left wall of the passageway. There were no holes in the wall to their right. Molly shivered as she realized that they were in a dungeon, and the cells were on the other side of the left wall. And she was willing to bet that they didn't have doors or bars or windows. They were just holes in the rock with air holes at the top. Andromeda or the asteroid had jumped the prisoners in and left them there with no food or water. But this was Hell. They couldn't die. They just sat there, hungry, thirsty, and alone in the darkness forever.

The mages huddled in the howling, hate-filled passage, shaking in awe and horror at the grim reality of a world without death or mercy.

"I wonder what they did to deserve this," said Diana.

"I don't know and I don't want to know." Micah whispered.

A single silver note slid gently through the screaming gloom. The voice that formed it was pure and sweet, and cut through the rage and hate like a sparkling mountain stream. It wavered for a moment and then split into two notes that soared in heart-stopping harmony.

Just when Molly began to ache from its vibrating intensity, it stopped.

Diana sank back on her haunches and whined, then threw back her head and howled. It rose up from deep in her chest and slammed into the prison walls. It thundered with rage and grief, but a brilliant thread of savage joy and passion spiraled around it. It surged up to a deafening peak and then ended with a piercing yip.

"Well, so much for sneaking into the castle," Micah whispered into the eerie silence.

"What was that all about?" Molly asked Diana, who yawned hugely, exposing a mouthful of wicked-huge fangs. The yawn ended with a low whine.

"There is now one fewer soul in the dungeon than when we came in. Whoever it was must have 'seen the light.'" Micah said, and headed for the blank stone wall at the other end of the passageway,

Diana was already there, sniffing it, although Molly had no idea how she could smell anything in here except the overpowering stench. After going over it twice, Diana rose up on her hind legs, and bracing herself against the wall, she looked over her shoulder at Micah and Molly and woofed.

Okay, fine. Diana was gonna do this one. Molly grabbed Micah and pulled him to the ground. When Diana was satisfied that her companions were as safe as they'd ever be in this place, she gathered up her power and willed the wall to open. A door shaped rectangle appeared. The rock inside it glowed, sparkled, and disappeared with a flash, revealing a stone stairway that spiraled up into the darkness.

"I can't stand it in here a second longer. Let's go. Quick before it closes," Molly said.

For once, no one argued.

Diana dashed through the door and up the steps with Micah and Molly close behind. They didn't stop until they came to a sturdy wooden door with iron hinges and a door knob.

It was locked.

Molly's patience was totally gone. She grabbed the door knob, shoved some energy into it and twisted. It turned, and when she pulled on the door, it opened, creaking and groaning like they'd awakened it from a deep slumber. Micah snagged her elbow and pulled her to one side so Diana could push past, nose quivering.

Nothing stirred in the huge, musty smelling room. The mage-light cast dancing shadows across casks and wine racks filled with dusty bottles. Cobwebs straight out of a third-rate horror movie draped down from the walls and ceiling and across a jumble of old furniture, discarded rugs, huge chests bound in rusting iron, a bird cage, and dozens of other cast-offs. They followed Diana, who followed her nose through the maze of stuff to a straight, simple, wooden staircase that ended in another door, which was also locked. When Molly opened it, it creaked even louder than the one downstairs, setting her teeth on edge. If that was the basement they'd just come through, then this was the main floor and the door was a perfect alarm. She was sure it could be heard all over the castle.

They stepped into an empty passage. At one end was a pantry lined with shelves of cans and small boxes and bags, and beyond that was a gleaming kitchen, filled with all the latest appliances. They headed the other way, toward a finely finished wooden door with ornate iron fittings. The walls and floor were still the same gray stone of the cliff face and the lower levels, but it was cut into smooth blocks that fit perfectly into one another. Molly reached out with all her senses and gasped in terror as she immediately encountered a dark, malevolent presence that permeated everything. Waiting and watching, like a cougar ready to pounce.

The door opened on well-oiled hinges, revealing an impressive three-story entry hall. Dozens of large, colorful tapestries covered the stone walls and a huge, intricately patterned carpet covered the stone floor. To their right was a wall, and to their left, the length of a spacious living room away, a massive stairway of dark, gleaming wood plunged gracefully down into the hall from the second floor.

Every nerve and brain cell in her body screamed, "Don't go in there!!!"

Yup. Definitely a bad idea.

But it was the only one she had.

38

Molly

olly dropped her pack by the door, snapped up her shields, and stepped into the hall. Diana nudged past her, ears back, fangs exposed, and vibrating with barely suppressed growls. Micah was a strong, protective presence on her left. She wished that she could stop, just for a second, and look at them and memorize them, in case this was the last time she'd see them alive; but she was too busy scanning the hall to take the risk.

And then she felt it. The horrid thing that was haunting the castle was on the second floor near the top of the staircase. Micah and Diana felt it too. They both paused and looked back and up toward the second floor. But they couldn't see the top from here. The three mages turned in unison and slowly backed up until the top step came into view. There was nothing there except an awesome, floor-to-ceiling stained glass window of angels and demons ripping and tearing at each other. The subject required lots of red glass, which scattered blood-red morning sunlight across the landing and down the gleaming, wooden steps.

A starburst of electric-violet light flashed, and Andromeda—it had to be her—stood at the top of the stairs surrounded by a snapping, snarling, milling pack of dogs. The light through the stained glass turned her short, red hair into a fiery halo that curled around her cap of two back-swept, iridescent raven's wings. But it was her intense, steady gaze that sent a rush of adrenaline coursing through Molly and raised every hair on her body. This was the stare of a warrior mage in fighting mode. She recognized it because she'd slipped into it accidentally once during a particularly intense practice session, and Master Lieu had just spent weeks teaching her how to get there on command—body relaxed, but hardwired into the brain, ready to move in less than an instant; brain in hyper-drive, so quick that time...slows...down. It was called "in the flow." In this state, a warrior's leisurely move looks quick, and her quick moves are too fast to follow.

Why would Andromeda be in the flow?

That was simple, she was ready to fight.

But how would she even know how to get there? Surely Gram would have told them if she was a warrior mage.

Shit.

Molly dropped into the flow.

Micah touched her arm. "Bad news, Miss Molly. Hold that face. Keep looking at Andromeda. Don't look surprised." He spoke so softly she could barely hear him. "There are two souls in that body. One is probably Andromeda. The other is definitely Tamerlane."

Molly's guts turned to ice water and her brain screamed "Run! Now!" But she couldn't because she was paralyzed with fear. In a flash, she was back in the moonlit forensics lab with a knife stuck in her intestines, staring with horror into the hungry, hate-filled eyes of Tamerlane, her beloved mentor, as he held her wrists in an iron grip and sucked the life out of her. Pain, grief, and betrayal burst out of the mental closet she'd shoved them into months ago. They wrapped themselves around her heart yet again and squeezed.

There was now no doubt in her mind that Tamerlane was behind the deaths of the First and Second Webmasters and Denzel. She wasn't quite sure how he'd managed it, but he had.

She needed to kill him...again.

If she didn't, he would not only kill her, but also Micah, Diana, Gram, and the entire Mage Web.

But if she killed him, she would also be killing Andromeda.

She had no option. It was either her own life and the lives of those she loved or Andromeda's.

With grim determination, she shoved the painful emotions back into their closet along with all the horror she felt at having to kill an innocent mage. They were distractions.

She focused, gathered up her power, and sank deeper into the flow.

"Spread out. Back up. Follow my lead," she said.

She felt, rather than saw, her friends follow her and fan out as she backed away from the foot of the stairs. Her eyes were fixed on Andromeda, whose knee-high, black leather boots were tapping, one slow step at a time down the magnificent staircase. Her knee-length, low-cut, copper satin dress clenched with a black leather corset swished and rustled like the whispers of restless spirits. She moved like a warrior, but her muscles lacked the high tone and precise contours of a warrior. Tamerlane was trapped in a woman's weak, untrained body. And he didn't know that Molly knew he was there. And he was unarmed. And she had help. The hounds, trailing behind Andromeda like a white shadow, looked dangerous, but Diana could handle them easily.

They might just have a chance against the immensely powerful monster her teacher had become.

"It would have been easier to jump onto the barbican. I would have let you in." Andromeda's voice was soft and smoky.

Yeah, right. Asmodius had jumped onto the barbican and he was dead.

"What happened to Asmodius?" Molly barely recognized her own voice. It was an octave too low and filled with menace.

"He had an accident," Andromeda replied, gesturing down to a bronze stand filled with spears. Her boots tapped sharp and slow and ominous as she continued down the stairs.

And the hounds followed, clicking and pattering on the hardwood steps.

Molly heard Diana's growl and Micah's savage curse.

But her eyes were locked on Asmodius.

His sleek, powerful body was impaled on a boar-hunting spear, drenched in blood and draped limply over its crossbar. He was most definitely dead. As she stared at her friend's corpse, breathless with horror, her mind slipped back to the time, just last summer, when she and Asmodius had toured the armory in King Alexander and Queen Flora's palace in Damia. Asmodius had explained that the reason a few of the spears had cross bars was because they were used to hunt wild boar, who were so fierce and so strong that without that bar to stop them, they'd continue running down the spear and gore their attacker.

Asmodius had been fierce and strong.

A cruel but fitting weapon to use against him.

Angrily choking down a sob of grief, she looked into Andromeda's cruel, remorseless eyes and grabbed Flick from its pocket between the worlds.

"You are so dead."

Andromeda, who was now stalking toward them over the stone floor, threw back her beautiful head and laughed a truly villainous laugh.

"Oh, I think not!"

A huge, sizzling ball of magic fire appeared in her hand, and she hurled it straight at Molly's head.

It came toward her, a spinning, crackling mass of violence. Her plan was to wait till the last possible moment and duck, but that moment never came. Micah hit it with a small, focused dart of light, knocking it away from her toward Diana, who leaped high in the air and into its path.

The werewolf and ball of magic collided and hung suspended. She turned back to Andromeda just in time to see her deflect one of Micah's well-aimed knives. Molly was totally not worried about Diana. Werewolves are magical creatures, and Tamerlane had just given her a huge dose of magic. She would grow even stronger now. Molly heard Diana's claws click as she dropped to the floor and felt the even more intense buzz of pure power that now surrounded her.

"Kill!" Andromeda snarled, pointing at Diana. A sword appeared in her hand. Fortunately, it wasn't Death Dancer, Tamerlane's magic sword.

As the dogs howled an unearthly howl and surged toward the werewolf, Molly bounded toward Andromeda and Micah threw another knife. The fraction of a second it took to deflect it gave Molly just enough time to take the offensive. She closed with a quick lunge that put Andromeda's timing off as she sidestepped Flick. She only just managed to parry Molly's next slash, but countered with a quick, vicious jab, which Molly avoided easily. And so it went, lunge, parry, slash, parry. In their heightened state, they were moving quicksilver fast. To someone in normal time, they would be a blur, so Micah wouldn't be able to help. Her strategy was to wear down Andromeda's untrained body. It was the only way to get the opening she needed to slash her head off, because this was the only way to kill Tamerlane.

The hall echoed with clashing swords, snarling dogs, and the occasional crack as Diana grabbed one of the pack and snapped its neck. The area soon became an obstacle course. Molly found herself sidestepping dead and wounded dogs and avoiding the chairs and table in the center of the room. But her opponent was tiring. Andromeda's responses were not quite as quick, and once she just barely managed to recover from her own lunge in time to parry a slash from Molly that would have decapitated her. Molly gathered up her strength and pushed harder. She felt no fear, and her trained body rejoiced in the challenge. But one of the many things that Tamerlane had taught her was to resist the urge to ecstasy that came with intense sword play; to stay focused at all times, notice mistakes, and make use of them. This was fortunate, because soon, when Molly was sure her opponent had reached the end of her strength, Andromeda ducked a slash, grabbed a chair and shoved it toward Molly, who sidestepped it, and came in fast.

This was the chance she'd been waiting for.

Andromeda's guard was totally down.

She'd never get her sword up in time to parry.

And she was off balance and wouldn't be able to dodge or duck the killing blow.

Molly swept her arm out to begin the slash.

"Molly, stop! Now!" Micah snatched her wrist and held it fast.

No!!!! shrieked every muscle, every nerve, and every sinew in her body. *Kill! Kill while you can. Or die!*

No!! howled Flick. *I want blood!*

But her heart remembered.

It remembered that she trusted Micah.

Trusted him with her very life.

So, instead of twisting out of his grasp and completing the blow, she listened to her heart.

And somehow managed to stop the raging beast that she had become.

Andromeda stood still as death, holding her sword defensively in front of her chest. But its position and her body lines were all wrong. She no longer stood in a fighter's stance. Her eyes were round with shock, but her jaw was set in determination. This was not Tamerlane.

"Tamerlane is gone," Micah said, holding her tight as she leaned against him, gasping for breath, and telling her muscles to relax.

Good thing we stopped, said Flick.

Yeah, you've had enough blood, and probably enough horrid stories to keep you entertained for years. Molly squeezed Flick's silk-cord-wrapped hilt affectionately and slipped it back between the worlds. And even though what she really wanted to do was throw her arms around Micah and sob in relief, she moved out of his comforting embrace and stood up straight.

"Welcome back, Andromeda," she said. "Where's Tamerlane?"

"Tamerlane?" the Warden's eyes went round with horror. "It was Tamerlane?"

Molly nodded.

"Oh gods!" Andromeda sobbed.

"I don't know," she finally said. "One second he was here, shoving me back into a dark corner of my brain and fighting with you, and the next second he vanished." She dropped limply into one of the chairs and let the sword fall from her hand. It landed with a thud on the carpet.

One dog remained alive, snapping and snarling and lunging at Diana, who kept batting it away with a paw the size of its head.

"Dasher, leave it," Andromeda said. The dog whined and padded over to its mistress, where it dropped to the floor panting. "Good boy," she said, caressing his head and patting his flanks until his tail thumped on the floor. The Queen of Hell gazed sadly around at the bloody, mangled corpses that had once been her pets. "They were sweet dogs before he took control of them," she said.

The asteroid was already starting to work its magic. Sparkles were beginning to dance around their bodies. The exhausted mages watched in fascination as each corpse became a glittering mound of green and then gold that shifted and swirled in beautiful, mesmerizing patterns. After quite some time—Molly had no way of knowing exactly how long, but the patches of sunlight on the stairs had moved up a step—the mounds slowly morphed into dog shapes and the sparkles began to fade, revealing six living, breathing, snoozing dogs. Just before the sparks dimmed to nothingness, they flashed into bright white light that surged into each dog. Their eyes drifted open, glowing red with life and intelligence, and Molly caught her breath in wonder. As they staggered drunkenly to their feet, Andromeda dragged herself out of the chair and moved among them, patting and stroking each one, fondling their red ears and paws and calling them by name.

"Oh, jeez," Molly said. "You named them after Santa's reindeer!"

"It seemed like a good idea," their mistress replied with a grin. "There were eight of them and their personalities fit the names perfectly." She headed back to her chair, and the dogs followed, nudging and jostling each other, tails wagging and ears erect. When she sat down, they clustered close around her, sank down on their haunches, and gazed calmly at Molly, Micah, and the werewolf—totally different animals from the snapping snarling pack that had attacked them just a short time ago.

"However," Andromeda continued, "now there are only seven. Blitzen is missing."

"Shit!" Molly said. "I know what happened to Tamerlane! He threw that chair to distract us, and Blitzen was probably right beside him. All he had to do was touch him, transfer into him, and jump. There were so many dogs, and we were so caught up with what was happening, that we didn't notice when one disappeared."

The four mages contemplated this in stunned silence, until Micah said, "And we'll never know where he went. A brilliant escape. Brilliant because, as far as he knew, we had no way of knowing it was Tamerlane we were fighting and not Andromeda. He left right when Molly was set to cut off her head. In fact, he probably set the whole thing up that way. You would have killed her and we all would have assumed that it was Andromeda and not Tamerlane who had gained control of one of her prisoners and start killing off the mages.

"We would have thought that she'd gone crazy or something, up here in Hell, all by herself surrounded by monsters," Micah continued. "We'd have figured we'd caught the killer and never looked further."

But Flick would have known she wasn't a killer and would have told me, Molly thought.

"Until he started killing again," Andromeda replied.

"Yes, but he would have had plenty of time to find a new and even better place, settle in, and amass the resources he needed," said Micah.

"Well, he'll still be able to do that because we have no freakin' idea where he is!" Molly said.

"Like I said. Brilliant!"

"You don't have to look so happy about it," Molly said.

"Genius is genius. Ya gotta admire the guy."

"No I don't. And he's not a guy, he's a monster."

"True that," Micah replied. "But his soul is magnificent. You should see it."

The Queen of Hell regarded Micah intently over steepled fingers. "You must be one of Hades' agents. Lucky for me that you were here."

"At your service, Your Majesty," he said, bowing gracefully before her. "But I'd rather you kept that intelligence under your raven's wings."

"I understand," she said with a sad smile, "Your secret is safe with me."

"But wouldn't the asteroid have brought you back to life like your dogs?" Molly asked, pulling them back to the original subject.

"Actually, no. The Hounds of Hell were created by the asteroid to be companions to the warden, so they are immortal. But I've never been through the Gate, and the asteroid has no other strong link to my soul, so it will heal me and keep me healthy, but it can't bring me back to life. If I don't have a fatal accident or get killed, my body will slowly wear out and I will eventually die. As far as I'm concerned, this is a blessing."

Molly thought of all the souls doomed to spend eternity here and could only agree.

"So you really did save my life," Andromeda continued. "If you hadn't come and freed me from Tamerlane, once he'd learned enough about how things work in my kingdom, he would have killed me and taken over my body. Hell would have become an evil eternal's stronghold. A perfect place from which to take over the Mage Web. You three have done both me and the Web a great service this day. I will gladly grant you any favor that is within my power."

"We came to find Asmodius," Molly said.

Andromeda gazed over at the corpse hanging from the spear and her face clouded with grief. A tear tracked down her cheek and dropped onto her breast.

"May we take his body back to Estelle?"

"Ah, Estelle," Andromeda breathed the words like a prayer. A flood of emotions washed over her lovely face—rage, grief, and, at last, peace. She remained silent for some time and wept more tears. Molly and Micah sank into the closest chairs and Diana sat on the carpet. The three young mages watched the floor and gave their hostess space.

—

After some time, Andromeda sighed, rubbed her hands over her face, and focused once more on her guests.

"Of course you may take his body home. And there is a chance you can take it back alive, united once more with his spirit and soul."

"What?!" Hope surged through Molly with a fierceness that took her breath away.

"When Tamerlane killed Asmodius, he wanted to make absolutely sure that he stayed dead. So he threw a stasis field around his corpse and kept it off the asteroid's surface on the iron spear. His plan was to take it back to your world, remove the field and dump it somewhere far away from Portland. My hope is that the stasis field went up so quickly that it trapped Asmodius's soul while it was still hovering beside his body." She turned to Micah, her body tense with hope.

"It did," he said.

"Okay, we have a chance." Andromeda said. But she kept a white-knuckled grip on the arms of her chair.

Molly went limp with relief.

"This floor was drenched in Asmodius's blood—not just blood from a wound, but life-blood. Asmodius died here, which gives the asteroid a strong connection to him. My spirit flows through every part of Hell. That's how I keep track of things. You might say the asteroid and I have a very close working relationship. I may be able to convince it to bring him back to life."

"What needs to happen? Can we help?" Molly was vibrating with energy born of hope and wanted to be doing something—anything.

"First, we need to pull him off that spear." The Queen of Hell regarded the warrior mage intently. "Can you help me with that?"

"No problem," said Molly, although she dreaded touching the cold, lifeless body of her once powerful and ever-so-alive friend.

As it turned out, she didn't have to. Andromeda helped her lift the spear and Asmodius's quite hefty body out of the brass stand and pulled it off while Molly held the spear steady. She was relieved to see that his eyes were closed. She couldn't imagine looking into those once vividly alive amber eyes and finding them dead. And she avoided looking at the still glistening blood that coated the entire upper end of the weapon. The stasis field had done its work. The blood was so fresh that it was still bright red and wet and smelled sweet, meaty, and metallic. She was barely able to stave off the nausea that was threatening to well up from her belly, turn her legs to jelly, and narrow her vision to a tunnel. She knew that sequence well. She couldn't let it happen. Asmodius needed her.

Hell's Warden hugged the bloody corpse close as she moved off the carpet to the stone floor. She knelt and laid him down, motioning Molly to kneel opposite her. The sensation of the solid stone digging into her knees cut through her emotional control. Molly took a shuddering breath and wept, pouring out her rage, grief, love, and hope, her tears splashing onto the cat's sleek, shining fur. She looked up into the Warden's eyes. They blazed with life, but it was a totally alien sort of life. Molly could find no love, no hate, no fear, no desire. Only a deep, abiding, watchfulness. But those emotionless eyes were filled with tears that flowed freely down onto the furry body beneath her bloody hands. Hands that glowed with the strange, inhuman power of the asteroid.

"She's removed the stasis field," Micah whispered.

Molly watched, transfixed.

Could Andromeda really bring Asmodius back to life?

39

Asmodius

There was no form. Only nothingness. A vast darkness. There were no boundaries, no time, no thought, no sensation. Only void, and spirit moved across its face.

—

A spark splashed into the void, wet and hot. And then another. And another. They rained down with unbearable intensity, bringing sensation where before there had been nothing.

—

And then there was form.

A vast, penetrating intelligence seized that form, giving it definite shape and sentience where before there had been none.

Egad! Where am I and what's happening?!

Asmodius screamed as living power sizzled through all his nerves and brain cells.

At least he tried to scream. His body wasn't responding.

Millions of electric ants scrabbled feverishly through the maze of his nerves.

He felt them shaping and enlivening his organs.

They converged on his heart and it began beating, rhythmic and warm. Filled with love and healing. He lay in complete contentment as that amazing warmth pulsed through him with each steady heartbeat.

And with each beat, his soul flowed gently into him.

He wasn't quite sure how he knew it was his soul.

He wasn't even sure what a soul was.

But it was definitely his soul.

Scent flooded into his nose and gushed into his heart. The sweet, spicy scent of Elizabeth—no, not Elizabeth, Andromeda. He was in Andromeda's entry hall. He remembered it now—the solid, earthy smell of the stone floor, the Turkish carpet that smelled of old wool and dogs, the musty, dusty scent of the family tapestries. And then came the smell of spring forests and cinnamon sticks. Molly was here!

His heart pity-patted with joy. They were here. Two of his favorite people.

"That's not Asmodius!" Molly gasped.

"Um, actually, it is," replied his beloved.

There was a jolt, like gentle lightning, and his eyes opened.

Everything was a blur, which came into focus with maddening slowness. Andromeda's beautiful beaming face and sparkling green eyes swam into view and then Molly's equally lovely, but horrified face.

He could move his fingers and toes now.

Wait! He didn't *have* fingers and toes. At least not anymore. He had paws.

"I don't understand! This can't be Asmodius!" Molly's voice was filled with panic.

He ran his tongue over his teeth and discovered a flat even surface.

Where were his beautiful fangs?

He discovered he was belly up. His tail should be between his legs.

He tried to move the tip of it, but it wasn't there.

Where was his long silky tail? What would he do without a tail to flick in amused annoyance, to lash in anger, and to curl around his nose on cold winter nights?

The realization flashed into his brain like a beam of sunlight wrapped in rainbows and joy.

He was a man again!!!

Oh shit! Am I naked? Molly's here. She can't see me like this!

"Don't worry, you have clothes on," Andromeda said.

A moment of relief, and then another thought.

But do they look good? This is an important moment, I want to look good.

Andromeda laughed a snarky laugh. "And I can guess what you were just thinking. Yes, you look marvelous. Black designer jeans and a black cashmere sweater. No shoes and socks, though. And, yes, you are still as incredibly handsome as ever. A bit older, though."

Andromeda had always been able to read his mind. One of her less admirable traits.

"Tell me what happened to Asmodius!" Molly pleaded.

"The Webmasters turned him into a cat. But he still had human DNA, so that's what the asteroid worked with."

"What?! Why?!!"

"That's a story that needs to wait until Asmodius can help me tell it. Be patient."

The former cat raised his hands in front of his face and wiggled his fingers and touched each one to its opposing thumb. And then did it again. And again. Hands were quite marvelous things.

His lips moved and his cheeks scrunched up and his eyes squeezed a little bit shut.

After a bit of thought, he realized that he was grinning like an idiot. Rats! There were definite advantages to his more immobile cat face. But it couldn't be helped. He couldn't stop grinning.

"Welcome back, my darling. You have no idea how glad I am to see you!"

Asmodius gazed up at her and grinned even harder. He wasn't going to try and say anything for a while. Speech was going to take a little practice.

"Molly, you need to help me massage him back into his body." She began stroking his face, tracing around his lips and down the bridge of his nose and around his eyes and ears. It felt wonderful, and the memories of what a human face felt like and how it moved came flooding back.

"Start with his hands and arms and then do his feet and legs."

Asmodius surrendered to his still-present cat instincts and basked happily in the attention.

But what had happened? Had he been asleep? And why wasn't he a cat anymore? His brain was mush, but he spoke to it severely. It grudgingly perked up and began muttering memories.

Ah. He'd been dead.

—

"Asmodius, you can't just lie there looking goofy anymore. You need to start practicing your speech."

His eyes shifted, and he groaned in horror to see Micah and one of the largest, blackest, scariest werewolves he'd ever seen— that must be Diana—staring at him in avid amazement.

"That's a start," she said. "Now say 'Ahhhh.'"

Asmodius glared at her. The last thing he wanted to do was mumble like a moron in front of all these people.

"We'll stop massaging you if you don't say 'Ahhhh.'"

"Mmph," said Asmodius.

"Okay, we'll start with 'Mmmmm.'"

40

Molly

Once they were sure Asmodius would totally recover, they'd left him and Andromeda to his speech lessons. With their hostess's permission, Molly headed back toward the kitchen, grabbed her pack, and followed Micah and Diana upstairs to find bedrooms and, more importantly, bathrooms. The first door to the right opened onto a bedroom with a full bath. Molly pulled Diana's cell phone and some clothes that hadn't been ripped to shreds and drenched in demon blood out of her pack. She tossed them on the bed and left so Diana could become human, wash, and dress, and, of course, call Adam. She'd found her own bedroom and bath, taken a much-needed shower, and rooted through her pack again for something to wear. Then she'd sprawled on the bed and called her grandmother. By the time she'd told her the whole story—well, almost the whole story, Gram really didn't need to hear the violent, gory parts—her grandmother was in tears. Molly could hear her sniffing, and the tremor in her voice when she'd said, "Thank the gods you are all safe. I can't wait to see Asmodius!"

After the call, she'd snatched a few hours of sleep.

A soft breeze stroked Molly's cheek as it filtered in through the huge, open entry hall door. The last rays of the setting sun dappled the lush, green courtyard garden and slanted into the hall, warming the gray stone walls with their golden glow. The round coffee table was spread with a large platter of bloody, rare steaks, baked potatoes with all the fixings, a colorful salad, a bowl of fruit, and a plate stacked with brownies still warm from the oven.

Molly sank back in her chair, chewing contentedly on a piece of steak. If only Gram and Adam were here, life would be perfect. She and Micah, Diana, Andromeda, and Asmodius were all sitting around the table, plates on their laps, devouring their meals. Everyone except Asmodius. He stared in distaste at the plate Andromeda had fixed for him—cut up steak, a small portion of potato with a dollop of sour cream, and a few lettuce leaves and veggies from the salad.

"You're not a cat anymore, my dear. You need to start getting used to human food," Andromeda said. "Try a piece of the meat."

"I know I'm not a cat anymore." Asmodius glared over at her. "And quit hovering!"

The Queen of Hell gazed at him happily as she sank back in her chair and bit into an apple wedge.

Molly decided that this Asmodius was even better at glaring than the cat.

He started to pick up a piece of meat on his plate, froze, grabbed a fork, fumbled with it until he was holding it right, then stabbed savagely at the bloody morsel and put it in his mouth. He chewed slowly and carefully, like he was afraid he'd bite his tongue, and favored everyone with another glare.

"Don't you have anything better to do than watch me eat?"

Molly grinned and went back to devouring her meal. Exactly what the cat would have said. His eyes were still amber and blazed with the same power and intelligence, he still moved with a cat's quickness and grace, his handsome face remained vaguely cat-like, his wavy, close-cropped hair was almost black, his clothes were black. Everything about him was familiar.

The five mages concentrated on their meal in comfortable silence. Diana had methodically demolished two large, raw steaks and was reaching for her third. Micah and Andromeda were the only ones who paid any attention to the salad. Asmodius picked at his last few pieces of meat. He hadn't touched his tiny sample of vegetables. Finally, he growled softly—it wasn't the same as the growl the cat used to have, but Molly was glad that he could still growl—and plunked his unfinished plate down on the table in disgust.

"I know everyone wants to hear about why I was turned into a cat, but before we start down that road, I'd like Andromeda to explain how Tamerlane got hold of her body and how a demon managed to escape from Hell and murder two adepts."

"Three," Molly said. "The Second Webmaster was killed yesterday."

"Oh dear," said Asmodius, "Gabriel was a good, kind man. What a loss." His face darkened for the briefest instant, and he slumped slightly. Most people wouldn't have noticed, but, because she was used to ignoring her mentor's face and watching his body for cues about his mood, Molly recognized his sadness.

"And Nysrogh didn't really escape. He's back in Hell. We saw him," Micah said.

"Even stranger," Asmodius said, and turned back to Andromeda. "Tell us how this came to be."

"I don't know for sure how Tamerlane got control of my body," she said, and sat forward in her chair tucking one foot up under her knee. "I woke up one morning about three weeks ago and found that I was trapped in what felt like the basement of my brain. I could see my bedroom ceiling, hear the hounds' heavy breathing, feel the bed under my body, and smell the lavender scent of my sheets, but it was like they were a long way away. When I tried to look at something besides the ceiling, my eyes wouldn't move, and when I tried to turn my head, it was like I was paralyzed. I threw the covers off, and got out of bed. But I hadn't done any of those things. Someone or something else was controlling my body.

"I panicked, but my heart didn't race, and my breath didn't come in gasps. Instead, my voice said, 'Good morning, Andromeda, and thank you for lending me your body. The reason you're not dead is because I need you to show me how to run the asteroid. We wouldn't want any master criminals escaping, now would we?'

"I was beyond horrified! Some bastard had stolen my body and taken over my kingdom and was demanding that I tell him how to run it. My first impulse was to tell this monster exactly what I thought of him, and that there was no way I was going to help. But, on second thought, if I didn't help, he could make serious mistakes that could destroy the asteroid or cause my charges even more suffering or allow one to escape. And, of course, I wanted to live as long as possible—because I had no doubt that when I was no longer useful, the beast would shove me out to die. But as the days went by, I almost wished he'd kill me. With no control over anything except my own thoughts, and therefore nothing to do but think in ever narrowing circles while he took over my life, I was slowly going mad."

Remembering her horrible captivity took its toll. Andromeda wrapped her arms tight around her chest and seemed to shrink in on herself. Tears flowed freely down her cheeks.

"It was terrible," she whispered as she rocked slowly back and forth in her chair. The sight of an adept reduced to this state made Molly shudder. When all this was over, she was gonna ask Aunt Althea to spend some time with Andromeda and help her heal. Molly could only imagine what Hell's Mistress had been through, but she knew from her own experience with deep trauma that Andromeda was gonna need help. The four mages sat silently while she worked through her memories.

Night had engulfed the asteroid, and the red planet, like a malignant, evil eye, shone through the demons and angels in the stained glass above the landing. Its light flowed down the gleaming stairway in a bloody cascade. Alfred, Andromeda's butler and jack-of-all-trades, shuffled in bearing a tray of mugs, sugar and cream, and a large thermos in one hand, and a silver candelabra with six flaming candles in the other. He reminded Molly of Lurch, the Addams family butler. After setting the candelabra in the middle of the coffee table, the tray in front of Andromeda, and removing the empty meat platter, he looked over at his mistress with concern.

Off in the distance a creature howled.

Andromeda sighed, wiped away her tears, and blew her nose with a spotless white handkerchief that she produced out of thin air. "That will be all, Alfred, we'll clear away the rest when we've finished."

After the butler had made his slow, dignified exit, she sniffed one final sniff and squared her shoulders in determination. "Who wants coffee?" she asked. When everyone had been served, she continued her story. "A few weeks ago, Tamerlane began remodeling the stairway up through the cliff. You saw the results."

"Yeah, we almost didn't make it," Molly said. "But we figured out that he did it so Nysrogh, and only Nysrogh, could get to the room with the bars."

"Exactly. Several days ago, Tamerlane summoned Nysrogh up to that room."

"How?" Micah asked.

"As warden I can compel any of my charges to do practically anything. I've never used this privilege, it's just a safety measure.

Tamerlane forced me to tell him how to do it." The color had drained from Andromeda's face and her expression turned grim.

Molly was sure that Andromeda hadn't parted with this knowledge easily.

"After he'd summoned the demon, we ventured down past the dungeon to the room on the other side of the bars and waited. Finally, the door opened and Nysrogh stalked in. Even without his magic his eyes usually glowed blue, but now they were blank holes. Tamerlane took a cobalt-blue vial out of my pocket, uncorked it, and drank its contents. Almost immediately, my brain started to fuzz over. We lay down on the cot, and Tamerlane made Nysrogh touch my shoulder—he could barely reach it through the bars. Just as I slipped into unconsciousness, Tamerlane left. I can only assume that he went into Nysrogh. Unfortunately, I couldn't make use of my freedom. My brain was so fried that all I could do was sleep."

"Oh gods!" Diana said, her features a mask of horror and anger. "He gave you a tincture of *Valeriana oblivia*! That stuff is just evil. It totally knocks out your magical ability. At first the effects only last a few hours, but with repeated use, it does permanent damage."

"Yes. He made me take it three times, and the grogginess lasted a bit longer with each dose." Andromeda shivered. "It was awful."

"That explains everything," Molly said. "Once Tamerlane was in Nysrogh's body, the demon could do everything that an eternal can do. That's why he could jump into Denzel's study without being invited—Tamerlane had probably been there dozens of times. And that's why he could throw fireballs at us. Even though Nysrogh's magic was gone, Tamerlane's wasn't."

"When Tamerlane came back," Micah said, "he'd have Nysrogh touch you again and he'd transfer back into you while you were still asleep. You were safe because you were behind bars and just out of the demon's reach. Then he made the demon go back down the stairs and into the valley. Brilliant!"

A door slammed at the back of the castle, and everyone except Andromeda jumped to their feet. Paws pattered and clicked in the passage between the kitchen and entry hall, and The Hounds of Hell surged into the room, a panting, jostling, white tide tipped in crimson. They greeted each of their guests with friendly enthusiasm and lots of tail wagging. Molly kept an eye on the coffee table—especially the candles and brownies—but, somehow, nothing got swept off. However, everyone except Diana kept the dogs at arms' length and gave them only a few tentative pats. Their muzzles were covered with blood, their eyes blazed red with insane ferocity, and they reeked of death. Only the werewolf had absolutely no problem with this.

After their blessedly quick greeting, the dogs leaped for their mistress.

"There you are, my darlings! Did you have a good hunt?" Andromeda reached with joy for each terrifying beast, called it by name, stroked its gory head, fondled its ears, thumped vigorously up and down its muscular body, and told it what a good puppy it was. Then she pointed to a rug beside the main door and said, "Go lay down." They all padded over to their spot and collapsed in a heap.

"What do they hunt?" Micah asked.

"Anything that happens to be in their way. There are deer up in the hills. That's where they usually go. My charges know the hounds hunt on the night that our planet, Aries, is full and stay inside."

"I'm so sorry you lost Blitzen," Diana said. "Your hounds are such beautiful, intelligent animals. I hate to think of one being under that monster's control."

"Oh, I haven't lost him," Andromeda replied with a grin. "The Hounds of Hell are creations of the asteroid. They belong here and only here. Once Tamerlane leaves his body, Blitzen will immediately return."

"That's a relief!" Molly said. "He should be back soon then, because I can't believe Tamerlane will want to spend much time as a dog." She tried not to think about the unfortunate human he'd transfer into when he left Blitzen.

"I wish we knew where he was," said Diana.

"Gram said the Webmasters would do everything they could to locate him. But she didn't sound too hopeful. He could be any-where and any-time in the multiverse."

Molly sat in glum silence wondering when Tamerlane would try to kill the Third Webmaster, and what they could do to prevent it. Terror curled in the pit of her stomach as she remembered for the bajillionth time that Gram was the Third. Impatiently shaking away her fear, she stretched and said, "We still have brownies to eat, and, Asmodius, you promised to tell us how you got turned into a cat."

Asmodius reached over and took Andromeda's hand in his. Their eyes met, and volumes of love, unspoken agreements, and grief passed instantly between them. At least it seemed that way to Molly.

"That is not just my story. Andromeda and I will both tell it."

"But it's a long story. Where shall we begin?" she asked, passing around the plate of brownies and refilling coffee mugs.

41

Asmodius

"It begins, I think, in Geoffrey Gould's apartment, on the day I decided to be a pot smuggler," Asmodius said.

"What?!" Molly cried. "I can't believe the Web-masters turned you into a cat because you were smuggling pot. Half my friends smoke it."

"No, of course they didn't. Be patient. As I said, it's a long story."

It was, indeed, a long, difficult story. It was one of the hardest things he'd ever done. He didn't think he could have managed it if Andromeda hadn't helped—filling in or squeezing his hand at the difficult parts, reminding him of things he'd forgotten, and making sure the young mages understood that they had worked together to create the disaster that had happened.

He couldn't have asked for a better audience. All three of them listened with rapt attention, perched on the edges of their chairs, coffee and brownies forgotten. They only interrupted a few times.

When he mentioned Estelle, Molly said, "Wait! Was my dad around then?"

A familiar pain had surged from Asmodius's heart and shimmered all the way out his toes and fingers. Keeping his face unreadable, he closed his eyes and let it pass. Unfortunately, that particular pain always came back. This was, indeed, a night to touch and remember grief.

"Yes. He was four years old going on twenty," he'd said.

When they got to the part where they decided to summon a second-order demon, Molly and Diana had gasped and Micah slapped his forehead, fell back in his chair, and said, "D'oh!!!" And they'd all yelped in surprise and horror when they learned that the demon they'd called up had been Nysrogh.

Together, Asmodius and Andromeda told their story to its bitter end.

—

"And you know the rest," Asmodius said.

He settled back in his chair, clutching Andromeda's warm, solid hand, and reveling in the fact that they were together at last, and that, even after all these years, she still loved him. He swallowed down the tightness that had suddenly formed in his throat.

It was done.

They had told them everything.

Except for some of the more personal details, of course.

A weight that he hadn't even known was there lifted off his chest, freeing his aching heart and allowing a full, sweet, nourishing breath of Andromeda-Molly-Micah-Diana-dog-stone-and-burning-candle-scented air into his lungs.

But with his next breath came fear.

His dark secret was out.

What would Molly think?

42

Molly

Molly stared at the dark, handsome adept who was staring right back at her with eyes that glowed golden in the flickering candle-light.

Her heart was torn.

According to Andromeda, this was, indeed, Asmodius.

But was this *her* Asmodius?

A few days ago Asmodius had been a huge, magical black cat. A beloved teacher who had guided her through Damia on a journey that had transformed her from a depressed, angry teen into a warrior mage.

And just hours ago he had been dead.

And now here he was, a living man.

A man who had made huge mistakes that had led to a life of loss and bitter grief. A totally sexy man who was obviously in love with an adept who not only called up horrible demons, but also ruled over them with a satin-gloved fist of iron.

A man who wasn't the black cat she had known and loved.

And yet, the cat and the man were alike in so many ways. She had loved the cat not only for his intensity, power, and strength, but also for his beauty, self-centered vanity, and pride. And these were the very qualities that had gotten the man into trouble.

So why couldn't she love the man as much as she had the cat?

Because the man had a history—a human history of pride, driving ambition, love, and grief. He was no longer an inscrutable, mysterious cat.

Because a man like that wouldn't look at her and judge her the same way the cat had. That man would compare her to the other amazing and powerful humans he'd known.

And if she didn't measure up, she couldn't bear to see it in his eyes.

But wait.

If Andromeda and Asmodius were telling the truth (and why would they lie?), the Asmodius she had known and loved hadn't really been a cat. He'd been a man in a cat suit. So the man sitting in front of her was the same man who had cared for her, protected her, and snarled at her from the time they'd first met in Damia until he'd left for Hell.

Maybe this really was Asmodius.

And maybe it was okay that this really was Asmodius.

The uncertainty was crazy-making.

She set her mug on the coffee table with care. Her hands had been gripping it so hard she was surprised she hadn't crushed it. As they released it, they began to shake. When she stood up, her body creaked and complained like she'd been sparring for hours. Asmodius's face remained an unreadable mask of stone, but his hands were clenched into fists.

As Molly moved toward him and opened her arms, the mask dissolved and his face lit up with joy. And were those really tears shimmering in his eyes?

There was a flash of movement and Asmodius's arms were around her, holding her close. His clean, musky scent surrounded her, so familiar and so Asmodius—only now there was a hint of lime. And somehow, that was familiar as well. She felt his strong, steady heartbeat and every muscle in her body relaxed, her stomach unclenched, and joy rushed through her like a warm summer wind.

She knew that heartbeat as well as she knew her own. It was the same heartbeat she'd felt all those times when she'd curled around Asmodius's warm, furry body, clutching him tight in terror or grief or desolation.

And that heartbeat had always comforted her.

At last. She was sure.

This was her Asmodius.

⁓

After schlepping the dishes on the coffee table back to the kitchen, everyone headed for bed. Diana practically ran up the steps to her room, and would, no doubt, soon be on the phone to Adam, telling him Andromeda and Asmodius's tragic story. Asmodius and Andromeda, wrapped in each other's arms, climbed the elegant stairway ahead of her.

Micah was a potent presence beside her. Every cell in her body tingled and reached toward his violet-black aura. In mere moments she was gonna be shamelessly plastered up against him.

Not.

She kept going, one step at a time, gripping the polished wood banister and staring straight ahead. Micah had taken off his sunglasses, and she knew that if she looked into his eyes, she'd be lost. After traveling through Hell with him, she had come to know him much better. She now truly understood that he was a violent, dangerous man motivated by a completely different moral code than her own. A gang-leader, a criminal, probably a murderer, and to top it all off, an agent for Hades, the freakin' King of the Dead.

And no amount of love, time, or magic was gonna change that.

But then, she was a violent, dangerous woman too. And maybe she wasn't a murderer, but she was definitely a killer. Were they really that different?

And being with him felt so right, so natural. Like something that had to be.

They were at the top of the steps now and turning toward her room. What was she gonna do when they got there? Desire and fear and common sense fought it out in her head, making her dizzy and sick. Her arms and legs feel like they were filled with lead instead of rapidly pumping blood, and she was breathing like she'd just climbed Mount Everest instead of a set of stairs.

What if he kissed her? What if she kissed him? What if they didn't kiss? What if he came into her room?????? What if what if what if what if...

The only sound was their footsteps measuring out the distance to her door.

And then they were there.

Micah pulled gently at her arm until she was facing him. She could feel the tension in his touch.

She stared up at his thin, perfectly formed lips, terrified of looking up into his eyes.

Here she was, a warrior mage who had fought her way through Hell and killed more demons than she cared to count, afraid to look into the eyes of the man she loved.

Oh jeez, yeah. She did love him.

Shit!

She looked up.

Micah's eyes weren't endless black holes, this time. They were dark brown. But so intensely intense that it still felt like they were looking into her soul.

He must have been waiting to see her eyes and the feelings behind them, because the moment she looked up, he sighed and stroked her cheek. Gently. Carefully. Like she was the most precious thing in the world. The touch sent a shiver of electricity ricocheting through her body like a pinball.

His kiss was soft, warm, and questioning. His hand rested lightly against her cheek. She could pull away if she wanted to.

But she couldn't.

Even if she'd wanted to.

His lips were lightning. Paralyzing her and holding her suspended in a jolt of pleasure.

She had no idea how long it lasted—forever, for seconds, it was all the same. She was in a place where there was no time.

When Micah stepped back, she had to lean against the door to keep from keeling over.

"Good night, Miss Molly," he said. "It's been quite the day."

Molly couldn't tell if the look on his face was deep despair or total ecstasy.

Or both.

43

Molly

The kitchen of Andromeda's castle was a comfortable mix of ancient and modern. The floor and walls were made from the same stone blocks as all the rest of the castle, but the floor had been smoothed and polished to a soft gloss, bringing out the stone's intricate patterns. Beautiful and totally functional. Micah was sitting beside her at the big oak refectory table, which was distracting, especially when he draped his arm across the back of her chair. Molly tended to be klutzy when she was distracted, so she was trying not to drop her coffee mug, which made her even more distracted.

There was a stone fireplace along one wall that was big enough to roast a cow, but today the spit was empty, and only a modest fire crackled contentedly on the grate. Andromeda, dressed in an outrageous steampunk creation involving a green leather corset studded with spikes and chains and buckles, a white satin shirt with flowing sleeves, brown leggings and brown knee-high boots with more buckles and chains, was tending a popping, sizzling griddle of bacon and a skillet of scrambled eggs on a stainless steel gas range large enough to cook for an entire castle-full of people. She wore no apron, but there wasn't a single spatter of bacon grease on her outfit. Neat trick.

The smell of freshly baked bread, spices and bacon permeated the room, making Molly's mouth water. Alfred had made cinnamon rolls last night and left them to rise, and Diana was taking the finished product out of the oven. As she opened the door, the hot air gently blew her black and silver-streaked hair away from her smiling face and brought a soft flush to her tanned, sharp-chiseled features. Cinnamon rolls were one of the few foods besides meat that she craved.

Asmodius pulled plates out of one of the oak cabinets above a gleaming stainless steel sink set in a long, stone counter-top that matched the floor. Crossing over to Andromeda, he set them beside the stove. And then he paused, hands resting on either side of the plates, gazing at the blank wall in front of him. Although he was wearing black jeans and a sweater, his slim figure and cat-like grace made him look like a fashion model dressed to the nines. His hands clenched into fists and he turned to Molly.

"I will come back with you to see Estelle," he said, "but I can only stay a few days."

"Why?" Molly said, clutching her mug.

But she knew the answer.

He was coming back here to be with Andromeda. He didn't need her or Gram anymore.

"I died here, Molly, and the asteroid refashioned me from the life-blood I spilled on it. Most of me is me, but some of me, the part that gives me life, belongs to this place. I can't be away from it for very long.

"So Andromeda and I have decided to share the ruler-ship of Hell. I need to come back here to learn how everything works and shadow her for a few months. Then she will leave for a much-needed vacation. After that we'll alternate. Part of the year I'll spend with you and Estelle and the other part here. You could pop in for a visit any time. Not many young ladies get to go to Hell and back whenever they want!" he added with an evil leer.

"Not many young ladies would *want* to go to Hell and back. But for you, I'll do it!" said Molly, her shoulders sagging in relief. He wasn't leaving for good.

"Actually, I pretty much already have," she added.

Laughter filled the warm, fragrant kitchen, but stopped abruptly as power thundered into the room. Molly jumped and dropped her coffee. With a sound like a gunshot, the mug crashed to the floor, exploding into a thousand pieces and spattering the creamy, brown stimulant everywhere.

Shit.

The room flooded with snapping sizzling energy. It sent tiny shocks up her arms and pressed against her chest, making her heart race with fear. Whatever was coming was big and danger-ous and angry. She reached for Flick and it slipped into her hand.

The energy abruptly coalesced and became a tall, slender woman. But her shoulders were broad, her arms rippled with muscle and she held herself like a warrior. Her long, silver-blond curls wafted back from her face in an unseen wind, and were held in place with a white headband embroidered with a silver, seven-pointed star. A sleeveless, white cotton tunic topped dove-gray leggings and serviceable gray knee-boots. The tunic was clenched with a wide, black belt fastened with a silver buckle. Thrust into that belt was a sword very much like Flick, except its scabbard and hilt wrappings were silver-gray. Molly couldn't see it from where she stood, but she knew that a white swan charm peeked out from under those wrappings.

Brigga stood directly in front of Asmodius, her fierce, steel-gray eyes snapping. She might not have been big, but she was, indeed, dangerous and furious. Molly had no doubt that a look from this goddess could kill. And that Asmodius was just a blink away from dead.

"Asmodius and I have some unfinished business," Brigga said.

"Lady! No! Please!" Molly begged, unconsciously holding Flick in strike position.

"Hush, Lass." And with a flick of her wrist she froze Molly and everyone else in the room in place. When Molly tried again to plead for Asmodius's life, she found that she couldn't make a sound.

Only Asmodius remained unfrozen. He sighed and looked Brigga straight in the eye, his face expressionless.

The memory of the day when Brigga had begun making Flick flashed through her mind like a nightmare video in fast forward.

In one swift slash to the Goddess's wrist, Asmodius had kept Molly from being Brigga's tool and, instead, made her a blood sister. She would never be the powerful pawn that Brigga meant to create, because when Molly died, a piece of the Goddess would die with her.

Brigga had come to seek her revenge.

Why had Asmodius done it? She would have gladly been the Goddess's slave and perhaps died an early death. Owning Flick was worth the price. Now she was going to lose Asmodius, right when she'd found him again.

Molly? Flick's voice sang with grief.

Yes?

You know I can't kill her. She made me and her blood is in me.

I know. I would never kill her either—even if I could. Grabbing for you was just a reflex.

I'm sorry, I like Asmodius and I'm glad he did it. He made me even stronger.

Yeah.

"Let's get this over with," growled Asmodius.

With a move that was almost too quick for even Molly's trained eye, Brigga unsheathed Brightwing, her fabulous sword, and on the down-stroke, slashed it across Asmodius's handsome face.

Bright crimson blood erupted from the wound and Asmodius's hands flew to his face. He fell to the floor, rolling in agony. A sharp piece of Molly's mug ripped across the back of his left hand and even more blood flowed. Molly sobbed and tried to bury her face in her hands so she wouldn't have to witness his pain, but she was frozen. Forced to watch.

Sparkling points of green light appeared and began dancing over the bloody wounds.

Of course.

The asteroid would heal him and everything would be fine.

Brigga pointed sternly at the twinkling lights and they stopped in their airy tracks like children caught stealing cookies. She closed her hand into a fist and twisted it quickly.

The energy shifted.

The lights resumed their dance.

Soon all the blood was gone and Asmodius rose to his feet, shaking with shock. He was alive and whole, but a livid white scar ran from the corner of his left eye down to the corner of his mouth. As he raised his hand to trace the line of it, Molly noticed that the wound on his hand had healed without a trace.

"There. That should teach you not to meddle in the ways of the Gods," Brigga said. "But it probably won't."

"My Lady, you are most merciful," said Asmodius.

"Bah! Just be glad my sister is so fond of you." She waved her hand and Molly found that she could move and speak once more.

She ran to Asmodius and hugged him tight. "I'm so, so sorry. You didn't have to do it!"

"Oh, but I did. And I'd do it again in a heartbeat," he whispered.

"I heard that," snapped Brigga.

"Molly, we have work to do. Queen Flora of Damia is heaping offerings of great lengths of the steel cable that I use to make my swords onto my altars and pestering me with pleas for help.

"We will need that one as well," she said pointing to Micah, who cringed.

Molly had never seen Micah cringe.

"Hades has given him permission to aid us. Both of you. Come stand by me. It is time to be gone."

So much for breakfast.

At least she'd gotten her coffee.

Well, most of it.

PART III

Damia

44

Alexander

ing Alexander I of Damia lounged in a padded chair in his bed chamber. Even though it was, at last, spring, it was a foul night. A roaring fire blazed in the fireplace, warming the room and making the polished oak floors, imported hardwood furniture, and colorful hand-knotted carpet glow in its golden light. His hunting dogs lay in a snuffling, snoozing pile by the door, except for a new addition who hadn't yet been accepted into the pack, and so lay a few feet away from them. Although his head was a bit larger than normal and his mouth was overly full of fangs, he was a lovely beast—big and fierce with a powerful chest. His color was unusual—pure white body with red ears, paws and eyes. A good addition to his kennels.

Alexander's sinews cracked and popped as he stretched luxuriously. He wasn't getting any younger, but he was still healthy and life was good. As he gazed into the dancing flames, he counted his blessings.

First and foremost among them was his wife, Queen Flora. Even in midlife she was still both lovely and loving. But their relationship ran even deeper than a normal husband and wife bond, or even that of a king and queen. Damia was the only kingdom that he knew of that still retained the mystical connection between the king, the queen, and the land. Dalot had given up the practice over a century ago. Their wedding day, with its elaborate ceremonies and festivities, had passed in a busy, colorful blur, but their wedding night was seared into his memory in intricate, unforgettable detail. At midnight, in a secluded forest glen, under a brilliant full moon, the priests and priestesses of Damia had invoked Dalot, the Great Father, into him and Dama, the Great Mother, into Flora. The raw power of the God had blazed through him, making new pathways and connections in his brain and filling him with a mystical, inhuman energy that, like a bolt of lightning, sought the earth. And Flora was Dama, the earth. Her beautiful body had become an extension of their land, and it called to him with a mysterious, irresistible force.

They had retired—quite precipitously, as he recalled—into a glowing white pavilion and made ecstatic love on a soft carpet of moss. His beloved new wife had become more than just a woman. She was his entire realm, his whole reason for being. She was Dama. And, as her consort, Dalot, he poured his love and power into her. She had gloried in that power and accepted it joyfully, joining him totally, permanently, and irrevocably to her, and therefore, to his kingdom. That sacred bond and their love was still as strong and comforting today as it had been then.

And their love had created a new life. A son and heir to carry on their line. William was a young man now. Strong, intelligent, practical, and well trained in the subtleties of ruling a country. He would make a good king. He wished he could see him more often, but that couldn't be helped.

Damia was prospering, due mostly to the peace treaty that he and King Louis III of Dalot, his former enemy and neighbor to the east, had forged two decades ago. No armies had ravaged the land in many years, and so, under Flora's care, the land had granted them one plentiful harvest after another, which meant that the farmers, who made up most of Damia's population, had become wealthy, which meant that his granaries and tax coffers were full. And Dalot was thriving as well. Its water-powered looms and forges were producing wool cloth and tools for export and for its people instead of uniforms and weapons. No wars meant uninterrupted trade, and Dalot's sheltered, deep-water ports were bustling with ships bringing in all sorts of wonderful things from all over the world. Alexander nestled his slippered feet more deeply into the warm thickness of the brilliantly patterned carpet from the far eastern realms. The surplus grain meant that his people could buy luxuries like this from Damian merchants who bought them in Dalot and trundled them over the Altaspina Mountains in great caravans. Because of the treaty, those caravans traveled safely, protected by both Damian and Dalotian troops.

The hardest part of creating peace had been convincing their subjects that their neighbors were allies, not the enemies that they had been fighting for centuries. But, as every effective ruler knows, the human mind is malleable. If you say something long enough, and if you say it loud enough, and if you get the priests to say it too, and if you make it fashionable, and most importantly, if you make it lucrative, you can convince most people that black is white and that bad is good. It hadn't been long before Damia and Dalot were firm friends. The rest had been simply crafting trade agreements, making sure the mountain passes were free of brigands, and then stepping back and letting people make money. Which, of course, he and Louis taxed.

But, unfortunately, once they had gotten everything running like clockwork, things were boring. Alexander was a man of action, a warrior king. He loved a good fight. But he was also a very intelligent, practical man. And war was bad for the kingdom and, of course, for his wife, who was his kingdom. So, he was stuck with peace. Things could be worse, he thought with a rueful smile.

The new dog stood and stretched, front legs flat and forward on the floor, back haunches high. Then he yawned, shook himself, and padded over to the King.

"Ah, come to say hello and be friendly, have you?" Alexander said as he held his hand out for the hound to sniff. The dog snuffled at the King's fingers, wagged his tail, and came closer. Alexander stroked his head, fondled his ears, and murmured the soothing phrases that dog lovers throughout the multiverse say to comfort and reassure their furry friends. But instead of panting happily and enjoying the caress, the hound went rock still and stared balefully up at him, eyes blazing with uncanny intelligence.

The King barely noticed as the hound backed away, lips drawn back in a vicious snarl, red eyes glowing with fear and hate, because his hand and then his arm were tingling and buzzing like thousands of tiny bees were crawling through them. And he definitely didn't notice the dog shimmer and vanish, because the bees had coalesced into a dark, stinging shadow that slithered and raced through his muscles, veins and nerves. It was a vile evilness, and he battered at it furiously, desperately trying to boot it out. But the thing was strong. It simply swatted him away like an irritating fly. Alexander continued to fight. He fought savagely, with all his heart.

He had to.

He had no doubt that if he let this thing win, he was doomed.

The thing soon ignored his increasingly feeble attacks and slithered easily through him, touching him with a sickening, intimate possessiveness. But he still fought on. Terror and rage gave him strength.

It wormed its loathsome way into his heart, and a monstrous wave of grief, hopelessness and desolation overwhelmed him. It was agony. Both physical and mental.

A merciful darkness descended, shoving him into oblivion.

—

Alexander awoke with a start and then froze into perfect stillness.

He was alive, but something was wrong. And he wasn't moving until he understood what that something was.

The light was dim, but bright enough to reveal that he was surrounded by stone walls and supported by a cold stone floor. It could have been one of his dungeons, but there was no smell of rot, unwashed humanity, chamber pots, or fear. In fact, it smelled like his bed chamber. And wasn't that the crackle of a fire? And that was the sound of a log shifting in the flames. Suddenly he was looking into those flames. Yes. He was safe in his bed chamber and this had all been a terrible nightmare.

He relaxed and raised his eyes to his family's coat of arms painted in beautiful detail above the fireplace. A red dragon coiled around a white unicorn on a green field.

But the view of the fire remained the same.

Even though he was sure he'd looked up, he was still looking into the fire.

But he was also looking at stone wall.

His body stood up.

He was still lying on the stone floor, but his body was walking around his bedchamber, looking at things, and picking them up and examining them like it had never laid eyes on them before.

And, horror of horrors, no matter how hard he tried, there was no way he could stop it or make it do something different.

His heart raced with panic, but the heart in his body continued to beat in a slow, steady rhythm.

This was his worst nightmare.

The Prophecy had come to pass.

Something had taken over his body.

WHAT ARE YOU? He screamed. His mouth moved and he could hear the words, but his real lips remained still and made no sound.

You're finally conscious. Good. I am King Alexander I of Damia and you are my adviser.

No! I'm *King Alexander and you are a thief.*

Unimaginable pain seared through him. Every nerve flamed white hot, and his entire body scream in agony. It went on and on and on. At first, he was afraid it would kill him, but soon, he was afraid it wouldn't. And then, as quickly as it had begun, it stopped, leaving him shaking and terrified, because he knew that even though the pain was gone, it could come back at any moment. It could come back any time the monster inside his body wanted it to. And Alexander also understood that the monster inside of him was incredibly evil.

And that monster now controlled his kingdom.

He had never felt so alone and so desolate.

Now, as I was saying, I am King Alexander I of Damia and you are my adviser. I don't need you, but like any adviser, your knowledge will help me rule more effectively. The moment you cease to be useful, or that I find I can't trust you, I will kill you.

A hand grabbed Alexander by the back of his collar and dragged him up to an open window high above the floor and he stared into an endless, black night sky. But it was unlike any night sky he had ever seen. There were stars, but they weren't in any of the familiar patterns. And they pulsed and moved in a most un-star-like fashion. An immense cloud of golden light in the shape of a lion stalked slowly past. It had an eagle's head with evil red eyes and cruelly pointed beak, huge bat wings, and a long, snake-like tail. A shape straight out of one of his most terrifying nightmares. He shuddered and looked away.

That is the astral realm. Your body is an astral body and belongs there. All I need to do is toss you out this window like so much trash, and you will be sucked into that blackness, never to return.

Do you understand?

Yes.

A fist came out of nowhere and smashed into his face, sending him crashing into the wall and tumbling back down to the floor.

Yes, Your Majesty.

Cold fury seethed through him. Wasn't it enough that this monster had robbed him of his body and kingdom? Did he really need to rub his nose in the fact that he'd stolen his identity as well?

Yes, of course he did. It was part of the process of breaking him, making him a compliant and willing tool. Although he did not employ torturers, King Alexander was quite familiar with the techniques needed to gain power and control over someone. He'd used them himself. Although not nearly so brutally.

And his body was no longer made of muscle and bone. No amount of abuse would kill it. So he could refuse to cooperate and suffer endless agony with no possibility of an end—until the monster got tired of torturing him, decided that he was no longer useful, and tossed him away.

Would he die then? Or would he wander aimlessly through that black, starry sky? Either way, he would never know what happened to his kingdom or his loved ones.

Refusing to cooperate was not an option. But there had to be other, more productive, ways to fight this evil, and he would find them.

A hand grabbed the front of his shirt and yanked him up like a rag doll while a fist slammed into his gut, paralyzing him with pain.

Say it!

Yes, Your Majesty.

Now leave us. The hand threw him crashing into the wall once more.

The King lay curled and shaking on the hard stone floor, waiting for the pain to subside and smiling grimly to himself. He had discovered a few of the monster's weaknesses. He was only able to read his captive's surface emotions and couldn't read his thoughts at all. Alexander knew this because he had been awake and thinking and feeling for quite a while before he'd actually called out, and his captor had replied, *You are finally conscious.* He hadn't sensed that his captive had already been awake. Also, his captor was extremely powerful, and extremely powerful people tend to be overconfident and underestimate their adversaries. He, himself, had made that mistake once—but only once. So he would continue to resist, but not for long, and then pretend to be broken and compliant. The monster would believe it, because, of course, his power was irresistible, and of course, this helpless man could never have held out against him. So, clutching his fury and determination deep inside him and allowing his pain and fear to scream out at the surface of his emotions, Alexander began evaluating his position and planning what needed to be done.

His thoughts were interrupted by his wife's quick knock on his door. The same sequence of taps he'd waited for almost every night of their marriage. The knock was a courtesy, she didn't wait for a reply, just opened the door strode toward him. Her waist had thickened slightly with age and her lush, wavy hair the color of ripe wheat fields was streaked with silver, but she moved with the fluid grace of a much younger woman and her perfect oval face was creased with laugh lines, but no other signs of age. As always, Alexander's heart quickened with joy at the sight of her. The monster plastered a smile on his face, but his heartbeat remained steady.

She'd come to say good night. Or, perhaps, spend the night with him.

Except she wouldn't be spending the night with him. She'd be spending it with a monster.

NO!!! RUN AWAY, MY DEAR. RUN AWAY NOW!!! He screamed and pounded furiously on his prison walls.

Be still! A fist slammed into his face, shattering his front teeth and filling his mouth with blood. Pain warped his vision and sent him to his knees. But moments later, the blood was gone and his teeth were back in his jaw, ready to be smashed again. The pain lingered, but eventually faded away.

Flora glided into his captor's waiting arms. She gave his body the same strong hug as always and walked to the window.

"It's a beautiful night," she said, as she always did. Except it wasn't. It was raining buckets.

"But not as beautiful as you, my dear," his captor replied.

Alexander was proud of his queen. Her shoulders only stiffened for the slightest moment. Even the sharpest eyes wouldn't have caught it if they weren't looking for it. But he had been watching for her reaction, And he was her husband. She hardly hesitated at all before turning and gazing carefully into the monster's eyes.

"You are so kind." If Alexander hadn't been looking closely, he would never have seen the quick glimmer of terror in his wife's beautiful, violet eyes.

"I stopped by to wish you good night," she said. "I'm going straight to my chambers. My headache is back."

"I'm so sorry you aren't feeling well. Get some rest, and hopefully you'll be better in the morning."

"Thank you, my dear. Good night." She squeezed his body's hand and strolled out the door.

Alexander groaned in relief, but he was more than relieved—he was ecstatic. However, the monster wouldn't expect him to be ecstatic, just relieved that he didn't have to watch impotently while his wife made love to another man. So he didn't laugh with joy and punch the air and scream "Yes, yes, yes!!!" He acted like a beaten man who had been given a temporary reprieve.

He and his queen had lived their lives in the shadow of the Prophecy. The night William, their son, had been born, which was the same night that the armies of Dalot and Damia celebrated the Peace Agreement, the young warrior mage who had saved their kingdom had a vision. She'd told both him and King Louis that one day, when the Prince had grown to manhood, King Alexander would break the peace and attack Dalot. Alexander,

Flora, and Louis all knew that visions of the future are unreliable because every present has many possible futures. But they were not so foolish as to completely ignore a warning that came from a warrior mage at such a significant time. They thought hard about why Alexander would break the peace that he had worked so hard to bring about. There were at least two possibilities. The first was the simplest and most likely. Times would change and something would happen that made it necessary to attack Dalot. This might even be in Dalot's best interest—Dalot might have been invaded by the Norse, their common neighbors to the north. But there was a second possibility. Something would happen to King Alexander that would totally change him. He would become a different person. So the three monarchs crafted a plan that would cover both possibilities. Prince William would be raised somewhere unknown to his father, and he would come and visit him at random times determined by his mother, but Alexander would never know until the Prince was actually there when this would be. Flora also feared that if her husband was gone and his body had been taken over by a stranger, she wouldn't know until it was too late to warn her son or protect her kingdom. So she and Alexander had made up a going-to-bed-ritual that they had performed faithfully for the past two decades. Flora would come to his chambers, give him a hug, go to the window. and say, "It's a beautiful night." And he would reply, no matter what the weather, "The stars are so bright." If he said anything else, Flora would flee the palace. Even if she did the obvious thing and joined her son, they would be safe, because Alexander had no idea where his son was. But if he continued to reply correctly, which would mean he most likely hadn't been taken over, and still decided to invade Dalot, Flora and William would have the choice of supporting his decision or fighting against him.

But the worst had happened. The monster had failed the test, and so Flora knew that her kingdom was being ruled by a stranger who would soon be invading Dalot. They had often wondered if the intruder would keep the King around to guide him through the intricacies of ruling the kingdom and dealing with the Damian court or if he would kill him. When she mentioned having a headache, it was her way of telling Alexander that she knew he was not in control of his body, but that she was hoping he was still in it.

Because Flora never got headaches.

The Queen would be long gone by morning.

45

Alexander

WHERE IS SHE?!!!

The pain struck like lightning. Sizzling along each and every one of his nerves with an almost audible hiss. It was immense and cruel and overwhelming. As Alexander fainted, he found himself marveling at all the different kinds of pain that he had experienced over the past few days. And each of them had seemed worse than all the others at the time it was tormenting him. His fury had turned to a cold, hard hatred of the beast that inhabited his body and a steadfast determination to do whatever he could to destroy it. The thing was evil and a danger not only to him, but to all living things.

When Flora had left his chambers that first night, the monster began pacing back and forth. Alexander could feel him testing the muscles of his body for strength and balance. Then he' went through the familiar forms that every soldier must master to fight with a sword. Alexander had never seen them done so quickly or so perfectly. His captor was blindingly fast and strong and drove his body to its limits. When his body could do no more, the monster had stood at the window, stretching his exhausted muscles and gazing at the rain streaming down the glass in shimmering cascades.

Alexander felt his body go still, and there was a feeling of movement. Neither up nor down nor forward nor back nor right nor left, but movement nonetheless.

The window disappeared and he was standing on a dock surrounded by the smell of water. A broad river slid gently past. It was a warm night, and a few stars glimmered against a dark sky. Huge buildings, many times taller than the palace, towered over the opposite bank of the river. They were studded with lighted windows that glowed like jewels in the darkness and reflected on the black water. He didn't have time to really look at them because the monster only glanced up for a moment and then surveyed the length of the dock. His view included some of the river, and Alexander was astonished to see not just one, but three huge bridges, each one larger and more impressive than the next. They were covered in lights. Lighted carriages, pulled by some unseen force, roared across them. The city hummed like a hive filled with hundreds of angry bees. But the hum was in the distance. The only sound on the dock was the river slapping and gurgling at its floats.

The beast moved in swift silence until he came to a heap of rags lying beside a big metal basket on wheels stuffed with plump, shiny black bags.

The heap of rags shifted and snorted.

This was a man, a homeless beggar.

The streets of Bontare, Damia's capital, always had a few, no matter how prosperous the country was. In fact, the last time he'd ridden through the city he'd come upon a blind man and had the unsettling realization that it was only by the grace of the gods that he wasn't blind and begging in the streets as well. He'd tossed some coins into the man's bowl and made the sign against evil. Surely the beast hadn't come all this way to give money to a beggar.

His hand reached down and grabbed the back of the sleeper's neck. Warm, vibrant energy shot up his arm and into his heart, which opened, swelled, and, with its next beat, sent waves of hot ecstasy coursing through him. The monster gasped and shuddered with pleasure. The feeling was like nothing Alexander had ever experienced. More potent and intense than making love, it strengthened and rejuvenated, making him feel like he was twenty again. His already excellent vision became even sharper, his mind kicked into pure lucidity, and sounds that he'd never noticed before were suddenly loud and clear.

Like that distant sound of footsteps stumbling along the dock.

The monster snarled and released the beggar. As the body slumped onto the dock, the King realized that the rush of pure ecstasy he'd just felt had been the life force of a man.

A man who was now a lifeless corpse.

There was that weird sense of motion, and he was looking at the rain coursing down his chamber window once more.

You killed him, Your Majesty! He'd said, barely able to keep the anger and loathing out of his voice. The monster was quick to find an excuse to inflict pain, and he'd had enough for one evening.

It was necessary, his captor had replied, as though he were talking about something as mundane as swatting a fly.

Why, Your Majesty?

To keep my body from aging.

That's my body, you miserable thief, he'd thought with quiet rage. And that life force belonged to the beggar. It wasn't yours to steal.

Will it live forever?

No, I will live forever. This body will only last another hundred years or so, then I will move into another one. Explain these documents on my desk.

How often will you need to kill someone?

A stinging blow smacked into his cheek, snapping his head back and sending lights flashing through his brain.

Explain these documents!

Fortunately, the work had been simple and routine, because Alexander was so stunned by what he had just learned that he would have had trouble focusing on anything more difficult. The thing that possessed him was capable of sucking the life out of people and probably anything else that was alive. He had heard tales from the outlying counties of Damia about vampires, people who weren't truly dead, but would rise from their graves and feed on the blood of their neighbors. When a village discovered that this was happening, they would unearth the corpse and drive a stake through its heart, pinning it down in its grave and keeping it from walking the night.

The beast within him was, essentially, a vampire that fed on life force instead of blood. Unfortunately, stopping this vampire would be more difficult than driving a stake through the heart of a helpless corpse. This vampire was a king. A person everyone respected and obeyed. A person who totally controlled an entire country. And when, or if, some perceptive person finally realized that their King was a monster and managed to slip past all the guards, and past the beast's lightning quick strength, and kill him, the evil would still not end. The beast's wicked magic and stolen life force would rejuvenate his body. Or it would take over another person's body—perhaps the body of its would-be killer, and no one would be the wiser. Everyone would assume they had solved the problem. But it would still be out there, feeding on the lives of innocent people.

And there would no end to it because the beast would live forever.

And it would never get caught. Because if it were really threatened, it could just fly away to another world. He knew this because it had just taken him to another world. Alexander had traveled through many countries during his life, and reveled in the feel of strange earth under his feet and the excitement of foreign sights, smells, and sounds. But the strangeness of the river-city had been different. It had been unearthly. Not of this world.

—

A sharp pain yanked Alexander back into consciousness. His body was paralyzed, and he could only watch in horrified fascination as an invisible knife sliced a thin, red line along the soft underpart of his right arm and down to his middle finger, and then another one parallel to it. Another line appeared, connecting the two lines at the top, and a strip of skin began to peel slowly away from his arm. Relentless, burning pain ricocheted through him, and he could do nothing but shriek helplessly as the monster pulled the first strip down and off his finger, and went back to his upper arm for a second strip. And then a third.

And then, the monster stopped.

Now tell me where she is.

Rage, impossibly intense and hot, consumed him, but he managed to float above it.

Who, Your Majesty?

Fingernails raked down the exposed flesh of his arm.

The Queen!

I don't know. He screamed.

The beast began peeling strips of skin from his other arm, and Alexander found himself almost wishing that he knew where Flora was so he could tell him and stop the agony. And, as the pain faded a bit, thanked the gods that he didn't.

Where is she?

I don't know! Brigga's blades, I'd tell you if I did.

How could you not know where she is? The beast asked as he began on another strip of skin.

She's the Queen. She doesn't always tell me where she's going.

Then where do you think she is? The beast continued peeling the skin from his arm and the King couldn't answer because he was screaming. But when his tormentor finally pulled the strip of skin off the tip of his ring finger and the pain lessened, Alexander was more than happy to talk.

She could be anywhere, Your Majesty. Anything to keep the pain from starting again. *She's magically bound to the kingdom. She knows every small part of it like she knows the palm of her hand. And her magic is so strong she can travel anywhere in Damia in an instant.* He could tell the thieving, sadistic bastard this much at least, and it gave him pleasure to feel his body's face being pulled into a worried frown. But his relief was short-lived.

Where is the Prince?

Wouldn't you like to know? My son would know something was wrong with me as quickly as my wife. You want them both dead, I'm sure.

I don't know, Your Majesty.

The beast began peeling a strip of skin off the inside of his thigh.

Then make a guess.

The last I heard he was in Dalot visiting King Louis, he gasped.

Is he still there?

I don't know, Your Majesty.

How can I find out?

One of your agents is due back from the Dalotian court today. You could ask him, Your Majesty

You had better be telling the truth.

Suddenly, Alexander was alone, lying as still as possible on the stone floor and shuddering in agony, the exposed flesh on his arms and leg burning and stinging as though he was being attacked by a thousand scorpions. It would heal quickly, but not quickly enough.

The beast sat on King Alexander's throne at the head of the palace reception hall. Sunlight poured in through the tall, arched windows that lined the long walls on either side, making the candles in the four huge chandeliers unnecessary. Lords and ladies and government ministers decked out in their dazzling finest, priests in simple black, brown and white robes, well-dressed merchants, and a few farmers in brown, homespun tunics and hose, and generals in red and white dress uniforms crusted in gold braid crowded the black-and-white marble tiled hall spread out before him.

Beside him, Queen Flora's throne remained conspicuously empty.

He stood and the hall went immediately silent.

"I've called you here to inform you that as of today, Damia is at war with Dalot."

Cries of protest and shock echoed through the hall.

"I have been informed by a very reliable source that King Louis, our trusted friend and ally, has captured Queen Flora and Prince William and imprisoned them in his palace."

The crowd roared with anger, but a few of them stared at the beast in disbelief.

Alexander screamed in helpless fury, but a fist smacked into his face, breaking his jaw and silencing him. The bastard was lying to his people. Alexander had never lied to them—conveniently withheld information, perhaps, but never lied—and so they would trust this monster who was pretending to be their King.

The truth of the matter was that his captor had met with his agent, whom Alexander had sent to gather information about Dalot's imports. The man had been surprised when his King had asked him if either Queen Flora or Prince William were at the Dalotian court, but had replied that he'd seen no sign of them. The monster had dismissed him, then flown down into the town, followed him into a dark, deserted street, sucked the life out of him, stabbed him with the agent's own knife, and flew back to his chambers. Quick, efficient, and untraceable. Guilt and grief had overwhelmed the King. His agent was dead because, in a moment of weakness, he had left him vulnerable to an enemy the man didn't even know existed. If his agent had a family, he vowed that if he ever managed to wrestle back his body, they would be given a generous monthly stipend. It wouldn't make up for the lost life, but it would ease his conscience.

The monster certainly knew how to work a crowd. He painted a heart-rending picture of the Queen, trapped in a foreign country, cut off from the strength of her land, and slowly fading away; and of the Prince, chained in a foul, dark dungeon. His people were furious now and screamed for vengeance and their rescue. But Alexander noticed his body's eyes follow a group of merchants as they turned and walked between the red granite pillars and out of the hall. They had businesses that took them to Dalot at regular intervals and probably knew that the Queen and Prince weren't in Dalot. Alexander's heart sank. He, himself, had told the beast about those merchants' businesses. They would all die mysteriously, and there wasn't a thing he could do about it.

Why is Dalot so important to you? Alexander asked as they stalked away from the reception hall, his people's angry voices loud in his ears. The beast had left his generals to do what they did best: organize a war.

I need the money.

Damia has plenty of money.

Not enough.

And there it was.

His beloved country and its neighbor meant nothing to this bastard. He would bleed them both dry and move on, leaving suffering, grief, and chaos in his wake.

Alexander didn't ask what he needed the money for.

He didn't want to know.

46

Alexander

hat will happen if I blow this?

The monster had removed the small, silver whistle and chain that King Alexander always wore around his neck and was examining it.

Alexander swam up out of a sea of agony. Every part of him was either on fire or being stabbed, even though he had no visible wounds. His body had forgotten how to turn off pain. The window was beginning to look really good. What chance did he have after all?

When he was able to concentrate enough to see what the monster was holding, it was all he could do to keep from crying out. The beast had finally noticed Mardoc's gift. Alexander remained silent and steeled himself for another round of torment, because he knew he shouldn't tell the bastard what would happen if he blew that whistle—at least not quite yet.

An invisible hand clamped his in a vice-like grip and shoved a knife tip between the nail and the quick of his forefinger.

Answer me!

His next finger met the same fate, and then the next. The King remained silent until all his fingers were mutilated and on fire with agony.

Answer me, damn you! The monster screeched and began gouging out chunks of flesh.

Alexander knew that normally this would eventually be fatal, and although he wasn't sure he could actually die from anything the monster did to him except pitching him out that window, he didn't want to take the chance. Much as he would like to escape the clutches of this demon, he wanted to kill him even more. To do that, he needed to stay alive. And there was also a faint hope. A hope so fragile that he didn't want to put it into words. But if things went the way he was hoping. He might, indeed, have a chance to save his kingdom.

I'll tell you! He gasped.

And he did. He told the monster exactly how to use the whistle and what it would do.

But he didn't tell him that the whistle had been a gift from Mardoc, god of war, on his coronation day; and that the birds he would be calling were the god's two ravens, Hither and Yon. He didn't mention it because the King had gleaned one simple truth from his encounters with the Damian gods: they never give anybody anything that didn't have strings attached to it. So if the gift is misused—or, sometimes, even if it was used correctly—it could twist in the user's hand. He was fairly certain that someone of the beast's magical abilities understood this as well, and would also know that since he was not part of the web of strings attached to the whistle, Mardoc would not take kindly to him using it.

And he didn't tell the beast that this was the third and last time that the whistle could be used.

They stood on the balcony of the top room on the palace's tallest turret. Below them, the red tile rooftops of Bontare sloped downhill to the city wall. Beyond the wall the early spring fields glowed an almost iridescent yellow-green, and the River Selene sparkled in the late afternoon light. Alexander loved this view and had spent many hours gazing at it and dreaming. But the beast barely glanced at the beauty that fed King Alexander's soul and filled his coffers. He was already blowing the whistle.

There was no sound, but the air in front of him shimmered; and Hither and Yon, Mardoc's two great ravens, appeared. They hung, fierce and silent, suspended on outspread wings. The beast motioned them into the room. Two sets of black wings flicked ever-so-slightly and they glided through the doors and onto the desk in the center of the room. Obsidian eyes tracked him as he sat at the desk.

"I need you to gather information."

The birds went still.

The beast laid his left forearm palm up on the desk, pulled his knife out of his boot, and made a cut just above the two small scars already on his wrist. Hither and Yon dipped their beaks into the wound and supped until their eyes gleamed as red as the blood on which they feasted and their jet-black bodies glowed violet with magic. The beast never took his eyes off them, and Alexander, realizing that this might be the last time he saw these amazing creatures, watched them with sadness.

The two ravens locked eyes with the monster, and King Alexander could almost hear him asking them to find Queen Flora and Prince William. A few seconds later, he felt his physical body slump and his eyes shut, leaving him blind to everything except his ghostly prison.

Seconds later, Hither and Yon popped into being in front of him, glowing in the twilight of the cell, and bobbing their heads in greeting. The King went weak with relief. He had been right to hope. Mardoc had made the gift to him, not the monster, and so the ravens had come to him. He whispered a fervent prayer of thanksgiving to the god of war.

You found me!

Of course. Said Yon. Its voice creaked and rattled like a rusty iron gate blowing in a phantom wind.

That is what we do. Croaked Hither. Its voice sent shivers down Alexander's spine.

Can you help me?

Help will come, Yon creaked.

Take heart now and pay attention, croaked Hither.

While Hither tapped a tiny hole in the King's dungeon wall with its beak, Yon taught him to become like smoke. *Simple,* the spirit bird said, *because your physical body is out there. In here, you are only as solid as you and the eternal imagine you to be.*

Eternal?

That is what the thing that possesses you calls itself.

A pleasant name for such an evil thing.

Yes.

Alexander found that, after a bit of instruction, he could, indeed, become like smoke or mist. And when at last he managed to pour himself through the nearly invisible hole in his dungeon, he was in his own body once more. Truly inside it, gliding along bones and muscles, nerves and sinews. He could also float outside of it and gaze down at himself, slouched and sleeping behind his desk. But it was like he was merely a spectator, just passing through. He still couldn't make himself lift even a little finger. The ravens told him to touch the spot he wanted to move, picture the movement, and concentrate.

Practice. Creaked Yon.

Be patient. Croaked Hither.

They also told him that even though he couldn't move his body yet, he could absorb its vitality and replenish his strength. Fortunately, this was easy to do, and the flood of sparkling energy that flowed into him eased his pain and raised his spirits.

Don't take too much. Yon creaked and clicked.

He will notice. Croaked the Hither.

Suddenly they were standing on the desk once more, bobbing and bowing to the beast.

Then they leaped into the air and vanished, leaving behind a faint whiff of ozone.

—

At dawn, the monster was back in the tower room pacing through the soft golden shafts of sunlight that slanted in through the balcony doors.

Where are they? You said they would come.

A fist smashed into the King's face, breaking his nose and bloodying his upper lip.

I don't know, Your Majesty. They always came to me first thing in the morning to report their findings.

The beast lifted the whistle to his lips and blew it once more.

There was a snap, like a tiny explosion, and Alexander was gratified to feel his lips and fingers burn with pain.

The silver whistle had disappeared.

47

Molly

 razor-sharp wind howled and danced through a land-scape as desolate and colorless as the moon's surface. To either side, the barren ground sloped down. Gradually at first and then steeply, plummeting toward the lowlands. On one side, farmland and forests in new, spring-green colors stretched on and on, and a large, silver river ran through them. On the other side, steep slopes of dark evergreens and small, fast-flowing streams plunged into a narrow plain. At the edge of the plain a coastal city embraced a large, well-protected harbor.

Molly shivered. She was dressed for Andromeda's cozy kitchen, and the air bit through her T-shirt. Micah was wearing his leather jacket because he never went anywhere, even a nice cozy kitchen, without it. He opened it up and pulled her inside its warmth. She was immediately surrounded by the bristling black-violet aura of a nervous gang-lord mage and the scents of leather and peppermint. She slid her arm around Micah's waist and sighed happily. She should have been ecstatic, even in this godsforsaken place; but unfortunately, Molly wasn't just shivering from the cold. Dread was running clammy fingers up and down her back.

She'd been here before.

"Oh jeez, Micah, we're in the Altaspinas, the mountain range that separates Damia from Dalot, and any minute now a soldier is gonna come out from behind one of those rocks and challenge us, so you're gonna have to lose the shades."

"How could you possibly know that?" Micah took off his glasses and shoved them into his pocket.

"Last summer, when I was in Damia, King Alexander signed a peace treaty with his neighbor, King Louis of Dalot. This was a big deal because the two countries had been enemies for ages. At the banquet celebrating the treaty, King Louis's wine steward brought out some bottles of what he called Peace Wine to toast the agreement. It made everybody mellow and peaceful, but another effect was that if a mage drank it, they would fall into a deep trance and dream a dream about the future of the peace treaty. But King Louis didn't say anything about that because he didn't think there were any mages at the banquet except Asmodius. Well, I drank the toast, tranced out, and ended up here. This is really close to Prince William and Queen Flora's camp. They're mustering troops against King Alexander, because he's gonna invade Dalot and break the treaty, just like in my dream. When I told the kings about the dream, none of us could make any sense of it. I mean, it was King Alexander who pushed for the treaty in the first place, why would he break it now? And he's a good man, I can't imagine his son and wife turning against him like this, and I don't even want to think about what they're gonna ask us to do."

"Halt. Who goes there?" A soldier stepped out from behind a boulder with his sword leveled at them. His uniform was minimal—just an old, gray coat with a grubby white sash with a red dragon coiled around a white unicorn bracketed by two yellow crowns.

"Got it in one," whispered Micah as Molly stepped away from him and stood so the sentry could see her empty hands and Flick tucked away in her belt.

"Friends," said Molly. "Please tell Queen Flora that Molly Adair is here and requests an audience."

The man just stared at her with his mouth hanging open as the color drained from his face.

"Lady Adair? You look jus' like the pitchers they drew of you when you called up a dragon and saved our country. But that were over twenty years ago," he finally managed to say. "And now here you are, not a day older'n when you left. This can't be."

"But it is. Please let the Queen know I'm here. It's important."

The man blinked rapidly as he processed this information, but he still didn't seem convinced.

"Is that yer magic sword?" he asked, gazing at Flick and dropping his sword point. "And where's yer dragon?"

Molly was freezing and anxious to see Queen Flora and the sentry was still staring at her sword, his brow crumpled with puzzlement. With a growl of impatience, she kicked his feet out from under him and snatched his sword. The next moment, the man was on his back on the ground with his sword point gently touching his throat. He stared up at her in surprise and fear. He swallowed hard, and his Adam's apple pressed against the sword point.

"Alright, maybe you are who you say you are. That was a slick move and you know how to handle a sword."

"You are going to get up and take me to the Queen. Now!"

The sentry led them to a rock outcrop about the height of two men. "Dragons and unicorns!" he said. The rock in front of them shimmered and a door appeared. Deliciously warm air wafted up a stone stairway that led down into darkness. Their guide headed down the steps.

"Wait!" Molly said, touching his shoulder. "Let's make this look right." She gave him back his sword and pushed ahead of him, pulling Micah behind her.

"Much obliged, m'lady," he said as he came down the stairs after them. "I surely wasn't looking forward to the endless jests about being captured by the people I was supposed to capture." And then he shouted, "Brigga's Blades!" His voice echoed down the stone steps. "That's the password," he said in a much softer voice.

The rock wall reformed behind them, leaving them in twilight which got brighter as three softball-sized mage lights came zooming toward them and stopped, forming a circle above their heads and filling the stairwell with golden light.

Another soldier waited at the bottom of the stairway. His uniform was cleaner and neater, and there were rank insignia above the top crown on his sash. "What'cha got here, Wil?" he asked, looking at Molly and Micah in surprise.

"Yer not gonna believe this, Cap'n, but this is Lady Adair. She saved us once. Maybe she's come to do it again!"

"You're right. I don't believe it. Lady Adair would be in her late thirties or early forties by now. Your prisoners can't be older than twenty."

Another officer strode toward them. This one wore a real uniform with lots of gold insignia on his white sash. He moved with the ramrod straight back and quick precision of someone who has spent their life in the military. His blond hair was going gray at the temples and smile lines creased his tanned, weathered face. He glanced at Molly and then skidded to a halt.

"Molly!?" His eyes went wide with wonder. "Is it really you?"

Molly's jaw dropped as she recognized a much older version of the young field cadet she'd fallen in lust with last summer. The Damian army had arrived at The Gap just as Molly was saving Queen Flora from Philip Fuller, Alexander's traitorous Minister of Finance. The quartermaster had drafted Field Cadet Gavin Shears into serving the Queen's needs. There had been no other women at the Wall except the camp prostitutes, and the quartermaster had reasoned that since his father was a tailor, Gavin would know something about women's clothing and hopefully, something about dealing politely with women. Queen Flora had sent him to Molly with one of her gowns to alter so she could wear it at the Peace Celebration.

"Gavin!" Was all she could manage to say as bittersweet memories rushed in. She had said her regretful farewells to this man less than a year ago, and now here he was old enough to be her father.

Field Cadet Shears, who was now probably General Shears, didn't seem to be doing any better. He stared at her like he was seeing a ghost.

"Still as young and beautiful as you were twenty-three years ago," he said, never taking his eyes off her face. "How can this be?"

Molly knew exactly how this could be, but she was still having problems wrapping her mind around it. Gavin must be in total shock.

He reached toward her hesitantly. "May I touch you? I need to assure myself that you are real."

With a sob of joy, Molly stepped past his arm and hugged him tight. He still felt as strong and solid and loving as when she'd kissed him goodbye, but now it felt like she was hugging her father. Tears streamed down her face. Maybe it had been more than lust after all.

"See, Cap'n, I told ya so!" said the sentry.

She finally managed to step back, pull herself together, and say, "I serve the Goddess Brigga, and she came to me and said Queen Flora needed help again, and that Micah and I were to come with her. She brought us forward to here, the time and place of my vision. Remember when I fainted at the banquet? And I had that dream and had to tell King Alexander and King Louis about it? Well, I think this is what I was dreaming about. If my dream came true, King Alexander is going to break the treaty and invade Dalot, and Queen Flora and Prince William have organized an army to stop him."

"Lady Adair foresaw this?" asked the Captain.

"You knew this was goin' ta happen?" the sentry gasped.

Gavin turned to his men and said, "I knew Lady Adair fainted at the banquet and that she talked to both kings, but I didn't know what she told them. I was not privy to that conversation. But obviously, both kings and, of course, Queen Flora knew. And, obviously, this is privileged information and must go no further. If I hear even a breath of it in the ranks, I will know where it started, and it will not go well with either of you. Understood?"

Both men nodded gravely, eyes wide with awe and fear.

"Can you get us an audience with the Queen?" Molly asked.

Gavin looked past her to Micah, and then back to her, a question in his eyes. Micah had assumed his gang leader "This is my turf, stay off," stance and was staring daggers at Gavin. Molly shot a warning glare at Micah, hoping he would back down and be nice. Then she took his hand and stood beside him.

"Gavin Shears, meet Micah Ortiz, a close friend and mage who has come to help you with your problem."

Gavin met Micah's glare, and shook his hand. Neither one spoke. Molly somehow had no doubt that this man, who had spent years commanding soldiers, looked through Micah's posturing and understood he was dealing with an insecure, angry, jealous, and dangerous young man. She hoped he would come to appreciate Micah's good points too.

He turned back to Molly. Was that disapproval she saw in his eyes? But then he smiled and said, "Of course. Her Majesty will be glad to see you."

—

Gavin led them through a maze of tunnels dotted with golden mage lights drifting along in random, eye-pleasing patterns. The tunnels looked like they had been molded into being by the earth herself. The walls, floor, and ceiling were smooth almost to the point of being shiny, but not flat. And there wasn't a square corner to be seen. They swirled and glittered with the patterns of the rock and the occasional vein of crystals.

"This is gorgeous! Where did those lights come from?" Molly asked. "They're so bright—it's almost like daylight down here. And the air is warm and fresh. Not like a cave at all."

"The Queen makes them. Don't ask me how. But, you're right, they're almost as good as sunlight. It means the men don't have to go topside so often. The floors are heated by hot water that comes from deep in the earth through a system of aquifers cut into the rock, and the air stays fresh because a system of vents to the out-side keeps it circulating. There are also hot-and-cold-water springs down here that give us all the water we need. Her Majesty has a way of talking to the earth and rock and it does whatever she says. I suspect that she made all this before she and Prince William began recruiting their army."

"Amazing!" Molly said as they followed the tunnel into a huge cavern filled with beautiful stone tables and benches. One end of the room was a huge fireplace. A fire blazed in a part of it under a whole pig turning on a spit. Other fires heated cauldrons filled with a garlicky, spicy-smelling something. Molly's mouth watered and her stomach rumbled and complained that it hadn't had breakfast. A few dozen men stood at the tables that lined the other walls. Some were chopping vegetables and some were washing wooden trenchers at several sinks that actually had running water. Others were just hanging out at the tables. They all turned to stare at Molly and Micah.

"This is one of eight kitchens," Gavin said. "It's surrounded by the sleeping areas and baths of the units it serves." He pointed to several smaller tunnels leading off from the kitchen/dining area.

"When did you begin recruiting?"

"About a month ago. The Queen came to Prince William and me and said it was time."

"How many troops?"

"We're almost full. The caverns hold about six thousand men."

He led them down the continuation of the tunnel which began on the other side of the kitchen, stopped after about twenty feet, and placed his hand flat on a smooth, inward curve of the wall. The area around his hand shimmered and disappeared, revealing a spiral staircase. As Molly followed Gavin up the steps, the tight, circular motion, swirling stone patterns, sparkling crystals, and wandering mage lights messed with her mind. Her dazzled brain gave up trying to follow the glittering, intricate patterns and twinkling lights and simply floated in blissful peace. She was almost sorry when they reached a broad landing in front of an arched oak door.

Gavin knocked softly.

"Come," Molly recognized Queen Flora's high, sweet voice.

"Wait here," said their guide as he went through the door.

Moments later, he ushered them into a large, light-filled room. The stone walls, and high ceiling gleamed and glittered like the inside of a jewelry box. Deep, plush carpets in an intricate floral design covered the floors. A gleaming oak desk, a matching conference table littered with a pile of rolled up charts and a few rocks, and a scatter of comfortable chairs completed the room. The light came from a huge window that overlooked the land of Damia, with its patchwork of fields and forests and the River Selene running down its center. The scene pulled at Molly's heart, and she stood for a moment and gazed down on the country that had come to mean so much to her. She was pretty sure that that large, dark patch of forest straddling the river was the Wildwood, where Tamerlane's cottage was and where she had first learned to use a sword.

"Welcome, Lady Adair," said the Queen.

Molly spun around, cheeks hot with embarrassment.

"Forgive me, Your Majesty," she said, curtsying till her butt almost touched the ground. "I couldn't resist. Your kingdom is beautiful and full of memories, and I was so surprised to see it, that I had to look." Asmodius had once told her that she must never turn her back on royalty. There were many reasons for this, he had said. The man was a total cynic.

"Of course, my dear, I understand. Who would expect such a marvelous view in a cave? But my rooms were formed, literally, in the mountain's side. Just open up an outside wall, and there you have it." She gestured toward the view and then touched Molly's shoulder, signaling her to rise.

"Your Majesty, this is Micah Ortiz, a friend and fellow mage," Molly said, turning to Micah, who was beside her. She hadn't had time to tell him what to do in the presence of royalty, but, to her immense relief, he followed her example and bowed low enough to honor a Queen. Asmodius had taught her court etiquette when they had been at the King and Queen's palace in Bontare. He had explained that the level and length of a curtsy or bow was determined by your status as compared to the person you were honoring. And if you didn't get it right, people were scandalized.

"Come, be seated," the Queen said, gesturing to two green velvet upholstered chairs that looked out the window and took a chair facing them. Even with her face in shadow, Molly could see the faint age and stress lines etched into the corners of her eyes and mouth; and her golden, wheat-colored hair was streaked with silver. But the years had treated her kindly, and she was still a strikingly beautiful woman. Molly could feel the same gentle, loving power that had healed and comforted her when she had been a troubled, angry stranger to this land.

Only now that power was even more potent.

"Gavin has gone to find my son. He will want to meet you." The Queen paused. Her expression was both puzzled and hopeful. "It is a joy to see you again, my dear, but why are you here?"

"I'm here because you prayed to Brigga for help. She heard your prayers and brought Micah and me forward in time. We're here to give you whatever assistance you need. But you seem to be doing just fine on your own. I'm guessing that my dream came true and King Alexander is going to invade Dalot and you and Prince William are gathering an army to stop him?"

"You are correct."

"What made King Alexander decide to break the treaty and attack his ally?"

"I don't think he did decide to break the treaty."

"But it looks like he has," Molly said.

"Let me explain," replied the Queen. "After you left, Alex, Louis, and I kept trying to make sense of your vision. We understood that people and times change, and that perhaps, in the years to come, it would be in Damia's best interest to invade Dalot. But if this were so, then why would both William and I be so opposed to it? The only thing we could think of was that Alex would have changed, wouldn't be himself. I know him so well, and I was confident that I could spot any changes. But what if he were actually possessed by someone or something that was clever enough to hide its presence?"

Molly's initial feeling of dread came back with a vengeance. She was definitely not having good feelings about where Queen Flora's story was headed.

"We wanted to make sure I would notice in time to escape, so we made a plan. Every night before we went to bed, I would walk to Alex's bedchamber window and say, "It's a beautiful night." And he would always answer, "The stars are so bright." Except, one night, about two months ago, he didn't. So I fled and came here, to these caverns which, unbeknownst to him, I had created to shelter and hide the army we might one day need. I got word to William, who, as usual, was away from court, to meet me at a certain place. I brought him here and explained about your vision and that it had come to pass. We decided to muster an army and oppose him."

The Queen's face was a mask of tragedy. As the reality of their situation began to sink in, Molly realized what a difficult decision this had been. If they had decided to do nothing, their people would be ruled by someone or something who had taken over King Alexander's life and stolen his kingdom, most likely for personal gain. The impostor would squeeze every last copper they could from the kingdom and its people and move on, leaving behind a shattered, vulnerable, and poverty-stricken country. And their lives would be in constant danger. As two possible heirs to the throne, the Queen and the Prince would be a rallying point for opposition and therefore a threat to the false King. So Queen Flora and her son had decided to oppose him. If they lost, they would be killed in battle or executed as traitors; and if they won, Alexander—or his body, and the being who had possessed it— would be killed in battle or executed as a traitor. It was a lose-lose situation.

"And this is what Alex wanted us to do," the Queen continued, "We discussed it endlessly. He reasoned that only a very powerful, very evil mage would be able to steal another person's body, kingdom, and life in this way, and that as soon the Evil One realized that William and I knew that Alex was no longer Alex he would kill us, for obvious reasons. My husband could not begin to imagine watching his body killing his wife and son. He also guessed that the mage would not have the interests of his kingdom in his heart. So he begged me to protect myself, our son, and our kingdom, and to do everything in my power to stop the invasion of Dalot—even if it meant his death, which it probably would. If an evil mage took over his body, he said, the part of him that was Alex would be gone anyway. He would be dead already."

There was a soft knock on the door.

"Come," said the Queen.

A young man entered the room followed by Gavin. He looked exactly like King Alexander, with blue eyes and a hawk-like nose, but his crisp, wavy hair was the color of ripe wheat and his eyes were a violet-blue instead of piercing ice-blue like his father's. He stalked into the room with an aggressive, don't-mess-with-me attitude—totally not his father's firm, confident gait. A deep, vertical line creased the skin between his brows, and a hint of petulance flickered around his lips. All in all, Molly recognized an angry, insecure twenty-something. A classier and, hopefully, more innocent version of Micah Ortiz.

"Hello, my dear!" Queen Flora held out her hand to her son, who took it and stood beside her protectively. "Prince William, this is Lady Molly Adair and her fellow mage, Lord Micah Ortiz."

The Prince stared in amazement at Molly and bowed.

"My Lady, this is, indeed, a pleasure. But shouldn't you be a bit older?"

The Queen's musical laugh rippled through the room.

"She hasn't had time to age, William. She'd been home from Damia less than a year before Brigga heard my prayers and brought her forward in time to protect our kingdom once again."

"The pleasure is all mine, Your Highness," Molly replied, curtsying to the Prince a bit less deeply than she had to the queen. Out of the corner of her eye she saw Micah do the same, but his bow wasn't nearly as deep as Molly's curtsy, and he was staring daggers at the Prince. She shifted uneasily as the handsome prince gazed at her in awe, totally ignoring Micah.

"How can we help?" she asked.

Her heart ached for the queen and her son and twisted with fear whenever she thought about what had happened to the king, but she hadn't a clue how to make things any better.

"I'm not sure," replied the Prince, "but I can show you our plans and perhaps you will be able to think of something."

He headed for the conference table. By the time everyone else had gathered around it, he'd unrolled a map of the long peninsula that Damia and Dalot occupied. There were the two mountain ranges: the Coronas in the north that divided Damia and Dalot from Norseland, their mutual enemy; and the Altaspinas, with Damia to the west of them and Dalot to the east. Bontare, Damia's capital, was in the northern part of the country and Brithhaven, Dalot's capital, was in southern Dalot, just a bit north of The Gap, a wide pass through the Altaspinas. Two decades ago Molly and her dragon had prevented a war there and King Alexander had talked King Louis into a peace treaty—the one he was now planning to break.

"The King has pulled together Damia's army with unexpected swiftness and is marching south," said the Prince as he weighted the huge map down with stones and followed the River Road south with his beringed index finger. "That window over there faces north, and we were able to actually watch his troops approach. Our agents report that they will probably make camp here tonight, about a day's march north of The Gap. And we are here." He pointed to a spot in the Altaspinas southeast of where the king would be camping.

"We have been in touch with Louis's agents for the past six weeks or so," the Queen said. "He has known that the King would march south probably before the King himself knew."

Molly noted that neither the Queen nor Prince William called the King "Alex" or "my husband" or "father." To them, their beloved husband and father was dead, and the man ruling his kingdom and commanding his army was the enemy. This, more than anything else, made her grieve for the true King.

Tears stung her eyes.

She had liked and admired him.

"As soon as he knew, King Louis began to gradually pull his troops south, a few units at a time, toward The Gap, the only place where a large army can cross the Altaspinas. He also began gearing up for war. Before his enemy had even started for The Gap, King Louis's troops were armed and ready to go there as well. Most of them are encamped at The Gap now, but he has troops watching all the passes in the south in case the King splits his army and sends part of it over one of the smaller passes to attack the Dalotian army from the rear. We have also been watching from this side, and he hasn't done that. So tonight, we will give the signal for King Louis to move the rest of his troops into The Gap.

"And we have a little surprise planned for the Evil One. Tomorrow we will march our troops through the Altaspinas to these two outlets." He pointed to two circles near The Gap on the Damian side of the mountains. "When he has moved his army into place here," he pointed to an array of lines just south of the circles and opposite the lines indicating the Dalotian army, "our troops will come out of the tunnels under the cover of night, and array themselves here." His finger traced a line behind the Damian army. His ruby ring flashed red with defiance. "Mother and I will be front and center, easily recognizable under our standards. This should cause some problems for the King because he has been telling our people that King Louis is holding us captive and this whole war is about getting us back. We are counting on a large portion of the troops deserting and joining us. Perhaps, between King Louis's army and ours, we will be able to capture and kill the impostor without a fight."

Molly could see that this was the best use they could make of their small army, and it might work. But if it didn't, King Louis would be forced to attack, and there would be a blood bath, with Damians killing not only Dalotians, but also other Damians, and maybe even friends and family. And with the rebel force attacking from behind, Damia would most likely lose and they would be at the mercy of the Dalotians. Would King Louis be willing to give the Queen and Prince their country back? Or would he do what any sensible king would do and seize the country for himself and imprison the heir to the Damian throne and his mother? And, if the impostor was who she thought it was, Molly had no doubt that he would escape.

Not a satisfactory conclusion.

"But I've just realized!" The Prince's enthusiasm cut through her musings. "With you here, our chances of a bloodless victory are much greater. You can call up your dragon and no one would dare oppose us!"

Shit! She'd been afraid of this.

How could she convince this desperate man that calling up her dragon for almost any reason except to save her life was totally not a good idea.

And, unfortunately, her life wasn't in danger.

Dragons are short-tempered and testy, and calling one up for any lesser reason could be fatal—if not for their human, then for everyone else within the angry dragon's range. But, because a dragon's life is tied to its human's, it doesn't mind being called on to save itself.

And dragons are power personified. And Riada was Molly's power. But they are astral beings. Riada's power was meant to strengthen Molly's astral body, which would then strengthen her physical body. She didn't belong in the material realm. It would be a wrongness, a disruption in the order of things. So using a dragon as a physical weapon, even for a good cause, was a step down a long, slippery slope toward becoming as bad as the people she was threatening. Since a dragon is by nature power hungry and completely amoral when it comes to human ethics, it needs very clear moral guidance from its human. Molly shuddered as she remembered Phillip Fuller, the Minister of Finance who had tried to take over Damia. He'd not only been a terrible role model for his dragon, but also hadn't been able to keep it in check. The dragon went rogue, killing hundreds of innocent people before Molly finally killed Fuller.

It was most fortunate that her world didn't have enough magic to materialize a dragon.

A surge of power swept into the room with an almost audible roar and Brigga appeared in their midst. She stood, hands on her hips, silver-blond hair wafting out from her face in an unseen breeze, and raw power sizzling and snapping around her. Molly breathed a sigh of relief.

Brigga would tell her what she was supposed to do.

"That," said the Goddess, glaring at Prince William, "is a verra bad idea."

The hapless royal's face went white as his pristine shirt and his mouth formed a surprised and terrified "O." Queen Flora smiled at her Goddess and curtsied low. Everyone quickly recovered themselves and followed suit.

Brigga gestured impatiently for everyone to rise.

"I have a much better idea," she said and strode toward the map on the table. As she approached, the intensity of her power caused Gavin and the Prince to back away from her. But Molly, Micah, and Queen Flora knew from experience that even though the presence of the divine was uncomfortable, it had never harmed them, so they filled in the places beside Brigga.

"When all three armies are in place, King Louis will send a messenger with a proposal to the eternal."

"Tamerlane! I knew it!" Molly groaned.

"Yes." Turning to Queen Flora, Brigga continued. "The creature who now possesses your husband's body calls itself an eternal because it can live forever. Unfortunately, this is because it feeds off human lives to restore itself and when its body wears out it simply takes over another body. It has superhuman strength, quickness, and intelligence, and has no trouble recouping from even lethal injuries. The only way to kill it is to set it on fire and burn it completely to ashes or cut off its head. And this particular eternal is also an adept mage, which makes it even more dangerous because it's a magic user and can teleport within this world and between worlds."

The Damians stared at the Goddess, eyes wide with terror, but she ignored them and continued.

"The messenger will say that, to spare the lives of his people and those of Damia, King Louis requests that a duel by swords be fought to determine the victor. The side whose champion kills the other's champion wins the war and therefore both countries."

"King Louis would never agree to risk his kingdom like that!" said Prince William. A look of horror spread across his face as he realized that he'd just contradicted a goddess. "Er... begging your pardon, My Lady," he added quickly, and bowed.

Queen Flora stepped forward and put a comforting hand on her son's arm.

"Actually, there have been several precedents for a contest of champions in the history of Damia and Dalot. And, of course, the losing king chose to fight instead of give up his country. But his army lost morale not only because its champion had been defeated, but also because their king had broken his word. In all the contests that I know of, the army whose champion was defeated always lost the ensuing battle."

Molly's heart sank. She, of course, would be Dalot's champion. And Tamerlane, because he could never resist a fight and because he knew that no human could defeat him, would be Damia's champion. She would be fighting the man who had taught her almost everything she knew about fighting. A man she had once loved like a grandfather. And to make things even worse, he would be in the body of King Alexander, a man she was quite fond of, and husband to Queen Flora, of whom she was even fonder. Her vision began narrowing to a tunnel and her legs started getting rubbery.

As if from a great distance, she heard Brigga explaining to the Damians why the King would gladly accept this offer. Molly, of course, would be Dalot's champion and, with the Goddess's help, would kill the eternal, who, of course, would be Damia's champion.

Yeah, right. She made it sound so easy.

This was her worst nightmare.

She knew first-hand how lethal Tamerlane was. And she wouldn't have Micah and Diana to help her. Of course, he would be in King Alexander's aging body. But the King had been a swordsman and was probably still in good shape. And his reach was much longer than hers. Even with Brigga's help, how could she possibly win? And then there was the other unspeakable thought. What if Alexander was still trapped in his body with the eternal like Andromeda had been? If she did manage to win, she would be killing him too.

Molly shuddered and decided that she'd rather be back on Hell fighting demons.

After Brigga explained her plan, everyone stood there in silence, eyes round with fear and awe. It was, however, a very active silence. Even though they all knew that it wasn't open to discussion, Molly could almost hear the questions, objections, and rebuttals running through everyone's minds and bouncing off the crystalline walls. Finally, Prince William asked, "How will Lady Adair get to King Louis in time?"

"The same way she got here," said Brigga.

48

Molly

Olly, Micah, and Queen Flora materialized beside King Louis's huge, banner draped pavilion. No one had noticed them, so they took a moment to get their bearings. The afternoon sun blazed in a seriously deep-blue sky dotted with a few fluffy clouds. Mountains towered over them in the north and south. They were in The Gap, the broad, flat plain that sliced through the far southern end of the Altaspinas. The Dalotian camp was a buzzing hive of activity, with soldiers in blue uniforms bustling around every which way, intent on their preparations for tomorrow's battle. Far to the north, Molly's sharp eyes could just make out the blur of red and the sparkle of sunlight glinting off armor that was the approaching Damian army. Closer in, the barren, black line that Riada had burned into the ground two decades ago contrasted sharply with the brilliant green of the plain, forming an unmistakable boundary between Damia and Dalot. A temple nestled in glorious splendor at each end of the line. They had been built from the rubble of the wall that Riada, Molly, and Queen Flora had gleefully smashed to bits. The Temple of Dalot was the natural, gray of the stone it had been built from. Its square base soared up into a cluster of graceful towers with peaked roofs that drew the eye skyward. Dama's temple was a dome with six huge, arched gables supported by massive stone pillars. The whole thing was painted in geometric patterns of mossy greens, blacks, buttery yellows, and blood reds. It looked like an exotic flower blossoming out of the earth.

Molly was lost in memories when an officer with lots of bling on his uniform walked past and jumped in surprise when he saw them.

"Your Majesty!" he said, bowing to the Queen and looking totally confused. "What a pleasure!" Molly could tell from his expression that it definitely wasn't. But then his face relaxed.

"Allow me to escort you to King Louis." Molly could almost hear his unspoken thought that this wasn't his problem, best to let the royals sort it out themselves. He led them to the front of the pavilion and scratched a quick rhythm on the door flap.

"Come!" called a brisk voice from inside.

The officer stepped inside the tent and said, "Your Majesty, Queen Flora of Damia requests your attention."

There was a pause, and even from her position outside, Molly could feel the air inside the tent bristle with question marks and exclamation points.

"Show her in immediately."

The officer swept the door flap aside, and with a low bow, gestured them into a spacious room filled with light that beamed through the pavilion's colorful banners and creamy white canvas. A densely woven carpet in a complex geometric design covered the grass under a group of ornately carved wooden camp chairs. Micah's fingers twitched almost imperceptibly, weaving lines of energy around the perimeter of the tent in a spell that Molly suspected would make anything said inside unintelligible to anyone outside.

"Thank you, General Worthing, that will be all."

Even before the door swished closed behind the general, King Louis III of Dalot bounded out from behind a huge, gleaming wood table layered with maps and lists and over to Queen Flora. His wheat-colored hair was streaked with silver and his blue-violet eyes twinkled in a face deeply lined and leathered by decades of sun. But he moved like a man in his thirties, and he wore his silver battle armor like a second skin over his blue tunic and leggings.

"Flora! What in all the gods' names are you doing here?" He caught up both her hands and looked worriedly into her eyes.

"I came to let you know that there's been a change of plans," the Queen replied, squeezing his hands gently before she let them go and gestured to Molly. "Lady Adair has come to our aid once more."

King Louis stared at Molly in a mix of amazement and terror.

"Impossible!" he whispered as he backed away from her.

"It's quite possible," Queen Flora said, catching his arm and turning him to face her. "The Goddess Brigga brought her forward in time because she is the only one who can help us against the evil monster who has stolen Alex's body." She quickly explained about the eternal's superhuman and supernatural capabilities in precise, painful detail.

"Then we're doomed," Louis said, sinking into a chair and holding his head in his hands. "I've seen what mages can do—they fling balls of fire and call up dragons. They can weave spells of protection for their troops. And, no doubt, a cartload of other things I don't even know about. My intelligence sources tell me that our armies are evenly matched, but with his magical abilities, we could never hold out against him. And even if by some small chance we did win, he would still escape and we would never know where he was, or who he was, or what he was doing."

"Louis, stop it!" said the Queen, shaking her fellow monarch none-too-gently by his shoulders. Molly stared in astonishment. Kings and queens didn't yell and shake each other.

Or did they?

King Louis just glared at Queen Flora and rolled his eyes. These two were used to arguing and snarling at each other. With their matching wheat-gold hair and violet-blue eyes they could be siblings. Or, perhaps, cousins?

And she and Micah were the only other people in the tent; and they were neither Damian nor Dalotian—in fact they weren't even from this world. The royals didn't have to keep up appearances.

"Quit being such a pessimist!" the Queen continued, stamping her foot. "Listen to Lady Adair. She can explain."

Oh fine. Now it was suddenly her job to convince this powerful man who had obediently turned toward her, his face grim and full of doubt, that they at least had a fighting chance.

She gathered her wits about her and began.

"The monster in King Alexander's body used to be my mentor, an adept mage named Tamerlane. And, like me, he was a member of a worldwide association, or web, of mages that works to improve their skills, train their children, and protect the people of our world from mages who misuse their power. Tamerlane's already killed two of the Webmasters and one of their assistants. He intends to kill all the mages so he can gain control of our world. He's here because he needs the wealth of Damia and Dalot to accomplish this. With Brigga's help, there's a good chance that I can kill him. And I know how to make him stay dead."

The King sighed and massaged his forehead with one hand. "I never used to believe in magic and certainly not creatures who could suck the life out of a man with a single touch. And, frankly, I was happy in my ignorance. Then I began dealing with Flora and Alex, and my life got...more complicated." He rang the silver bell on his desk. An aide appeared immediately and was ordered to bring refreshments. Molly's empty stomach gurgled in anticipation.

"We haven't been introduced," said the King eyeing Micah curiously.

"Your Majesty, this is my colleague and fellow mage, Lord Micah Ortiz," said Molly as Micah bowed low. "He has talents that are necessary to our success."

"Then I am glad you are here," said the King, gesturing to the chairs. "Let's sit and be comfortable." They made small talk until the aide brought in a tray of cold meats, cheese, bread, and pickles and what looked to be some kind of fruit juice. It was all Molly could do to wait until the King and Queen helped themselves before she loaded up her plate, and began chowing down. Everything was delicious, and yes, it was some kind of fruit juice. Life was suddenly doable again.

She was just reaching for seconds when King Louis turned to her and said, "Now, tell me how you intend to kill this monster and make him stay dead."

The Queen took pity on the hungry teen and explained Briga's plan while Molly filled in the last of the empty places in her stomach.

"It might work," he said, and then turned to gaze intently at Molly. "If it doesn't, you will be dead. You are risking your life for us. Thank you."

"No need to thank me," she replied, wondering if all kings and queens were able to make you feel like a defenseless but cherished child just by looking at you. "Tamerlane is the Web's problem that, unfortunately, became your problem. We need to make it right—if we can."

"Nonetheless, we are grateful. Now, let us put our heads together and work out the details, so that your risk will be less risky."

◆

After Queen Flora had jumped back to her army, the King summoned his own armorer, swore him to secrecy, and had him measure Molly for a Dalotian uniform to wear tomorrow. He had wanted to add full armor, but Molly insisted on a simple chain mail shirt. At Molly's request, he also provided the young mages with the brown, homespun leggings and tunics worn by servants and peasants throughout Damia and Dalot. They would be a perfect disguise.

There was plenty of time left in the day, and, since the King needed his tent back and they needed to stay hidden from the monster's spies, they did a series of line-of-sight jumps up into the forested slopes above The Gap. Molly was happy to see that, under the influence of the Queen's magic, the areas that had been clear-cut to fuel the wall-builders' campfires were once again lush forests. After calling Estelle and Diana and telling them about Tamerlane and Damia, they watched with growing concern as the Damian troops arrived and set up camp. The army was huge and well disciplined.

When they jumped back inside the pavilion, King Louis hustled them into his dressing room, pointed out the two nests of blankets and a large tray of snacks that he'd ordered, supposedly for himself, and headed out to have dinner with his generals.

Sitting cross-legged on the blankets, they munched through their dinner, talking about anything except tomorrow morning. When they'd finished, Micah said, "I'm going to jump over to King Alexander's pavilion and check to see if it's really Tamerlane in his body and if Alexander is still there. I don't know about you, but I think we need to know this before tomorrow. I don't like last-minute surprises."

"Then I'm coming with you," Molly said, putting her hand on his shoulder.

"No, you're not. If by some freak chance we're caught, it'd blow the whole plan. But if I go alone and get caught, it'll be easy to escape and even if he sees me, Tamerlane probably won't recognize me. Nobody around here really looks at servants."

He vanished before Molly could argue.

"Be careful," she whispered to the pile of blankets beside her. She flopped back and punched her make-shift bed in frustration. Micah was right, she needed to be sure it was Tamerlane she'd be fighting, and she needed to know if King Alexander was still in his body. If he wasn't, so much the better. But if he was, she still wanted to know. And finding that out was a job for Micah.

And only Micah.

She sighed unhappily as her thoughts wandered toward tomorrow's fight. There was no way around it. If Tamerlane was in King Alexander's body, she would need to kill him. And if King Alexander, a man she admired and who had been kind to her, was still in his body, she was gonna have to kill him as well. Tears stung her eyes as she slowly came to grips with the fact that the King and Queen of Damia had filled the void left by the death of her parents. And she had always looked upon Tamerlane as the grandfather she'd never had. So tomorrow she would be fighting her father and her grandfather. And if she won, she would have killed them both. But, she told herself sternly, Tamerlane was not her grandfather. He was a monster so totally evil that he couldn't be allowed to survive. Unfortunately, the only way to kill him was to kill someone she cared for.

Molly had no problem with fighting. In fact, she thrived on it. She loved the excitement and challenge of a good fight. Everything became more vivid and alive and power sang through her. But she wished that all her fights could be with worthy opponents, and that they all ended with a winner and a loser that walked away from them alive and unharmed.

Unfortunately, she was Brigga's agent, and the Goddess had other ideas about what fighting was for. Fortunately, so far, when she'd had to kill it had felt right. At least as right as taking someone's life could ever feel. And not just because if she hadn't, whoever she was fighting would have killed her. And not just because whoever she was fighting somehow deserved to die. And not just because Brigga wanted that person dead. There was no logical, reasonable explanation. It had just felt right. She suspected it had something to do with her training as a warrior mage. Master Lieu had been teaching her not just how to ground, center, and focus her mind like Tamerlane had, but also how to be aware of and open to the multiverse on all its levels.

Killing King Alexander felt wrong. And not just because he was a good man and she was fond of him. Somehow she knew that he wasn't supposed to die, at least not yet. And that if she killed him, something inside her would warp and change, an innocence and goodness would be lost.

And she would have trouble looking at herself in the mirror.

She shuddered and pulled her thoughts back to the present.

She also knew that Tamerlane would cheat and use magic. So she wove a super-strong shield spell that she could call up quickly. Brigga would also protect her and give her strength and speed.

Molly hoped it would be enough.

She was glad that Brigga had promised to have at least four Web adepts in place tomorrow to shield the two armies and to help out in any unforeseen emergencies.

Micah appeared beside her, and all thoughts of the coming day disappeared in a whiff of leather, peppermint, and cool, fresh air. In one quick, gentle move he reached out and cradled her tight against his body and kissed the top of her head.

"It's Tamerlane," he whispered. "And King Alexander is still in his body."

The words jolted through her.

She was trapped.

She wanted to scream and beat on things, but that wouldn't help.

Instead she wrapped her arms around Micah and sheltered in his tight embrace.

"I'm afraid," she whispered. "I'm not afraid to fight, and I'm not afraid to die. I'm afraid that when the time comes, I won't be able to kill King Alexander."

49

Alexander

t was not an auspicious day for a war. Storm clouds were blowing in from the west and piling up against the Altaspinas. Thunder rumbled ominously in the distance, and discontent rumbled through the Damian army. Flora and William's troops had appeared, as if by magic, out of the morning mists, sandwiching them between two forces and making the Damian soldiers wonder why they were fighting at all, since their beloved Queen and Prince were obviously not Dalot's prisoners and obviously not on the King's side.

And so the monster had been receptive to King Louis's challenge of combat between a Damian and Dalotian champion to determine the outcome of the war, asking only for a few minutes alone to make his decision.

"Does Dalot have any warrior mages?" he'd asked Alexander when the messenger had left.

No.

Then why is he making this challenge?

Why indeed? Their forces seemed to be fairly equal, and Alexander was fairly certain that King Louis knew all about the position of the rebel Damian army and that he didn't know that a powerful mage had stolen his body. As far as Louis knew, his chances of winning were more than good.

There are no Damian warrior mages either, your Majesty. King Louis is confident that his champion will win because every year we've held the Damian-Dalotian Games, the Dalotians have won all the swordsmanship events.

What was Louis playing at?

Then King Louis has a surprise coming. I will be Damia's champion. I doubt that there is a swordsman anywhere on this godsforsaken world that can beat me.

⌁

The clouds were so thick that it was nearly dark. Far to the west lightning flickered, followed by booms of thunder. The weather matched King Alexander's mood. The thieving bastard was going to win a bloodless victory. And even if King Louis chose to fight instead of give up, his army would be so demoralized by the loss of their champion that the Damians, supported and protected by the eternal's supernatural powers, would win. His wife and son would be captured, and he would be forced to watch them die.

The monster strode confidently away from the Damian army and toward the black line, where the combat would take place. In the distance, the Dalotian army stood in silence, a mass of blue that glinted silver with each flash of lightning. Out of the twilight, a Dalotian soldier strolled toward him. As he came closer, the King realized that he was actually quite small.

What was Louis thinking?

The soldier was almost within fighting distance when the King realized that he was actually a she. And that the Dalotian champion was none other than Lady Molly Adair, the warrior mage who had saved his kingdom almost two decades ago. And she hadn't aged at all.

A miracle!

But then his heart fell. Even if she did somehow manage to kill the monster, he would still recoup and either escape or take on a new body—maybe even King Louis's. There was no winning.

"It's time for you to die, Tamerlane," she said. Her face was a terrifying mix of rage and grief. "And this time you're gonna stay dead.

"Your Majesty, please forgive me."

Hope flared inside him once more.

She knows I'm here. And she's a mage. Perhaps she really does know how to make the bastard stay dead.

The monster laughed an ugly, terrifying laugh. "I very much doubt that you'll be any more successful than the last two times you've tried."

"Three's a charm, dirt-ball."

"Yes, this time I will finally finish *you*," he said and reached for his sword.

The world slowed to almost a stop, like it always did when his captor drew his sword and practiced the forms. But with his left hand, the bastard reached for something else. Alexander spotted it because he had existed for weeks in that no-man's-land between physical reality and what Flora called "the other reality." He could now see things in that other reality—like sparkly and sometimes not-so-sparkly lights flashing around people and spells being spun out of pure colors of light. He had watched the monster spin many nasty spells and either use them immediately or store them in his aura.

It was one of the stored spells that the evil mage reached for. A demonic hand shaped from black malevolence outlined in ghastly green light. It made Alexander shudder just to look at it, not only because it shimmered with mindless cruelty, but also because he knew it would grab, twist, and destroy anything it touched.

The monster threw it straight at the tiny mage's heart and whipped his sword downward in a stroke that would cut through the base of her neck and down through her chest. If the hand didn't kill her, the sword would.

But Lady Adair was moving just as fast as his captor. With a seemingly casual flick of her left hand, she surrounded herself with sparkling points of every imaginable color of light. The spell slammed into this fragile-looking shield and burst into multicolored fireworks, which were absorbed by the shield, making it flare up even brighter and stronger than before.

She tapped aside the sword that was whirring toward her neck, ducked under it in a quick pirouette, and slashed at the monster's rib cage. Because he had been so sure his blade would hit home, he wasn't prepared for her counter-strike and was barely able to recover quickly enough to parry the blow. Alexander gasped as her blade slid off the monster's sword and smacked into his shoulder. He felt cold rage fill his heart as the beast took the offense and began beating back the tiny mage. She was an amazing fighter, but the King was a good enough swordsman to know that she was still out-matched. He had to do something to even the odds. She was his best chance, and he was determined to make the most of it. It was time to use the skills that Hither and Yon had taught him and that he'd been practicing so diligently.

He slipped through the raven's hole and out into his arms, his legs, his heart, his brain, and his guts. Only then did he begin drawing tiny amounts of life force out of his body and into himself. The fizz and vitality were almost overwhelming and, as always, he was tempted to fill up with it and lose himself in ecstasy. But he resisted and only drew in a portion of his body's reserve strength. If the bastard even suspected that he was draining him he'd chuck him out the window in one quick thought and he wouldn't be able to help Lady Adair save his wife, his son, and his kingdom.

There was a flash of blinding light and the monster and his opponent both looked up in surprise. Alexander watched in awe as one strand, then two, then many strands of blue-white light blossomed from a single searingly bright point above his head and snaked outward. Other lines flashed and flickered off them, creating a blazing spiderweb that extended over the entire battlefield.

The air sizzled and reeked with the bitter sharp stench of lightning. The storm had arrived and he realized that he was watching a lightning flash in slow motion. Thunder boomed, so loud it slammed into his chest. As the sound went on and on, an enormous black dragon materialized in the center of the brilliant web, wings outstretched, neck ruff extended, and its immense, wicked head raised in a roar that eclipsed even the thunder. Screams of terror rose up from both armies.

The dragon glared down at the panicked Dalotian army that was falling over itself in its haste to retreat and breathed a gout of orange-red dragon fire that would have incinerated several battalions. But an array of blue shields snapped up just in time, and deflected the roaring inferno up into the clouds.

Only mages could turn away fire like that. Where had they come from?

The rain began.

It pounded down in sheets, hissing and spattering like a living thing.

The dragon roared in frustration as lightning tore bright furrows in the twilight clouds and thunder crashed in response.

The eternal renewed his attack on the tiny warrior, his sword cutting through the air in an arc that would slice off her head and send it flying toward the Dalotian army. She ducked just in time and lunged forward, the point of her sword headed for the monster's evil heart. He used the momentum of his swing to twist out of its path, pivoted completely around, and slashed down at her. She parried it easily, but the beast closed in with a series of quick strikes. Rain soaked his hair and ran into his eyes. It turned the ground slick and treacherous. The lightning made long periods of light followed by long periods of darkness and deafening thunder.

Another dragon exploded into being with a heart-stopping roar. Very few people had been fortunate enough to see one dragon, let alone two. They were astounding, beautiful creatures, and Alexander wanted very much to observe them before he died. And so, since his captor was occupied and couldn't look up and Lady Adair was, hopefully, safe for the moment, he drained a bit more energy from his captor and decided to risk leaving his body to watch them.

Just for a moment.

The King hung like an invisible mist above the wet green battlefield. To his left was the Dalotian army and to his right, the Damian army. Directly below him, the two champions fought in a vicious blur of arms, legs, and cruel glinting steel. Above him, the first dragon was dropping rapidly, foreclaws extended, ready to grab the tiny warrior. But the new dragon zoomed in silently and, at the last possible moment, extended its wings. There was a sharp crack, like a canvas sail unfurling in a high wind, as the dragon stopped suddenly in mid-air. Its feet swung forward and smashed into the side of the first dragon sending it tumbling. With a roar of rage, it righted itself and streaked toward the newcomer, who was also black, but its ruff and wings shimmered with rainbows of light. And it was much smaller than the first dragon. It didn't stand a chance.

But wait.

He knew this dragon. He'd watched it fight another dragon and terrorize the Dalotian army into a truce. And he'd actually ridden it in a glorious night reconnaissance over the Dalotian camp. It belonged to Lady Adair.

Which meant the other dragon belonged to the beast.

Which meant that if Lady Adair's dragon died, she would be weakened and most likely be killed. And not only would the monster be free to destroy both Damia and Dalot, but there would also be a wicked dragon at large preying on innocent folk in both countries. He'd seen it before. Alexander wracked his brain for a way to help the brave little dragon.

Lightning flashed and thunder boomed, and a third dragon hung suspended above the first two. It was huge and red and remained utterly silent. The first two dragons didn't notice it.

Greetings, Alexander. The red dragon's voice vibrated through him, a collage of feeling and sound and the smell of earth and blood and smoke and water. I am your dragon.

But I don't have a dragon.

Do not contradict me, human. I have been your dragon since the moment you were crowned King of Damia and will be with you until the moment you die. I am Belarian, the Dragon of Damia.

The King was suddenly gazing down through torrents of rain at the black dragon as it swooped with deadly precision toward the fleeing rainbow dragon. In wonderment, he felt his hands become claws tipped with talons twitching in anticipation of a fight to the death. Wings extended up from his shoulders, holding him suspended. He realized with a surge of awe and elation that he was now one with the mythical Dragon of Damia.

Welcome. Be still and observe. It is time to destroy this wickedness.

They dived straight for the black dragon, weightless, the air tugging at scale and wing and ruff, heart racing with savage joy. The King felt a sharp tug on his shoulder muscles as Belarian stopped with a snap of his wings and raked its foreclaws viciously down the black dragon's back. Scales and deep red blood erupted from the wound, filling the air with a hot metal reek that was quickly washed away by the rain. With a well-timed flick of their wings they headed upward, back claws lashing downward, shredding the base of the black dragon's wings. It roared in surprise and agony as it struggled to stay aloft.

Lightning flashed all around them, and thunder cracked and boomed.

Lady Adair's dragon shot straight up, back flipped, and rolled. A breathtakingly beautiful move that sent it streaking back toward its pursuer. Its mouth opened wide, exposing vicious fangs twice the size of broadswords, and snapped closed on the black dragon's exposed throat, cutting off its deafening roars of pain.

The evil monster vanished in an explosion of foul-smelling black smoke.

The two remaining dragons floated in suspended silence for a few moments as the rain sluiced away the smoke; and in those moments, Alexander felt his dragon's mind somehow slip into sync with the rainbow dragon's. Although he was not privy to what went on between them, he felt Belarian fill with intense happiness and contentment, as if he had been at last reunited with a dear old friend or, perhaps, made a new one. And then, in fierce, heart-stopping harmony, they bugled their triumph and began an intricate swooping, soaring, ecstatic dance.

After weeks of imprisonment and torture, being one with this mighty dragon while he was doing the dizzying loop-de-loops of a victory dance was pure joy. Fiery, earthy dragon energy flooded into him and soothed his tortured soul. He sighed with pleasure as his entire being sang with his dragon's exultation. Snow-capped mountains and broad green plains circled each other in dizzying spirals as Belarian alternated between weightless free fall and heaviness as he climbed upwards.

But all too soon, the dance was finished.

I have done all that I can.

I have made it possible for you to save our kingdom.

Lightning flashed and thunder crashed.

—

Alexander lay surrounded by the stone walls of his dungeon once more. He was back in the bubble of the two fighters. Nothing existed for them except their opponent and the next move of their deadly dance. They were both tiring, each was bleeding from several small wounds and each was watching for the other to slip on the slick, rain-drenched grass or fail to recover from a parry or block fast enough. But Lady Adair was tiring more quickly. Alexander cursed himself for his selfish romanticism and drained a bit more of the monster's strength. He should never have left the fight. She could have been killed before he'd had a chance to help.

He'd been buying himself time.

Time to live.

Time to fly with the dragons.

The tiny warrior fought with a grim determination, her movements swift and precise, darting in under the beast's longer reach and skipping out past his whirring blade. A dangerous, tiring way to fight, but she seemed almost charmed. A closer look with his inner sight showed him that, indeed, she was.

An aura of sparkling silver and gold surrounded her.

An aura that reformed itself into an image of the Goddess Brigga.

And that image glared into his eyes, and a commanding voice that wasn't a voice echoed through him.

NOW!!! You must do this quickly.

The words latched onto him, giving him the strength and courage he needed to help the champion not only of Dalot, but also of Damia. Rapidly, yet gently, he sipped more life force to give him strength and to weaken the beast and positioned himself in his sword arm. He had practiced moving his body during the few hours at night that the beast slept. It was difficult, but he'd finally mastered it. Because he couldn't risk waking him, he had only done slight movements of his fingers and toes. This was going to be a much bigger move, and the beast wasn't asleep. The King would have to push against him. And he would only have one chance. If his captor so much as suspected that he could escape his prison, he would kill him immediately and without a second thought.

King Alexander was not a patient man, but he managed to wait for just the right moment to act. Lady Adair stepped in, her blade slashing up and to her right. A stroke that would have cut through the side of his rib cage and into his heart. But, of course, the beast stepped back and her blade streaked harmlessly past him, leaving her wide open and unprotected, which gave the beast a crucial moment to use to his advantage. His blade slashed across and would have decapitated her, except that Alexander was ready. As soon as his arm began the stroke, he shot all his strength into it and pushed up so the blade angled skyward, passing harmlessly over Lady Adair's head.

The beast howled with rage, and a huge clawed hand burst into his prison, ready to grab him by the throat and fling him out into oblivion.

But it never touched him.

He had given the tiny warrior time to complete her return stroke, which glided through his armor like a table knife through butter, between his ribs, and into his heart.

As darkness washed over him, King Alexander prayed that Lady Adair truly understood what she was dealing with and would be able to make him stay dead.

50

Molly

There was stillness.

Except for her rasping breath as she struggled to fill her oxygen-starved lungs, the rumble of distant thunder, and the hiss of rain washing red blood into green grass.

So much blood.

She was covered with it. The King was covered with it. It had gushed for one crimson moment out of his death wound.

The fight was over.

But he wasn't dead.

Molly stared down on King Alexander's face in horror as the fixed rage and fury of the eternal in his last few moments of life softened into calm repose.

The healing had already begun.

Killing someone who was trying to kill her was doable, but now she was gonna have to hack off the head of the man who had just saved her life.

Like an ominous flock of ravens, five mages, all dressed in black, materialized in a tight circle around her and the fallen King. They stood in brooding silence as Molly gazed into each of their eyes. Micah's, Gram's, and Asmodius's faces were a curious blend of joy that she was alive and grief for her grim task ahead. She was pretty sure that tears were streaming down Gram's face, but they were lost in the pouring rain. She realized with a start that the small, muscular Asian woman with black tats writhing up her arms, black leggings netted with silver spider webs, and a short black dress must be Ashara, the demonologist who had helped to banished Nysrogh. She'd be at least sixty by now, but she could have passed for a thirty-something. Her eyes held sympathy for Molly, but also grim determination. She had no idea who the man with piercing blue eyes and shaggy eyebrows was until he spoke.

"I am Theophilus Peregrine. After the loss of three colleagues and dear friends, I am now the Second Webmaster." He glared at Molly as if she were the enemy instead of the eternal. "I command you to do your duty to your fellow mages. Kill that monster while you have a chance!"

Molly glared up at the adept in outraged contempt. So this was Theo's father. She finally understood why her archenemy at Grant was so messed up. Unfortunately, the asshole was correct. She had to do this. If she didn't, Tamerlane would kill King Alexander—and it would probably be a slow, painful death. Then he would destroy the Web and take over her world and it would be all her fault.

But did any of them truly understand what it would do to her if she murdered King Alexander? She could already feel the guilt and grief worming their way into her heart, turning it grim and bitter.

Not an easy decision, but an obvious one.

She focused and planned the stroke that would end the life of a monster and the life of a friend. But as she raised Flick, a hand grabbed her wrist.

"Wait!"

It was Adam. And beside him was Diana. Their faces were tense with equal measures of fear and hope.

At her feet, Molly sensed, rather than saw, the King move.

"He's coming to. I can't wait!"

"STASIS FIELD. STAT," snapped Ashara.

The five adepts' hands moved in an intricate pattern and a brilliant blue bubble shimmered around King Alexander, who promptly froze. The field was so over-the-top-strong that Molly was sure even a psychically challenged, unimaginative accountant could see it. Hope washed through her, turning all her exhausted muscles to jelly. She would have toppled over if Micah hadn't appeared at her side and propped her up.

All the mages turned to Adam, who said:

"There's a better way to do this."

51

Molly

ell's Gate loomed over them, grim and black as banished hope. Moloch's body was gone. The asteroid had erased all trace of him—even the arrow. Molly shuddered as she watched the human and demon figures carved into the Gate writhe and twist down one side and up the other. The last time she'd stood here it had been midnight, and misty red planetlight and golden torchlight had rippled over its surface. She'd thought the play of light and shadow had made the figures seem to move, but she'd been wrong. Today was a cloudy late afternoon—not a single, slithering shadow in sight and the figures were busy as ever. She shuddered again, and Micah put his arms around her and shielded her against the raw power that pounded out of that dreadful portal.

Her body had run out of adrenaline, and the wounds on her arms and a nasty slash across her chest were screaming with pain. Every muscle ached and shook. A familiar tingle buzzed through her, and she looked down to see sparkling green lights spiraling up from the ground and dancing over and into her body. Thank the gods for the asteroid. She would be fit and pain-free in a few minutes.

And Micah would still have his arms around her.

The cliff, with Andromeda's castle perched on top, shot up on her right. On her left sprawled the central plain, which still looked like a war zone—scorched, gouged-up land littered with trash and the ruins of tiny houses. Off in the distance, there were more houses that looked to be in better shape. But not a human or demon stirred on the tortured field—probably because The Hounds of Hell were sitting on guard in a wide circle around them. Molly counted eight.

Blitzen was back.

"I don't care if the Librarian, and the Warden, and the First, are okay with this, I'm not!" Theophilus Peregrine's angry voice pulled her attention back to the mages gathered at the Gate and reminded her that her Grandmother now controlled the Web. "As a Webmaster, I took a solemn oath to never abuse the power of Hell's Gate. It's for imprisoning powerful and dangerous criminals, not snatching people from the jaws of death. The Web isn't in the God business. Once we make one exception, we'll be asked to make others. Where will we draw the line?"

"This is not an exception!" Andromeda stood at the feet of the frozen King and glared at the Second Webmaster. Her crown of raven's wings and red curls swept back and up from her face. Green eyes glittered dangerously from behind a deftly drawn mask of eyeliner and eye shadow. A cape of black feathers swirled around a red leather corset clenched over a gorgeous black damask dress. One foot, encased in a black knee-high boot, tapped impatiently. "We are, indeed, imprisoning a creature too dangerous and too powerful to be kept in a normal prison. It is simply a happy coincidence that an innocent man's life will also be spared. A man who suffered grievously because the Web bungled their first chance to kill the eternal. A man who saved the life of one of our mages at the cost of his own.

"We owe this man his life.

"And allow me to point out that you are now in Hell and have no jurisdiction here. I don't give a flying fart whether you're okay with this or not. I'm taking my prisoner!"

She raised her arms, palms parallel to the ground, over the King trapped in the stasis field. He rose a few inches off the ground and glided into the Gate, midway between its sides. The Gate thunked, as if someone had thrown a huge switch inside it, and brilliant blue light beamed from every inch of its inner surfaces and focused on the body inside it.

"Remove the stasis field," Andromeda said. It was barely visible within the Gate's blue inferno.

All of the adepts, except for the Second Webmaster, who stood apart from the group, arms crossed over his chest, raised their hands and, with a few deft movements, released the field. Raindrops that had been suspended in it splashed onto the King's body, which relaxed and drifted down onto the ground and over onto its back.

"This is it," Micah whispered into her ear. "I hope King Alexander manages to kick Tamerlane out of his body. Otherwise, we're screwed." Molly's stomach twisted in fear. What if King Alexander wasn't strong enough and he was the one who got kicked out?

The King lay deathly still, bathed in the Gate's piercing blue light. They kept watch for a space of several breaths, and then a sound that felt like honey and gold vibrated out of him. It took Molly's breath away and brought tears to her eyes as it swelled into a sweet, dizzying crescendo that poured itself out into everything.

It was the sound of magic.

She knew this from her very core.

Rays of violet light so deep they were almost black and so bright they hurt her eyes flashed out from the King.

And were gone the next instant.

And so was the heart-stopping music.

They all gasped and clutched at their hearts, because they knew they had just witnessed the stripping away of both King Alexander's and Tamerlane's powerful, beautiful, and precious magic. Witnessing such a cruel mutilation tore at Molly's heart, but she realized that it wasn't a totally bad thing. Without his magic, Tamerlane would lose his advantage over his prisoner. King Alexander now had a fighting chance.

The King's body stiffened and arched until only his head and heels touched the ground. His face clenched with painful effort. Micah's arm tightened around her and she held onto him in an agony of hope and fear. Their grip on each other was so tight that it would have been impossible for either of them to breathe, but they didn't notice because they were holding their breaths.

The King convulsed and then lay still as a corpse.

A scream tore through Molly's heart. There was no sound, just an avalanche of terrible rage and desolation.

And it didn't stop.

It went on and on, ripping through every nerve in her body. Molly doubled over, then went to her knees and screamed till her throat was raw, but she could barely hear herself.

The awful keening amped up and up...

And then stopped.

Molly sobbed into the soft, comforting quiet and staggered to her feet. The other mages didn't look a whole lot better than she felt. There was a profound, shocked silence, then they all looked at Micah, who said:

"King Alexander won."

And Tamerlane was now a disembodied spirit, isolated from the multiverse and doomed to Hell for eternity. Molly's monkey brain began to think about what it would be like to suddenly be without a body—forever. No more sweet, hot coffee to coax you awake after a night of healing sleep, no more beautiful sunsets, no more long morning runs with the wind soft and cool on your face and your muscles loving the rhythm and pull of the movement, no more passionate kisses. No more passion, because there would be no magic, no true connection with anything. Would Tamerlane be able to at least sense the other inmates? Or had they condemned him to an eternity of dark nothingness?

She groaned and throttled her busy brain. It was too horrible to think about, but a glance at the other mages told her that that was exactly what they were doing as well. Gram and Asmodius had moved to either side of Andromeda and held her close. The three of them stood still as statues, their faces etched with grief. Adam and Diana were locked in a tight, terrified embrace. Ashara's mouth made a perfect "O" of horror. The tough, demon-fighting adept had tears streaming down her cheeks. She was probably remembering the time back in Andromeda and Asmodius's place when Tamerlane had helped her send Nysrogh back to the Abyss. Even Theophilus Peregrine had bowed his head and was scrubbing his face with his hands, as if to simultaneously rub away the guilt and cover his eyes. Micah's arms tightened around her once more.

"Oh gods, what have we done?" he asked.

"Quit sniveling and answer his question, lass!" Brigga's voice resounded inside Molly's head. The Goddess seemed almost gleeful about what had happened. And if Brigga was happy, then so was she.

"I'll tell you what we've done," she replied. She said it loud and proud so everyone could hear her, because they all needed to hear this. "We've saved King Alexander's life and who knows how many thousands of other innocent lives. We've spared many more thousands of people a shitload of suffering. And we've saved the Web."

Micah's grip relaxed and his sigh sent delicious shivers rippling through her as it swept past her ear. She leaned back against him and said softly, "Remember Moloch. Tamerlane has a chance."

Andromeda glanced over at them and winked.

The sparkly green lights were already dancing over and into the King's body, followed quickly by golden ones. His color had returned to normal. Tension drained from the mages and most of the grim horror melted away from their faces as they watched the healing. It was some time before the lights finally sank back into the ground, but no one moved or spoke until every last sparkle was gone, the Gate had powered down, and Andromeda helped King Alexander to his feet.

He tottered away from the grotesque, black arch like his body was a stranger to him, placing each foot carefully in front of the other, as if he were unsure of his balance, but still savoring the feel of solid ground beneath him. He looked around like a man newly born, taking in each new thing with rapt attention. Molly noticed that his gaze lingered on the Hell Hounds a bit longer than anything else. At last he turned to Andromeda and asked the obvious question.

"Where am I?"

"You are in another world. We took you here to free your body from the creature who possessed you and to heal you."

"You have my sincere gratitude. You have saved not only my life, but also my kingdom and my family. Unfortunately, I don't feel like I'm really alive. Nothing seems to matter. It's like I'm wrapped in a thick coat of fleece. Nothing can touch me and I can't touch anything. What's wrong with me?"

"Nothing permanent," Andromeda said. "It's the effect of this place. Once you are back in Damia with your wife and son you will begin to feel better. But you have been through weeks of horrible trauma at the hands of a monster, and it will take some time to heal from that. The mages will offer help..." she scowled at the adepts as if to say *You will offer this man as many sessions as he needs with your best healer*, "and I strongly suggest that you take them up on their offer. I know how important this is because I too have been possessed by the same creature. It was an unspeakably awful experience that no one except someone who has also been through it will understand. Once you are stronger, please call me with this." She reached into her bodice and pulled out a silver chain. From the chain hung a small silver whistle.

"Where the blazes did you get that?" asked the king. He stared at the whistle like he was drowning, and it was a life preserver floating on a stormy sea.

"Two not-so-little birds brought it to me," she said with a grin and dropped it into his outstretched hand. "It would be an immense help for both of us to be able to talk to each other about our experience. I can be with you as soon as you call."

Epilogue

lexander and Flora stood in the King's bedchamber, wrapped in each other's arms and gazing out past the rooftops of Bontare onto the surrounding fields. A brilliant pearl of a full moon floated in a black velvet sky, dimming even the brightest stars. It painted the world with dazzling silver and left impossibly dark shadows in all the places it couldn't reach.

It had been a difficult week. Flora had been able to bring them both back to the capital ahead of the troops, which had been fortunate because the beast had left their kingdom in shambles.

Thank the gods for his Queen.

She had called everyone in the castle and all Bontare's public officials together and told the story of how they had tricked the evil eternal, making it possible for Lady Adair, with Brigga's help, to save the kingdom once more. Alexander was amazed and gratified that his subjects believed her and understood that their real

King had returned and had had nothing to do with the eternal's atrocities.

Without her help and support he would never have been able to soothe all the anger and hurt, provide some sort of compensation to those who had lost property or loved ones, get the accounts back in order, and rehire the cooks, housekeepers, and other castle workers who had fled the castled in terror of the monster.

The mages had been kind enough to send a healer to help him get himself back together. She had been an immense help, but he still woke up screaming in the night and he couldn't work for nearly as long as he used to. He touched the tiny silver whistle that he always wore. It would be a while before he was ready to summon the Queen of Hell.

But these were small things compared to what might have been. He sighed contentedly as Flora snuggled deeper into his arms.

"It's a beautiful night," she said.

"The stars are so bright," he replied, eyes burning with tears of gratitude as he tilted her chin up and gently kissed the corner of her eye, her cheek, and her lips.

—

Pot roast? Was that pot roast she smelled? It wasn't anything like Gram's pot roast, which usually smelled burnt. This pot roast smelled totally amazing. Lots of caramelized onions and was that just a hint of vinegar? In fact, it smelled just like the pot roast Dad used to make. The sinking, sad empty feeling she always got when she thought about her parents settled into her gut. Molly groaned and looked over at the battered alarm clock by her bed. Five thirty. Almost dinner time. She flopped back onto the pillow and groaned again. Reaching for her phone, she began checking her messages. Then she noticed the date. Shit! It was Saturday. She'd slept for two whole days.

When they'd come home from Hell, Aunt Althea had met them at the door, trundled Molly up to her room, into a shower, and into bed. She'd been asleep before her head hit the pillow. Althea had probably snuck in a healing and knocked her out for two days.

Meddling mages.

So much for spring break. She had to be back in school Monday.

But right now, there was pot roast. And she actually felt pretty good. She pulled on the last pair of underwear and the last pair socks in the drawer—time to do laundry—a clean pair of jeans, and a T-shirt, and headed downstairs.

When she got to the dining room, she skidded to a halt. The table was draped in white and set with Gram's good china and crystal. Beeswax votive candles flickered cheerfully on either side of a centerpiece of tulips, daffodils, and ferns cut from the yard.

"Wow! Are we having company? What did you do to the pot roast, Gram? It smells great!"

"Happy Birthday!"

Her mouth dropped open in surprise. Oh jeez. She'd totally forgotten about her birthday. It was actually a few days from now, but even so, she couldn't believe she'd forgotten all about it. Gram and Asmodius stood beside the table grinning from ear to ear. At least Gram was. There was worry in Asmodius's eyes as he took a sip—actually, a gulp—from his wine glass.

"Asmodius made the pot roast. I think he did it in self-defense. He can't stand my cooking. And besides, he likes to cook."

Molly wasn't real excited about Gram's cooking either and, like Asmodius, often cooked in self-defense. But she would never tell Gram that. The image of her surly mentor happily puttering around the kitchen was a bit mind-blowing.

"Who'da thunk!? I'm gonna have to get to know you all over again."

"That's true," said Gram. "And before you get too far into that process, there's something you should know."

In Molly's experience, conversations that began with "There's something you should know" were seldom pleasant. And her family loved to keep secrets—until that awkward moment arrived and they suddenly became Something-She-Should-Know. Her parents had told her almost nothing about Gram. She'd met her when she arrived to tell Molly that her parents were dead. Asmodius had eventually told her that her grandmother was a mage, but only after she'd demanded an answer and done everything except twist his pointy ears. But he'd neglected to mention that she was the Third. And Gram hadn't told her that her parents had died because her father wouldn't listen to his mother, an adept mage, when she'd told him not to get on that plane with his wife and child.

"What?" she asked, glaring at the two adepts and steeling herself for more hard news.

Gram put her arm around Asmodius, who was looking distinctly uncomfortable, and said:

"Molly, allow me to introduce you to your grandfather."

"NO!" she cried. What about Andromeda? And they weren't even married. And it had been hard enough imagining her parents locked in a passionate, sexy embrace, but Gram and Asmodius?!

Impossible!

She breathed in a shuddering breath as things began to swirl into a new shape. Not perfect, but somehow better.

And no wonder Asmodius looked so familiar as a man. His was definitely cat-like, but that hadn't been it at all. He looked like her father—or her father had looked like him—or whatever. Same height, same build, same coloring, same smile. But those intense amber eyes, the thing you really noticed about Asmodius, were completely different from Dad's.

Tears spilled down her cheeks at the thought of her father. But the achy, lonely, empty feeling was somehow softened. Because, standing right in front of her was someone who looked like him, and even, sort of, felt like him. Someone who had known and, perhaps, loved him. Someone who could talk to her about him. It was like being really sad but happy at the same time.

"See? I told you this was a bad idea." Asmodius had faded to a shadow of himself. The scar slashed across his cheek glowed ghastly white, and his face was a mask of tragedy. Gram looked devastated.

"No!" Molly said. "It was the best idea ever." In a flash, she had her arms around him, hugging him fiercely. "I'm so glad you're my grandfather. Why didn't you tell me sooner?"

"I just couldn't find the right time." His whole body was shaking and he sniffed.

Was Asmodius sobbing?

Molly thought back to the first time she'd met him. She'd just been dumped in Damia, exhausted and scared shitless. If the large, vicious black cat in front of her had told her he was her grandfather, she would have freaked. And after that, things got... complicated.

"And besides," his face was, indeed, streaked with tears as he stroked her hair back from her face, "I was afraid."

"You shouldn't have been. You know how much I love you.

"But there's just one thing.

"Can I still call you Asmodius? I don't think I can manage Grandpa."

"Of course."

Acknowledgements

Books are seldom written by solitary writers
hunched over keyboards in lonely garrets.
They are group efforts, and this one is no exception.
Many heartfelt thank-yous and kudos to:

Mike Howard and **Dick Seymour**, my intrepid first readers.
Your comments and suggestions were invaluable.

Jessica Morrell, my editor, for polishing my writing and telling me point
blank when a plot point doesn't work. You've made this a much better book.

Ron Root, for your final read-through and for
figuring out what to do with the backstory.

Rainbow Valentine's hilarious and informative podcast, "Disorganized
Crime: Smuggler's Daughter," by iHeart Radio, and **my husband**, for teaching
me everything I didn't already know about pot smuggling in the early 1970's.

Ted Balestreri, Kabbalist and magician, for making sure
I got the exorcisms and the invocations right.

Angie Heide, who told me that the "Family" is still alive and well
in Portland, and that many of them are possessed by demons.

The Mob Museum (themobmuseum.org)

Will Brown, for helping me design the killing stairs.

Becky Mellinger, my talented proofreader and niece, for catching my goofs.

Adam Forrest, my graphic designer, for creating
the wonderful demon drop caps
at the beginning of each chapter.

Todd LaVielle, my ever-so-patient son and webmaster. Without your
help, this book wouldn't have happened and my website wouldn't exist.

My family, for all your love and support. I can't
express how much they mean to me.

And last, but not least:

To the great Sumerian goddess, **Inanna**, for lending me her story.

About the Author

C. LaVielle began her grown-up life as a biologist because she is fascinated by people, plants, and animals and what makes them tick.

She became a wife, a mother, and a healer specializing in tarot divination and energy work.

She traveled to many marvelous, mythical places—from pyramids to temples to standing stones to cathedrals.

And became, at last, a writer.

She has discovered that magic is real. And it makes fantastic fiction.

www.ingramcontent.com/pod-product-compliance
Lightning Source LLC
Chambersburg PA
CBHW072009110726
47910CB00005B/1699